D0960263

Jan 20

The Polar Bear Explorers' Club

The Forbidden Expedition

Also by Alex Bell

The Polar Bear Explorers' Club

The POLAR BEAR

EXPLORERS' CLUB

Book 2

The Forbidden Expedition

Alex Bell

Illustrated by Tomislav Tomić

Simon & Schuster Books for Young Readers
NEW YORK   LONDON   TORONTO   SYDNEY   NEW DELHI

SIMON & SCHUSTER BOOKS FOR YOUNG READERS

An imprint of Simon & Schuster Children's Publishing Division

1230 Avenue of the Americas, New York, New York 10020

Originally published in 2018 in Great Britain by Faber & Faber Limited as *Explorers on Witch Mountain*

SIMON & SCHUSTER BOOKS FOR YOUNG READERS

is a trademark of Simon & Schuster, Inc.

For information about special discounts for bulk purchases, please contact Simon & Schuster Special Sales at 1-866-506-1949 or business@simonandschuster.com.

The Simon & Schuster Speakers Bureau can bring authors to your live event. For more information or to book an event, contact the Simon & Schuster Speakers Bureau at 1-866-248-3049 or visit our website at www.simonspeakers.com.

Jacket design by Chloë Foglia

Interior design by Hilary Zarycky

The text for this book was set in Granjon LT.

The illustrations for this book were rendered in pen and ink and digitally.

Manufactured in the United States of America

1019 FFG I First Edition

2 4 6 8 10 9 7 5 3 1

Library of Congress Cataloging-in-Publication Data

Names: Bell, Alex, author. ITomić, Tomislav, illustrator.

Title: The forbidden expedition / Alex Bell ; illustrated by Tomislav Tomic.

Other titles: Explorers on Witch Mountain

Description: First edition. I New York : Simon & Schuster Books for Young Readers, [2019] I Series: The Polar Bear Explorers' Club ; 2 I Originally published: London : Faber & Faber Limited, 2018. I Summary: Stella Starflake Pearl, Ethan, Shay, Beanie, and Percifal set out for Witch Mountain, where a fearsome witch has taken Stella's father, Felix.

Identifiers: LCCN 2018032960 I

ISBN 9781534406490 (hardcover) I ISBN 9781534406513 (eBook)

Subjects: I CYAC: Fantasy. I Adventure and adventurers—Fiction. I Explorers—Fiction. I Clubs—Fiction. I Witches—Fiction. I Kidnapping—Fiction.

Classification: LCC PZ7.B388875 For 2019 I DDC [Fic]—dc23

LC record available at https://lccn.loc.gov/2018032960

For Shirley and Fred Dayus.
Thank you for the warm welcome into your family—and for
raising the best man I have ever known.

Polar Bear Explorers' Club Rules

ALL Polar Bear explorers will keep their mustaches trimmed, waxed, and well groomed at all times. Any explorer found with a slovenly mustache will be asked to withdraw from the club's public rooms immediately.

EXPLORERS with disorderly mustaches or unkempt beards will also be refused entry to the members-only bar, the private dining room, and the gentlemen's billiards room without exception.

ALL igloos on club property must contain a flask of hot chocolate and an adequate supply of marshmallows at all times.

ONLY polar bear–shaped marshmallows are to be served on club property. Additionally, the following breakfast items will be prepared in polar bear–shape only: pancakes, waffles, crumpets, sticky pastries, fruit jellies, and donuts. Please do not request alternative animal shapes from the kitchen—including penguins, walruses, woolly mammoths, and yetis—as this offends the chef.

MEMBERS are kindly reminded that when the chef is offended, insulted, or peeved, there will be nothing on offer in the dining room whatsoever except for buttered toast. This toast will be bread-shaped.

EXPLORERS must not hunt or harm unicorns under any circumstances.

ALL Polar Bear Explorers' Club sleighs must be properly decorated with seven brass bells and must contain the following items: five fleecy blankets, three hot water bottles in knitted sweaters, two flasks of emergency hot chocolate, and a warmed basket of buttered crumpets (polar bear–shaped).

PLEASE do not take penguins into the club's saltwater baths; they *will* hog the Jacuzzi.

ALL penguins are the property of the club and are not to be removed by explorers. The club reserves the right to search any suspiciously shaped bags. Any bag that moves by itself will automatically be deemed suspicious.

ALL snowmen built on club property must have appropriately groomed mustaches. Please note that a carrot is not a suitable object to use as a mustache. Nor is an eggplant. If in doubt, remember that the club president is always available for consultation regarding snowmen's mustaches.

IT is considered bad form to threaten other club members with icicles, snowballs, or oddly dressed snowmen.

WHISTLING ducks are not permitted on club property. Any member found with a whistling duck in his possession will be asked to leave.

Upon initiation, all Polar Bear explorers shall receive an explorer's bag containing the following items:

- One tin of Captain Filibuster's Expedition-Strength Mustache Wax
- One bottle of Captain Filibuster's Scented Beard Oil
- One folding pocket mustache comb
- One ivory-handled shaving brush, two pairs of grooming scissors, and four individually wrapped cakes of luxurious foaming shaving soap
- Two compact pocket mirrors

Desert Jackal Explorers' Club Rules

MAGICAL flying carpets are to be kept tightly rolled when on club premises. Any damage caused by out-of-control flying carpets will be considered the sole responsibility of the explorer in question.

ENCHANTED genie lamps must stay in their owners' possession at all times.

PLEASE note: Genies are strictly prohibited at the bar and at the bridge tables.

TENTS are for serious expedition use only and are not to be used to host parties, gatherings, chin-wags, or chitchats.

CAMELS must not be permitted—or encouraged—to spit at other club members.

JUMPING cacti are not allowed inside the club unless under exceptional circumstances.

PLEASE do not remove flags, maps, or wallabies from the club.

CLUB members are not permitted to settle disagreements via camel racing between the hours of midnight and sunrise.

THE club kangaroos, coyotes, sand cats, and rattlesnakes are to be respected at all times.

MEMBERS who wish to keep all their fingers are advised not to torment the giant desert hairy scorpions, irritate the bearded vultures, or vex the spotted desert recluse spiders.

EXPLORERS are kindly asked to refrain from washing

their feet in the drinking water tureens at the club's entrance, which are provided strictly for our members' refreshment.

SAND forts may be constructed on club grounds, on condition that explorers empty all sand from their sandals, pockets, bags, binocular cases, and helmets before entering the club.

EXPLORERS are asked not to take camel decoration to extremes. Desert Jackal Explorers' Club camels may wear a maximum of one jeweled necklace, one tasseled headdress and/or bandana, seven plain gold anklets, up to four knee bells, and one floral snout ornament.

Upon initiation, all Desert Jackal explorers shall receive an explorer's bag containing the following items:

- One foldable leather safari hat or one pith helmet
- One canister of tropical-strength giant desert hairy scorpion repellent
- One shovel (please note this object's usefulness in the event of being buried alive in a sandstorm)
- One camel-grooming kit, consisting of organic camel shampoo, camel eyelash curlers, head brush, toenail trimmers, and hoof polishers (kindly provided by the National Camel-Grooming Association)
- Two spare genie lamps and one spare genie bottle

Jungle Cat Explorers' Club Rules

MEMBERS of the Jungle Cat Explorers' Club shall refrain from picnicking in a slovenly manner. All expedition picnics are to be conducted with grace, poise, and elegance.

ALL expedition picnicware must be made from solid silver and kept perfectly polished at all times.

CHAMPAGNE carriers must be constructed from high-grade wicker, premium leather, or teakwood. Please note that champagne carriers considered "tacky" will not be accepted onto the luggage elephant under ANY circumstances.

EXPEDITION picnics will not take place unless there are scones present. Ideally, there should also be magic lanterns, pixie cakes, and an assortment of fairy jellies.

EXOTIC whip snakes, alligator snapping turtles, horned baboon tarantulas, and flying panthers must be kept securely under lock and key while on club premises.

DO NOT torment or tease the jungle fairies. They *will* bite and may also catapult tiny, but extremely potent, stink-berries. Please be warned that stink-berries smell worse than anything you can imagine, including unwashed feet, moldy cheese, elephant poo, and hippopotamus burps.

JUNGLE fairies must be allowed to join expedition picnics if they bring an offering of any of the following: elephant cakes, striped giraffe scones, or fizzy tiger punch from the Forbidden Jungle Tiger Temple.

JUNGLE fairy boats have right of way on the Tikki Zikki River under *all* circumstances, including when there are piranhas present.

SPEARS are to be pointed away from other club members at all times.

WHEN traveling by elephant, explorers are kindly asked to supply their own bananas.

IF and when confronted by an enraged hippopotamus, a Jungle Cat explorer must remain calm and act with haste to avoid any damage befalling the expedition boat (please note that the Jungle Navigation Company expects all boats to be returned to them in pristine condition).

MEMBERS are courteously reminded that owing to the size and smell of the beasts in question, the club's elephant house is not an appropriate venue in which to host soirees, banquets, galas, or shindigs. Carousing of any kind in the elephant house is strictly prohibited.

Upon initiation, all Jungle Cat explorers shall receive an explorer's bag containing the following items:

- An elegant mother-of-pearl knife and fork, inscribed with the explorer's initials
- One silverware polishing kit

- One engraved Jungle Cat Explorers' Club napkin ring and five luxury linen napkins—ironed, starched, and embossed with the club's insignia
- One magic lantern with fire pixie
- One tin of Captain Greystoke's Expedition-Flavor Smoked Caviar
- One corkscrew, two cheese knives, and three wicker grape baskets

Ocean Squid Explorers' Club Rules

SEA monster, kraken, and giant squid trophies are the private property of the club, and cannot be removed to adorn private homes. Explorers will be charged for any decorative tentacles that are found to be missing from their rooms.

EXPLORERS are not to fraternize—or join forces—with pirates or smugglers during the course of any official expedition.

POISONOUS puffer fish, barbed-wire jellyfish, saltwater stingrays, and electric eels are not appropriate fillings for pies or sandwiches. Any such requests sent to the kitchen will be politely rejected.

EXPLORERS are kindly asked to refrain from offering to show the club's chef how to prepare sea snakes, sharks, crustaceans, or deep-sea monsters for human consumption. This includes the creatures listed in the rule immediately above. Please respect the expert knowledge of the chef.

THE Ocean Squid Explorers' Club does not consider the sea cucumber to be a trophy worthy of reward or recognition. This includes the lesser-found biting cucumber, as well as the singing cucumber and the argumentative cucumber.

ANY Ocean Squid explorer who gifts the club with a tentacle from the screeching red devil squid will be rewarded with a year's supply of Captain Ishmael's Premium Dark Rum.

PLEASE do not leave docked submarines in a submerged state; it wreaks havoc with the club's valet service.

EXPLORERS are kindly asked not to leave deceased sea monsters in the hallways or in any of the club's communal rooms. Unattended sea monsters are liable to be removed to the kitchens without notice.

THE South Seas Navigation Company will not accept liability for any damage caused to their submarines. This includes damage caused by giant squid attacks, whale ambushes, and jellyfish plots.

EXPLORERS are not to use the map room to compare the length of squid tentacles or other trophies. Please use the marked areas within the trophy rooms to settle any private wagers or bets.

PLEASE note: Any explorer who threatens another explorer with a harpoon cannon will be suspended from the club immediately.

Upon initiation, all Ocean Squid explorers shall receive an explorer's bag containing the following items:

- One tin of Captain Ishmael's Kraken Bait
- One kraken net
- One engraved hip flask filled with Captain Ishmael's Expedition-Strength Salted Rum
- Two sharpened fishing spears and three bags of hunting barbs
- Five tins of Captain Ishmael's Harpoon Cannon Polish

The Forbidden Expedition

CHAPTER ONE

STELLA STARFLAKE PEARL SAT down on her favorite ice bench in the backyard and sighed. Her recent expedition with her friends Beanie, Shay, and Ethan had been extensively covered in all the papers and expedition journals—not just because the four junior explorers had been the first to reach the coldest part of the Icelands, and not only because Stella was the first girl to ever be admitted to the Polar Bear Explorers' Club, but also because it turned out that Stella was actually an ice princess.

She looked over at the witch puppet she'd brought back with her from the Icelands. When she'd discovered it was a magical thing that could move around all by itself, she'd been delighted, but her adoptive father, Felix, had insisted on taking the puppet away and shutting it up in the top room of the East Wing.

From her position on the bench, Stella could now just

make out the pointed outline of the witch's hat as the puppet walked up and down the windowsill of the turreted bedroom. Every now and then the witch would stop and rap her wooden knuckles on the glass. The sound carried clearly to Stella through the frozen air, making her shiver.

"She won't be locked up forever," Felix had promised. "But we can't be too careful. This puppet is an exact likeness of Jezzybella. Not only did she kill your parents, but she tried her best to kill you, too. I've heard of witches making images of themselves and then being able to see through their eyes. If that's what this puppet is, then we can't have it anywhere near you."

Stella knew that what Felix said was perfectly sensible, and yet deep in her gut she couldn't help feeling that he was wrong about the puppet. Yes, it was a toy version of the witch who had killed the snow queen and king, but Stella had felt compulsively drawn to it back at the ice castle, and she still did somehow now.

The small, sad sound of the puppet rapping her tiny knuckles against the glass carried through the air once again, and she had to force herself not to run up to the turret to let her out. Felix had sent for a puppet expert from Coldgate, and until he arrived she would leave the witch where she was.

Stella smoothed out the powder-blue skirts of her dress and ran a finger lightly over the sparkly silver crowns stitched into the fabric. Her magical tiara had been put on display with other curiosities at the Polar Bear Explorers' Club, and word of the junior explorers' adventures had traveled fast. In the two weeks since she'd been back, gifts had poured in from people Stella had never even met. There had been dresses, lace gloves, beautiful boxes of pink jellies dusted with powdered sugar, tiny unicorn dolls, and more besides.

At first Stella had been delighted. Everyone likes getting presents, after all, and people send rather nice ones to ice princesses. But they send not-so-nice things too. Letters saying that ice princesses did not belong in civilized society, that they ought to stay out in the wilds of the Icelands, nursing their frozen hearts and casting their evil spells. Felix had taken those letters and tossed them straight onto the fire, telling her to pay them no heed and that everything would die down soon enough, but Stella still felt a cold little stone of worry about it, right in the pit of her stomach.

She was distracted from her concerns when her pet polar bear, Gruff, came lumbering over to her across the snowy lawn. Felix had rescued Gruff from the snow just like he had rescued Stella, and the great white bear had been her best friend for as long as she could remember. Visitors to the house were often startled by his enormous size—especially when he stood up on his back legs, which he did whenever he really wanted to show off and look fantastically handsome. He stood more than ten feet tall, towering over even the tallest man. He'd done this the first time he'd ever met Aunt Agatha—Felix's overbearing, bossy sister—who had let out the most terrible shriek and then fainted dead away in a cloud of petticoats and perfume. Stella had thought the screaming and fainting was terribly rude, especially as Felix had made Gruff look very handsome with a fetching bow tie he'd had specially made for the occasion.

Gruff shoved his black nose into the pockets of Stella's cloak in search of his favorite fish biscuits. She gave him a gentle shove and told him to sit. He flumped down obediently in the snow, and Stella rewarded him by tossing him a treat. The bear crunched it up happily, spraying crumbs everywhere, then licked Stella's cheek before lumbering off toward the lake. Felix had told Stella once that polar bears were very fast runners and could reach top speeds of twenty-five miles an hour, but Stella had never seen Gruff move any faster than a sedate lumber. This may have been because Gruff had been born with a twisted paw, but then again, perhaps he was just a big old lazy bear (which is what Stella really thought).

She stood up from the bench. There was no point moping around worrying. Felix always said that if you were feeling a bit anxious or upset, the best solution was to jump straight into doing something useful and/or fun. Preferably fun, of course, because fun things were much more effective at cheering up a person than a useful thing could ever be.

Stella glanced over to where Felix stood on the terrace, examining the glass fairy globe the fairies had given him the day before. Fairies were terribly fond of Felix, so it made sense that his explorer's specialty should be fairyology. There were several fairies flitting about him now—Stella could see the sparkle of their wings from across the yard.

Felix looked up and gave Stella a wave. She waved back and then settled herself down in the snow to make a snow bear. She would have much preferred to make a snow unicorn, but they were a lot more difficult and she had never managed to get one quite right. She put her gloved hand down, ready to scoop up her first snowball, when a crackle of blue sparks leapt from her fingertips.

She froze. There before her was a perfect, sparkling snow unicorn. It was no more than four inches tall, but Stella could see each individual strand of hair in its flowing mane, the twists in its white horn, and even a collection of fine, feathered eyelashes. The unicorn's beautiful snow eyes gazed directly at Stella, as if it could really see her—as if it was waiting for her to say something.

Stella gazed around in confusion. Had someone else come into the backyard and made the unicorn? But there was nobody around except for Felix, and even he couldn't make snow animals as detailed and perfect as that. And surely it hadn't been there just moments ago. One minute she had wished for a unicorn made of snow, and the next, sparks had shot from her fingers and one had appeared. Almost like magic. But Stella couldn't do ice magic. Not without her tiara. And that was miles away in a cabinet inside the Polar Bear Explorers' Club. . . .

Slowly, she reached out a hand toward the unicorn. As her fingertips got closer, she could have sworn that one of its ears twitched, just slightly—

The sound of breaking glass made her jump, and she snatched back her hand.

"Stella!" Felix shouted, and she was alarmed by the sound of panic in his voice.

She turned to look over her shoulder and saw that he had dropped the glass fairy globe, which lay in sparkling fragments at his feet. Stella clapped both hands to her mouth in dismay. Fairy globes were one in a million, and Felix wasn't likely to come across one ever again. What could possibly have caused him to drop something so precious?

"Stella, above you!" Felix shouted at the exact same moment that a monstrous dark shadow fell over her.

She looked up, and a cry of fear lodged itself in her throat. A gigantic vulture loomed over her like something out of a nightmare, its twenty-foot wingspan flapping out icy ripples of frozen air. It had bedraggled, dirty gray feathers, a long, stringy neck, and a completely bald head. Stella saw the sharp, hooked beak, the curled claws, and the cold gleam in its predator's eyes. If she had had her tiara she could have frozen the vulture, but without it she had no choice but to turn and run, her fur-topped boots kicking up great clumps of snow behind her.

The house seemed so far away. She was never going to make it. Behind her, the vulture let out a terrible squawk, which seemed to pierce the air. The next moment the giant bird swooped in so close that Stella could smell its damp, dirty feathers and the putrid scent of rotting flesh on its breath as it gave that screeching squawk once again, so loud that it seemed to slice right through Stella's eardrums.

She gasped as she felt the vulture's talons clamp down on her shoulders. Her boots were coming up off the ground, and she realized that the bird had caught her and was going to fly away and there was absolutely nothing she could do to stop it—

But then Felix crashed into her, and her cloak ripped free of the vulture's claws as he dragged her to the ground. Stella found herself pressed facedown in the snow, pinned there by Felix's weight as he shielded her from the vulture, which immediately tried to throw him aside. There was the sound of fabric tearing, and Felix's breath caught sharply in his throat.

Stella tried to push him off, because she didn't want his protection if it meant he was going to get hurt instead, but Felix was too strong and kept her tucked firmly underneath him as the vulture screamed into the air. The thought flashed through Stella's mind, clear as crystal, that the vulture was going to kill them both. There was no way they could fight it off, and there was no one around for miles. Even if one of the servants saw the attack from a window, Felix kept no weapons in the house, so there would be absolutely nothing they could do to help.

Suddenly she became aware of the ground trembling beneath her and looked up to see Gruff racing across the snow, faster than she had ever seen him move before, his huge paws kicking up tall fountains of beautiful, glittering ice. The great bear thundered up to them, putting his massive body between the humans and the vulture. His black lips pulled back in a ferocious snarl, and he let out such a deafening bellow of a roar that Stella felt it in the very ground beneath her.

She had never realized quite how many teeth Gruff had, or how cruelly sharp they were, and she had never seen him roaring and snarling in fury in such a terrifying way. The vulture squawked in alarm and drew back a little. Gruff stood up on his hind legs, towering at his full ten-foot height. He swiped at the vulture with his huge paws, landing a solid blow that sent the giant bird reeling farther into the sky.

Felix gripped Stella's arm, and she found herself being dragged to her feet. Then he scooped her up in his arms and sprinted back toward the house. Over his shoulder Stella saw that Gruff had thumped back down to all fours, but he was still roaring over and over again at the vulture, which had flown higher and was circling warily above.

Felix threw open the door to the library with one hand and set Stella down in the doorway. Worried for her polar bear, she tried to see past Felix, but he was already turning back to the door.

"Gruff!" he shouted. "Come on."

The polar bear turned and lolloped across the snow toward them. The vulture had flown so high now that Stella could no longer see it. The moment Gruff padded through the doorway, Felix slammed the door closed and drew across the bolts.

CHAPTER TWO

ARE YOU HURT?" FELIX asked, gripping Stella's arms and peering at her closely.

"N-no," she said. "No. I'm okay."

"Thank heavens!" Felix replied, squeezing her tight.

"Are you all right?" Stella asked, remembering the sound of fabric tearing.

"Yes. Of course." Felix let her go and threw his arms around Gruff's neck. "You big, wonderful bear!" he said. "You shall feast on blubber pies for a month, I promise!"

"What was that thing?" Stella asked.

Felix frowned and said, "I'll have to consult my books to know for sure. . . ." As he trailed off, Stella noticed that he'd turned an unhealthy shade of gray. She was about to ask again whether he was all right when suddenly he leaned forward, steadying himself against Gruff's broad side. "Stella, I don't want you to be alarmed," he said calmly, "but I'm afraid that blasted bird might have succeeded in scratching me a couple of times. Perhaps you would go and fetch Mrs. Sap from the kitchens. There is a chance I might require her assistance removing my shirt."

Stella walked around behind him and gasped. The vulture had shredded Felix's jacket and ripped straight through his shirt as well. She could see angry red welts all over his back. Smears of blood stained the white cotton, and Stella could see at a single glance that these were no mere scratches, but slashes deep enough to leave scars.

She felt tears fill her eyes but blinked them quickly away. She could cry and be terribly upset about it all later, but right now she had to go and fetch help. She turned toward the door, but before she could take a single step, it burst open and the housekeeper, Mrs. Sap, rushed in carrying the most gigantic rifle Stella had ever seen. It looked rather incongruous alongside the housekeeper's frilly hat and crisp white apron.

"Where is it?" she cried, pointing the rifle wildly around the room, her gray curls bouncing about her shoulders. "Where is that awful creature?"

"Good heavens, is that a rifle?" Felix asked.

"Now, I know your thoughts on guns, Mr. Felix, and that's all well and good, but living out here in the snow, one never knows when one might suddenly be faced with a yeti attack."

"Yeti attack!" Felix exclaimed. "My dear woman, the closest reported sighting of a yeti was miles and miles from this house."

"That's as may be, but haven't you just been attacked in the backyard by a dragon? I saw it with my own eyes!"

"That was a bone-eating vulture, unless I am very much mistaken," Felix said with a sigh. "Mrs. Sap, please do stop pointing that gun all over the place. You're likely to blow our heads off. The vulture has flown away. Gruff frightened it off."

Stella noticed that Felix put a little extra emphasis on that final sentence. Mrs. Sap had not been happy when Gruff arrived—not happy at all—and was forever disagreeing with Felix over things like whether polar bears should be kept as pets, or allowed in the house, or washed in the best bathroom in the massive claw-footed tub, or permitted to flop down on the four-poster bed in the guest bedroom whenever guests were not present (and sometimes even when they were, as Aunt Agatha had found to her dismay the last time she'd stayed. Really, anyone would have thought she'd discovered a hoard of horned baboon tarantulas nesting within the sheets the way she'd carried on about it).

"Felix is hurt," Stella said, bringing everyone back to the subject. "The vulture clawed at his back and ripped through his clothes."

Mrs. Sap huffed angrily. "If you hadn't banned weapons from the house, Mr. Felix, and thereby forced me to hide the rifle in the jam and preserves cupboard, then I might have gotten to it a great deal sooner and saved you from terrible injury."

Felix raised an eyebrow. "You might recall, Mrs. Sap, that the owner of the White Unicorn sent me a substantial bill for damage to the wood paneling of his pub's four-hundred-year-old walls after you attempted to participate in the darts tournament there last year. So I think we can all count ourselves extremely fortunate that the rifle was hidden beneath piles of jam."

Mrs. Sap huffed again but didn't say anything more as she set the rifle carefully down in the corner and bustled over to them. She gasped when she saw Felix's back, and made him sit down in one of the chairs.

"Merciful heavens, you look like you've taken a flogging!" she exclaimed. "The doctor will have to be sent for."

There was no arguing with Mrs. Sap once she decided on something, and in no time at all the doctor had arrived and was treating Felix upstairs. Stella found herself whisked away to the kitchen with the housekeeper and Gruff.

"You're a big old stinky, messy, slobbery thing, but you were superb today," Mrs. Sap said to Gruff, reaching up to pat him on the head. "Superb."

She settled Stella in the comfiest chair in front of the

stove with a steaming mug of hot chocolate and then fetched a whole roast chicken from the cool box and let Gruff have it all to himself. While the polar bear munched happily on the rug in front of the fire, Stella clutched the hot chocolate Mrs. Sap had given her but found she was too upset to drink it. She kept hearing the shriek of the vulture in her ears, the sound of fabric tearing, and then the image of Felix's blood-stained, ripped shirt swam before her. Before she knew it, tears had filled her eyes again, and this time she was quite helpless to stop them from falling.

"Oh, my duck," Mrs. Sap said, swooping down on her at once. "What a terrible morning you've had, you poor, dear thing."

She took the hot chocolate from Stella's trembling hands, then picked her up and settled her down in her lap, just like she used to when Stella was tiny.

"There, there," the housekeeper said. "You have a good long cry if you want to. Lord knows anyone else would be bawling their eyes out by now."

"Is . . . ? Is Felix going to be okay?" Stella asked in a shaky voice.

"Of course he is, my sweet. He's a tough old stick. This won't be the first time he's been attacked by some terrible monster, mark my words, not with all those expeditions he's been on." Mrs. Sap sighed. "Why you all want to go tearing off to unknown lands all the time, I'll never understand, but it's no use trying to talk sense to an explorer, goodness knows. They've just got maps and compasses and adventures on the brain, and that's that. But he's going to be absolutely fine. Those scratches looked a bit of a mess, I'll grant you, but they'll mend soon enough."

In fact, Felix couldn't walk properly for almost a week. Mrs. Sap was all for sending for Aunt Agatha to nurse him, but Felix said that he couldn't think of anything more appalling, and if the housekeeper had ever had any liking for him, then she would do no such thing.

"I am not an invalid," he said, "and I do not require nursing by my sister, or anyone else for that matter."

He confiscated the rifle for Mrs. Sap's own safety, which she was most put out about, and he also told Stella that she must not, under any circumstances, go outside for the time being—not even to visit her unicorn, Magic. Stella protested keenly, but Felix was adamant. There was no telling if the vulture might return, and they couldn't take any chances.

"But, Felix, I can't stay inside forever!" she said. "We've never seen one of those vultures in the backyard before, and they don't live around here, do they? It probably just got lost and is long gone by now."

Felix sighed. "That vulture came from Witch Mountain in the Icelands, Stella. I'm afraid it was no accident that it was here. Jezzybella must have sent it after you."

"But how would she know where I live?" Stella asked,

shuddering at the witch's name. "You don't think it might be something to do with the puppet, do you?"

"It could be. We'll have to wait until the expert arrives."

The puppet expert arrived just a couple of days later. His name was Sir Erwin Rolfingston, and he was a tall, thin fellow with a rather startling hooked nose and the pointiest black mustache Stella had ever seen. This was probably due to the fact that Rolfingston had a habit of twirling it constantly—like the pantomime villains Stella had often seen at the theater.

It took them a while to climb the spiral staircase to the top of the East Wing because Felix's back was still hurting him and he had to pause a couple of times to catch his breath.

"Are you quite well?" Sir Rolfingston asked, peering at Felix dubiously. "This is the second time you've stopped."

"My apologies. I'm afraid I injured my back recently, and stairs are still giving me a bit of trouble."

Sir Rolfingston sniffed loudly through his magnificent nose. "Hurt my back a few years ago," he said. "Got tangled up with a giant dancing puppet. Blasted nuisance, what?"

"Quite," Felix replied.

Stella moved closer to Felix so that he could rest his hand on her shoulder for balance, and soon enough they reached the top room of the turret. Felix drew the key from his pocket and unlocked the door. They all piled into the room before quickly shutting the door behind them in case the puppet tried to make a break for it.

Stella couldn't see her at first. The small circular space was filled with soft toy polar bears. Felix had ordered one for Stella's birthday a few years ago, and due to an unfortunate shipping error, had received one hundred bears instead of just one.

Stella was aghast to notice that one of the bears had been ripped open—presumably by the puppet. There was stuffing scattered everywhere and—worst of all—the bear fabric had been fashioned into a rug, stretched out on the floor, just like the skinned bear at the Polar Bear Explorers' Club.

"Bloodthirsty." Lord Rolfingston sighed, noticing the tiny rug. "Quite bloodthirsty." He glanced at Felix, twirled his mustache, and said, "You used to find singing puppets and dancing puppets and hopscotching puppets most frequently, but these days, I tell you, it's bloodthirsty puppets that seem to be all the rage."

"Where has she gone?" Stella asked, just before the witch puppet appeared from beneath a pile of polar bears.

The piece of wood her strings were attached to was suspended above the ground all by itself, as if held by an invisible hand. The witch tried to dive back into the mound of polar bears when Sir Rolfingston reached for her, but he moved with surprising speed and grabbed the piece of wood before she could disappear. In his grasp, the puppet had no choice but to dangle helplessly from her strings.

Stella peered at the witch, curious to see her again. From the tip of her pointed hat to the end of her crooked nose, the puppet was every inch the classic witch. She was carved entirely from wood, with real clothes and waves of frizzy gray hair that puffed out from beneath her hat. The strangest thing about her, though—aside from the fact that she could move around by herself, of course—was that both her wooden feet were horribly burned and scarred. At the snow queen's ice castle, Stella had learned from a magic mirror that a witch had killed her parents, presumably in revenge after they attached red-hot iron shoes to her feet in order to make her dance at their wedding. Even though this was just a puppet, the sight of those scarred feet made Stella feel sick with shame over what her birth parents had done.

Sir Rolfingston took one look at the witch—thrashing, kicking, and struggling in his grip—and said, "No doubt at all, this is an effigy spy puppet."

Felix sighed. "That's exactly what I was afraid of," he said.

"What's an effigy spy puppet?" Stella asked, although she feared she already knew the answer.

"It's a puppet version of an actual person," Sir Rolfingston replied. He sniffed and looked the puppet up and down. "They're magically linked, you see. Extremely rare.

Everything the puppet sees, the real witch sees." He glanced at Stella. "She appears to be extremely interested in you, what?"

He was quite right. The witch puppet kept twisting and turning against her strings, straining to get a proper look at Stella. When he set her down on the floor and let go, the wood remained suspended in the air, moving all by itself as the witch slowly turned around, her wooden feet clattering on the floor. She then walked straight over to Stella, reached up one gnarled hand, gripped the hem of Stella's dress, and gave it an insistent tug.

"Most peculiar," Sir Rolfingston said. "Where did you find it?"

"A snow queen's castle," Stella replied glumly as she pulled her dress free. Why had she brought the dratted thing home in the first place? Why hadn't she just left it at the back of the wardrobe where she'd found it? Then the vulture would never have come and Felix wouldn't have been hurt. She couldn't explain, even to herself, the weird pull that had caused her to put the puppet in her bag.

"Damned inhospitable places, from what I hear," Sir Rolfingston replied. "Nothing good ever came out of a snow queen's castle." Then he did a sort of double take at Stella, seeming to notice her pale skin, white hair, and ice-chip-blue eyes for the first time. "Upon my word, you're not the ice princess everyone's been talking about, are you?"

Stella looked back at him miserably, not knowing what to say. She was an ice princess, but she had absolutely no desire to be. In fact, even though she had always wanted to know where she came from, now she almost wished she had never gone into the snow queen's castle and found out her heritage. Who wanted to discover that their parents had been evil and that there was ice magic coursing through their veins that would freeze their heart solid and turn them cold and cruel if they used it too much?

"Stella is an ice princess, among a great many other things," Felix said mildly. "First and foremost she's a remarkable navigator, an intrepid explorer, a cherished daughter, an expert skater, a voracious reader, a loyal friend, and an accomplished maker of balloon unicorns."

Stella smiled at Felix gratefully. It was comforting to know that he, at least, didn't see her just as an ice princess. She was also pleased by his balloon unicorn comment. He had been patiently teaching her how to make them ever since they'd returned from the expedition, and although Stella's initial attempts had borne more of a resemblance to an ugly moose than a unicorn, they were now looking a lot more unicorn-like.

"Hmm." Sir Rolfingston peered at Stella dubiously. "Snow queens are known for having frozen hearts though, what?"

"Puppet experts are known for being maverick eccentrics, but where on earth would we be if we paid too much attention to stereotypes?" Felix said cheerfully. "Thank you very much for your assessment, Sir Rolfingston. Can I offer you some tea before your return journey?"

Sir Rolfingston glanced at Stella again and said, "Thank you, no. There's a prized collection of Bigfoot puppets awaiting my inspection in the Pinecone Mountains that I must get to urgently." He turned back to look at the witch puppet, which had wandered off to sit on her self-made polar bear rug, still watching them with her painted eyes. "A word of advice, though," he said. "Don't say or do anything in front of that puppet that you don't want the real witch to know about. You can guarantee she'll be watching everything."

CHAPTER THREE

S TELLA HARDLY SAW FELIX over the next few weeks. After Sir Rolfingston's visit confirmed that the bone-eating vulture had most probably been sent by the witch, Felix threw himself into a frenzy of activity. The giant birds were found in only one place in the world, and that was Witch Mountain, at the edge of the Icelands. Felix said that the witch must have fled there after killing Stella's parents, and he immediately began petitioning the authorities to go and arrest her so that she could be brought to justice for murder.

But as the days and weeks dragged by, it became increasingly apparent that the authorities weren't interested in traveling all the way to Witch Mountain to pursue a dangerous witch who'd committed a crime in the wilds of the Icelands ten years ago. Stella had a sneaky read of one of the letters left on Felix's desk while he was occupied with giving Gruff his bath.

Dear Mr. Pearl,

Thank you for your recent correspondence. Unfortunately, we must inform you that crimes committed within the Icelands are outside the jurisdiction of the Royal Justice Service. Furthermore, the Royal Justice Service will not involve itself in any murderous squabbles that break out between yetis, snow queens, ice monsters, or others of that ilk.

If you wish to have a magical person tried for magical crimes, we would refer you to the Court of Magical Justice, which is located in the wilds of the Black Spells Forest on the other side of the world. We must warn you that any journey to this court will be a grim challenge, fraught with peril and dangerous unknowns.

Thank you for your inquiry, and I am sorry that we cannot offer assistance on this occasion.

Yours sincerely,
Montague Rawnsley
Secretary to the Royal Justice Service

Stella took the opportunity to have a quick rifle through the other papers on Felix's desk and saw that there were many more letters like the first one. There was even a letter from the Court of Magical Justice, written on a heavy parchment scroll. It looked like it had been hand-delivered by a fire sprite, if the burned, blackened edges were anything to go by. This one stated that they would certainly be prepared to try the witch for her crimes, but that she would need to be physically present at the court in order for this to happen.

It all seemed rather hopeless, and Stella was starting to fear that she would be kept confined to the house forever. The bone-eating vulture had been spotted circling in the sky several times, and although it never came too close, Felix was sure that the second Stella stepped outside the bird would swoop down to carry her off to Witch Mountain.

"I'm sorry," he said to her. "I know you want to go outside and skate on the lake and see the unicorns and build snow penguins. But until we figure out what to do about the witch, it just isn't safe."

Stella knew he was right, but she absolutely hated having to stay cooped up in the house. Her hands burned to touch snow, and her skin ached to feel the delicious frostiness of cold, crisp air. She had always spent a lot of time outside, and it made sense that ice princesses were meant for the snowy outdoors, not toasty warm houses.

The orangery got very cold at night when the sun went down, so Stella took to spending a great deal of time in there with the pygmy dinosaurs Felix was studying. A tiny triceratops named Toby was new to the group, and although affectionate, he was very shy. Stella took the time to make friends with him so that he'd feel more at home. And, of course, she paid special attention to her favorite pygmy dinosaur, a T. rex named Buster.

But her days quickly became monotonous, and this was made worse by the fact that Felix had become very secretive about the witch and had stopped discussing her with Stella. She knew that he must have some kind of plan in mind, because Felix wasn't one to give up or to be told that something wasn't possible. She knew that he was applying all of his energy to solving the witch problem, so it was maddening that he just brushed off her questions whenever she tried to ask him about it.

Stella was absolutely delighted, therefore, when the magician and Ocean Squid explorer Zachary Vincent Rook arrived at their home, accompanied by his son. Ethan Edward Rook had been one of the junior explorers who had traveled with Stella to the coldest part of the Icelands on their first expedition, and although Ethan and Stella had not gotten along very well to begin with (mostly because Ethan could be terribly obnoxious sometimes), they had become good friends during the course of their adventures.

It was the first time Stella had seen him not wearing his black Ocean Squid Explorers' Club robe, but he was dressed no less formally in a rather somber-looking slacks, suit jacket, and tie ensemble. His white-blond hair was brushed carefully back from his pale, pointed face, as immaculate as ever.

"Goodness, you look like you're on your way to the undertaker's," said Stella the moment she saw him.

Ethan looked her up and down and said, "Well, you look like you're about to be crowned at a prom." He raised an eyebrow. "I've never seen you look like a girl before. How on earth do you manage with all those petticoats?"

During their expedition Stella had dressed the same as the boys, in pants, cloak, and snow boots, but now she wore a blue dress with sparkly unicorn-shaped buttons. Her long white hair was tied back in a high ponytail and decorated with matching unicorn hair clips. The dress did have quite a few layers of petticoats because Stella enjoyed the rustling sound they made when she moved, as well as the way they puffed out around her when she spun in a circle.

"You can do absolutely anything in petticoats that you can do in pants," she said firmly.

"I don't see how," Ethan replied dubiously, straightening his already perfectly straight tie. "Must be a terrible nuisance."

"No more so than a mustache," Stella shot back.

"I haven't got a mustache," Ethan replied. "Besides, it's the Polar Bear Explorers' Club who are obsessed with mustaches."

"Oh, let's not start squabbling about mustaches and petticoats the second you arrive. Come on, I want to introduce you to Gruff."

They found the polar bear in the smoking room, lying flat on his back in contented bliss in front of the fire.

"Good God, he's enormous!" Ethan exclaimed the moment he saw him.

Stella was used to Gruff's size and tended to forget about how huge he seemed to people who weren't accustomed to having a polar bear in the house. But looking at him now, she felt a big swell of pride over her pet and grabbed Ethan's arm to tug him over to the bear.

"For an animal that's supposed to live in the snow, he really likes fires," Stella said.

The bear opened one eye to peer up at her when she stopped beside him, but he didn't look like he planned on moving anytime soon.

"You big lazy lump." Stella poked him with her toe. "Get up and say hello."

"That's okay," Ethan said. Stella noticed that he was hanging back a little. "He can say hello from there. I have a history of being bitten by things, remember?"

It was an unfortunate fact that during the course of their last expedition, Ethan had indeed been bitten by a frosty, a cabbage, and a rather irritated goose named Dora.

"Pecked, too," Ethan said, clearly thinking of Dora. "If the geese, cabbages, and frosties are anything to go by, it can only be a matter of time before I'm seriously mauled by something again."

"Don't be silly," Stella replied. "Gruff has never bitten anyone in his life. He would never dream of mauling you." She went over to Ethan, grabbed a handful of fish biscuits from her dress pocket, and thrust them into his hands. "Here," she said. "These are his favorite."

"Oh." Ethan looked appalled. "Oh no, please take them back."

He tried to shove them toward Stella, but it was too late. Gruff had already rolled his big body over with a *thump*, and he was now standing up and hurrying eagerly toward Ethan. The magician froze as the polar bear pushed its snout into his cupped hands and happily crunched up all the fish biscuits with a lot of grunting and snuffling. Once he'd finished, Gruff gave Ethan a big wet lick on the cheek, and then, suddenly, his nose twitched.

"Oh dear," Stella said. "Ethan, you should stand back before—"

But that was as far as she got before Gruff let out a gigantic sneeze that absolutely covered Ethan in bear slobber liberally dotted with biscuit crumbs. It was on his shirt and dripping down his face, and there was even a little bit of it caught in Ethan's hair, causing it to stick out at the side.

Gruff snorted, turned away, and lumbered back to his spot by the fire. Even though the bear and biscuits had gone, Ethan remained rigid, his hands stuck out in front of him.

Stella couldn't help noticing that quite a few strings of drool hung down from his fingers too.

"Gruff isn't the tidiest eater," she offered. "Sometimes he sneezes after having his biscuits. Sorry."

"Stella," Ethan said through gritted teeth, "I am having the worst time of my life right now."

"Oh, you can be so boring sometimes," Stella said with a sigh. "If Shay were here he would absolutely love Gruff."

Stella had met Shay, her wolf whisperer friend, on the expedition too, and he had been very impressed when she'd told him she had a polar bear as a pet.

"I am not Shay Silverton Kipling," Ethan said in his haughtiest voice. "Magicians do not mess around in kennels with wolves, and we do not enjoy being covered in slimy drool. Please show me to the nearest washroom at once."

Stella sighed again but took Ethan to the bathroom, and

after much fussing and splashing around he came out looking perfectly neat and tidy once again.

"So, why has your father come to visit Felix?" Stella asked as they made their way to the kitchens.

Ethan shrugged. "I was hoping you might know. You don't think they're planning an expedition without us, do you? I caught Father studying a map of the Lost City of Muja-Muja the other day."

"I don't think so," Stella replied. "Felix is too concerned with the witch to be planning expeditions right now."

She proceeded to tell Ethan about the bone-eating vulture attack and the witch on Witch Mountain.

Ethan frowned. "Yes, Felix sent word about the vulture before we arrived. We saw it circling the house when we got here, but it didn't come after us."

"Felix thinks it wants me," Stella said glumly. "To carry off back to the witch. That's why I'm not allowed to go outside."

"This is bad," Ethan said. "Bone-eating vultures are extremely dangerous. Father says the only way to control one if you're not a witch is to fasten a magical cuff around its leg. Then it will do everything you tell it to."

"But that sounds perfect!" Stella said. "We just have to find one of these magical cuffs and the vulture problem is solved."

"Father had one once; I remember him showing it to me.

But it wouldn't really solve the problem, would it? The witch could just send another vulture, or come after you herself. And the difficult bit would be actually getting the cuff on the vulture in the first place. Father says only an absolute madman would even think of attempting it. You're likely to get your face ripped off in the process. Those talons are sharp."

Stella remembered Felix's bloodstained clothes and shuddered. He was fully recovered now, but she knew well enough how dangerous the bone-eating vulture was.

She sighed. "So, I'm doomed, then," she said.

"We'll think of something," Ethan replied. "You can't stay cooped up in here for the rest of your life, can you? It would be awful if you couldn't go on the next expedition with us."

Stella gave him a smile, but before she could say anything, they both clearly heard the silvery jingle of sleigh bells.

"Are you expecting visitors?" Ethan asked.

Stella shook her head. "I don't think so."

They walked a little farther down the corridor to the nearest window and peered out. A magnificent sleigh had stopped beside the front entrance, and they could see the Polar Bear Explorers' Club crest stamped on the side. Four beautiful zebra unicorns, with bells on their harnesses, stood before it, tossing their heads and snorting in the frosty air.

"There's only one person who has a sleigh like that," Ethan said.

And, sure enough, a moment later Algernon Augustus Fogg, the president of the Polar Bear Explorers' Club himself, stepped down from the sleigh, assisted by his liveried chauffeur. Stella had met him when she took the explorers' pledge at the club and was initiated as a junior member. He looked just as she remembered: plump, portly, and sporting an impressively whiskery mustache that still made her think of walruses. As they watched, Felix appeared on the steps to welcome his guest and usher him into the house. Stella noticed that the president kept glancing fearfully up at the sky, so she guessed that Felix had warned him about the giant vulture.

Her heart sank. "Perhaps they *are* planning an expedition to the Lost City of Muja-Muja," she said, though she couldn't believe Felix would really go off and leave her now. But why else would the president be here?

It wasn't unusual for the president to be invited to dine at the private homes of members, although he had never been to Stella's house before. She knew that the dinners were usually grand affairs, but Felix said the real purpose was always to butter up the president whenever an explorer wanted something from the club. What could Felix want?

"I have no idea," Ethan said when Stella voiced the question. "Perhaps we'll find out what's going on at dinner."

CHAPTER FOUR

THE DINNER TOOK PLACE in the grand dining room that Felix used only on special occasions. A long table took up most of the space, and a chandelier sparkled from the high vaulted ceiling. The sun was low in the sky, and light poured through the vast stained-glass window, which filled almost an entire wall. It depicted a glorious map of the known world, the various lands colored in jewel-bright glass. Monstrous whales and sea monsters joined the sailing ships on the sparkling blue seas, while hot-air balloons, airships, and dirigibles adorned the corners.

Stella had always adored maps and globes and compasses—pretty much anything to do with navigating, really—and had spent hours staring up at this window when she was little. Sometimes Felix would join her and point out the different lands he had been to, telling her about the adventures he had had there.

Stella had always rather thought that he'd made some of it up (or at least embellished it) in order to entertain her—like when he said he'd had a stint as a boxing champion in the Mysterious Salt Lands in his youth. During the course of the last expedition, though, she'd learned that Felix could, in fact, box, and now she glanced at the window and wondered what else might have been true. Perhaps Felix really had accomplished the tricky skill of eagle taming in the Stone Mountains and mastered the art of ice-cream making while apprenticed with a famous ice-cream family in the Marzipan Islands.

Stella was pleased to see that Ethan looked quite impressed by the window, even if he had been inexplicably unimpressed with Gruff and even less impressed with Buster, who'd bitten him—rather hard—on the finger the moment he was introduced. Stella therefore kept a tight grip on the tiny dinosaur when she presented him to the president of the Polar Bear Explorers' Club.

"This is Buster," she said proudly. "He's the naughtiest pygmy dinosaur in the orangery."

"Great Scott, how extraordinary!" the president exclaimed, leaning forward for a closer look.

Stella was pleased that the president seemed impressed by her pet, although she was a little confused by the way he looked at her. When they had met at the club before the last expedition, the president had been reluctant to initiate a girl into the membership, but he had not seemed to think very much of Stella apart from that. And after the expedition he'd been too excited and distracted by all of the discoveries to pay her much notice, beyond congratulating her on the discovery of the mustache spoon. Now, though, he looked at her with an expression that was almost . . . well . . . almost fearful. She did hope he wasn't going to make a big fuss about the whole ice princess thing.

"Dinner is served," Mrs. Sap announced, and they all took their seats at the huge table.

The president sat at the head, as was his right, and the others—Stella, Ethan, Felix, and Zachary Vincent Rook— took their places on either side. Stella put Buster on her lap so that he wouldn't run around under the table irritating everyone. She couldn't help noticing that there seemed to be quite a strained atmosphere between the adults. Felix was quiet and withdrawn, not at all his usual cheerful self, and Zachary Vincent Rook seemed distracted, cold, and superior (though that was nothing out of the ordinary). President Fogg looked like he'd rather be anywhere else.

As the main course was served, Stella caught Ethan's eye across the table and raised her eyebrow. The magician shrugged back. Then he put down his fork, cleared his throat, and said abruptly, "Have we got the wrong end of the stick, Father, or are you planning an expedition to the Lost City of Muja-Muja and completely failing to include us?"

Zachary put down his fork with a clatter. "I'll have none of your cheek, Ethan!" he said in a sharp voice.

The light in the room flickered into shadow suddenly, and Stella frowned and glanced toward the window.

"There is no expedition being planned," Felix said. "For the simple reason that we have been denied permission to mount one."

"Witch Mountain is not a suitable place for exploration," President Fogg said, scowling at Felix. "Besides which, it has already been discovered and put on the map."

"But no one has ever explored it properly, have they?" Stella asked.

"That's because it's terribly dangerous, girl!" President Fogg replied. "Only witch hunters dare venture there, and they bring back the most terrible reports. Full of murderous witches and bone-eating vultures and argumentative mushrooms. No person in their right mind would want to explore such a place. When Captain Archibald Primrose Perkins first discovered the mountain, every single one of his team met with a sticky end before they could reach the summit. It was only a lone jungle fairy who returned to tell the tale, as I understand."

"Well, the last expedition to the Icelands was pretty dangerous too," Ethan pointed out. "What with the rampaging yetis and carnivorous cabbages and frostbiting—"

"I'm sorry, but it's out of the question," the president snapped.

The room briefly flickered into shadow once again, too quickly for it to be a cloud passing the window. Stella couldn't help fearing that it was the vulture swooping overhead, hoping that she would be unwise enough to stick her head out of the window to be bitten off.

"My daughter can hardly stay a prisoner in this house for the rest of her life, sir," Felix said, interrupting her thoughts. "Something must be done."

"But be reasonable, man," the president insisted. "No one comes back from Witch Mountain alive. No one except witch hunters!"

"Since its discovery, no explorers have been to Witch Mountain," Felix pointed out. "And if they do not venture there, then they cannot come back alive, dead, or anything in between."

The door opened just then, and Mrs. Sap arrived, tottering under the weight of a massive pudding presented on a grand silver plate. Felix hurried to help her, and together they set it down in the middle of the table. Stella was delighted to see that Mrs. Sap had constructed a woolly mammoth entirely from chocolate, complete with a fudge tail and magnificent white chocolate tusks. Her mouth watered at the sight of it.

Buster also seemed quite interested and dragged himself up the tablecloth and onto the table before Stella could stop him. He didn't seem to quite realize that the mammoth was not a real creature, because he ran right up to it and started roaring ferociously.

"It will be frowned on, Pearl, frowned on most severely by the club if you organize an independent expedition," the president said, raising his voice to be heard above the roaring pygmy T. rex. "Besides, I'm sure you're overreacting. This brain-eating vulture will soon lose interest and fly off, and then everything can go back to normal."

"It's a bone-eating vulture," Stella felt obliged to say, because she couldn't bear it when people got animal facts wrong. "Perhaps you're thinking of the zombie vulture of Dry Gulch Valley," she added, so as not to seem rude. "They eat brains."

The president gave her another one of those odd looks, as if he wasn't quite sure what to say to her.

"The vulture will not simply fly away," Felix said. "It won't leave until it has what it came for."

Stella shuddered because she knew that Felix meant her.

"Are we going to eat this woolly mammoth cake, or is the dinosaur going to demolish it all by itself?" Ethan complained.

Buster was, indeed, busily taking a big bite out of the mammoth's leg, but no one else seemed particularly interested in dessert just then.

"Look here, Pearl, just because you once dabbled in a spot of wild-eagle taming in the Pebble Mountains, or wherever it was, doesn't mean that you're suddenly an expert on every large bird of prey in existence," President Fogg said. "The bird will lose interest and fly home, you mark my words. Birds don't have the brains to be determined; chances are you'll never see it again as long as you live."

Once again, the room suddenly went into shadow, only this time it was not there and gone in an instant. The gloom stretched on and on. Everyone else noticed it too and looked toward the window.

"Merciful heavens!" Felix gasped. "Everybody, duck!"

He spoke mere seconds before the beautiful stained-glass window shattered in an explosion of flying pieces as the bone-eating vulture burst through it in a shrieking tangle of feathers, talons, and claws.

CHAPTER FIVE

ENORMOUS DARK WINGS SPREAD in the now-open space where the window had once been. The bone-eating vulture was an appalling sight; it had cut itself when it smashed into the window, but it didn't seem bothered by the injuries. It opened its beak and gave another ear-splitting shriek before swooping into the room.

Zachary Vincent Rook and Ethan both began hurling magic spells at the vulture, Felix leapt to his feet, Buster charged down the length of the table roaring his tiny head off, Stella lunged after Buster, and the president of the Polar Bear Explorers' Club hid under the table.

The vulture must have had an anti-magic enchantment on it—just like the carnivorous cabbage plant Stella and her friends had faced in the last expedition—because the spells just bounced off it, seeming to have no effect at all.

The vulture headed straight for Stella, its tiny eyes fixed on her with a terrible focus. Buster now charged directly in front of her in an attempt to protect her from the huge monster. His roaring would, no doubt, have been extremely effective had he been a full-size T. rex but given that he was actually no larger than a kitten, it really wasn't achieving anything. And the fact that he had dark chocolate smeared all around his mouth ruined his attempts to be ferocious anyway.

Stella snatched up the tiny dinosaur in her hands just seconds before the vulture lunged, snapping its beak where the T. rex had been standing. She shielded Buster with her own body as she ran, but turned around in time to witness an astonishing sight.

While Ethan and Zachary continued to mess about with spells that were clearly doing no good, Felix leapt onto the table and ran down the length of it, china plates smashing under his boots as he headed straight toward the vulture. Stella watched in astonishment as he took a flying leap and landed squarely on the giant bird's back. The vulture screamed in protest, but Felix ignored it as he reached into his waistcoat pocket and drew out a shining silver cuff. In one quick movement, he reached down and fastened it firmly around the vulture's bony leg with a snap.

Stella knew at once that this must be the magical cuff Ethan had mentioned earlier—the one that would allow

you to control the vulture. She realized Zachary Vincent Rook must have brought it—that this was the reason for his visit. Relief washed over Stella, as she was sure that Felix was going to hop off the vulture's back at any moment and send the giant bird away.

But then Zachary Vincent Rook spoke from across the room. "Don't do it, Felix. I urge you."

Stella looked at Felix in alarm and saw that he was gazing straight at her, and she knew—she knew without him even saying anything. She remembered how Ethan had said that getting rid of the vulture wouldn't solve the problem of the witch, and then she thought of Felix arguing with the president about organizing an expedition to Witch Mountain, and she knew he was going to leave.

"Take me with you," she said, already starting forward.

But Felix was shaking his head. "Not this time, Stella," he said. "Be good and do as Mrs. Sap tells you. I'll be back before you know it."

And with that he wrapped his arms around the vulture's scrawny neck and leaned forward to whisper something in its ear. The giant bird turned awkwardly in the room, flapped up onto the windowsill, spread its wings, and took off into the sky.

"No!" Stella cried, dismayed.

Still clutching Buster, she ran to the window and scrambled over the sill, pieces of broken glass tearing at her dress. The snow compacted beneath her slippers when she leapt outside; the cold air soothed her skin and filled her lungs, and it was glorious to be out of the house for the first time in weeks. But Stella couldn't enjoy it because she was too busy searching for Felix in the sky. Suddenly, a tile fell from above and landed with a soft *flump* in the snow. Stella looked up and realized that the giant vulture was perched on the roof, waiting patiently as Felix retrieved a bag from one of the chimney pots. He must have hidden it there earlier. It probably had witch-hunting supplies in it. A great wave of anger surged through Stella, and she balled her hands up into fists.

"Felix!" she shouted. "Do not leave me here!"

"Don't worry, my dear one," he called back. "I traveled with a witch hunter in Cauldron Gorge for a time. She taught me all the tricks of the trade. I know what I'm doing."

And with that he hopped onto the vulture's back, and they took off into the sky, growing smaller and smaller, until Stella could no longer see them at all.

It took everyone some while to persuade the president of the Polar Bear Explorers' Club that the vulture had gone and it was safe to come out from beneath the table. When he finally emerged, he'd gone white to the lips, and his mustache was rather all over the place—the previously pointy tips bushing out quite alarmingly.

"It's an outrage!" he exclaimed. "I've never experienced such a dinner in all my life, never!"

"Felix didn't exactly invite the vulture," Stella pointed out.

"I will never dine here again," the president said, and Stella was pleased because that meant Gruff wouldn't have to be banished to the kitchens with Mrs. Sap. Indeed, if the president hadn't objected to the polar bear's presence in the first place, Gruff would have been in the dining room with them and probably would have seen the vulture off like last time. Stella couldn't help blaming the president, at least a little bit, for the fact that Felix had gone.

"Sir," she said, trying to make her voice grown-up and reasonable. "I would like to formally request that the Polar Bear Explorers' Club mount a rescue expedition for Felix."

"Request denied," the president snapped, brushing crumbs and bits of dust bunnies from his clothes. "If Pearl wants to tear off to Witch Mountain, that's his own affair. Anyone who goes after him will only perish as well. The Polar Bear Explorers' Club will have nothing to do with this madness."

"Well, can I have my tiara back, at least?" Stella asked.

She didn't know quite how she was going to do it yet, but she knew that one way or another she had to get herself to Witch Mountain to help Felix, and if she was going to face a dangerous witch, then she would rather have her magical tiara with her, even if it was risky for her to use it too much.

"The tiara is on display at the club," the president replied.

"The tiara is on loan to the club," Stella said. "It belongs to me, and I have every right to have it returned."

President Fogg heaved a great sigh. "Very well," he said. "You must contact the secretary, who will provide you with the necessary forms. Once they have been completed, stamped, and verified, the tiara will be released to you."

"And how long will that take?" Stella asked.

"About six weeks."

"That's too long," Stella said coldly. "You know that. I need it now."

"There are procedures to be followed, girl," the president said, not meeting her eye. "The Polar Bear Explorers' Club has rules and regulations for a reason."

Stella shook her head impatiently. She was getting nowhere, and they were wasting time. If nobody would help her, then she would just have to work it out by herself.

The president said he wasn't prepared to linger in a place where giant birds of prey were wont to come bursting through windows at any moment, and Stella was glad to see him go. Before he went, though, he slipped an envelope with a note attached to it onto the letter rack on Felix's desk. As his sleigh pulled away with a jingling of harness, Stella hurried into the study and picked up the note. It read: *For the attention of Mr. Felix Evelyn Pearl. Be warned and take heed, for the sake of your own safety.*

Stella wrinkled her nose. Be warned and take heed? That didn't sound very good. Perhaps it was some kind of warning about the witch? Thinking there might be some useful information in there, Stella picked up the envelope—which was fat with papers—and tipped its contents out onto the desk, only to gasp with dismay. The papers were not about witches; they were about snow queens.

There were profiles of snow queens going back more than a hundred years. Some had lived in the Icelands, while others dwelt in the snow deserts of the east or the snow canyons in the west. The profiles were pieced together from firsthand accounts, photographs snapped from afar, arrest warrants, and newspaper reports. But wherever and whenever they'd lived, there was one thing that the snow queens all seemed to have in common. They were cold, murderous, and wicked.

A letter from Wendell Winterton Smythe, the president of the Jungle Cat Explorers' Club, accompanied them. The paper was headed with elephants and parrots and smelled faintly of expedition-strength mosquito spray. Stella's heart seemed to turn to stone as she read it. It was an official complaint from the Jungle Cat Explorers' Club, in which the president went on at great length about what a travesty it was to have allowed an ice princess to become a junior member of an explorers' club, that it was an affront to all the other clubs, and dangerous to other explorers besides.

Stella wanted to deny it all, to insist that she would never do anything to hurt anyone, but then she remembered how she had almost let Ethan fall to his death during the last expedition after using the tiara had chilled her heart, and a creeping doubt settled around her.

She shuddered as she read about Queen Veronica, who'd frozen all the members of her household staff to make a statue garden; Queen Abigaila, who'd murdered her own husband with a poisoned apple; Queen Portia, who'd frozen an entire village in a vicious, unprovoked attack; and Queen Jessamine—Stella's own mother—who had tortured countless people with the red-hot iron slippers that forced the wearer to dance for her amusement.

The papers fell from Stella's trembling fingers. Hadn't there been any good snow queens? Surely they couldn't all have been villains—surely one of them, at some point, must have been nice, or at least not completely wicked? But then she thought of the enchanted castle that had been her parents' home, with its poisoned apples, deadly spinning wheels, and ghastly iron slippers; she remembered what the magic mirror had told her about how snow queens were supposed to have frozen hearts and that it would happen to her one day too. . . .

Stella shook her head and thrust all the papers into a drawer. She couldn't worry about this right now. She needed to work out how on earth she was going to go after Felix.

The door to the study opened just then and Ethan walked in, adjusting his collar with one hand and smoothing back his white-blond hair with the other.

"Father has left," the magician announced. "He has an engagement with another explorer, and it will take him at least a week to get to his home. He says to give you his regards, as well as his regrets that he allowed Felix to talk him into selling him the magic cuff." He sighed. "He says he never would have let him have it if he had known about the poisonous rabbits."

"What poisonous rabbits?" Stella demanded, rather afraid that the situation was about to get even worse.

Ethan rubbed the back of his neck. "There's been reports from some local trader that Jezzybella has been paying a pirate to bring them to the mountain for her. And apparently, if you so much as touch a poisonous rabbit, that's it." He snapped his fingers. "You've had it. I heard President Fogg tell Father before he left, but he says he never got the chance to tell Felix."

Stella stared at him, appalled. "But this is terrible!" she exclaimed. "Felix adores rabbits. He simply adores them. If any of these poisonous ones come hopping up to him, the first thing he'll do is get down on his knees and try to stroke it!"

Felix would be well aware that Jezzybella herself was

dangerous, of course, but no one expected a little fluffy bunny to be able to kill them, even on Witch Mountain.

"It's a rotten business," Ethan said. "Now, look, I convinced Father to let me stay to keep you company while Felix is away—"

Stella scowled. "I don't need you to keep me company because I'm not staying here! I'm going after Felix."

Ethan opened his mouth to reply, but Stella held up her hand. "It's no use trying to talk me out of it," she said. "That witch killed my parents. I won't sit back and do nothing while she kills Felix, too. I just won't. Besides, Felix doesn't know anything about the poisonous rabbits. And I'm sick of cowering indoors." She lifted her chin a little higher and said, "Ice princesses don't cower indoors, and explorers definitely don't cower indoors. I'm going to Witch Mountain to rescue Felix, and there's nothing you, or anyone else, can say or do to stop me."

Ethan raised an eyebrow. "Have you quite finished?" he asked with a sniff. "That was a completely unnecessary speech." He lifted his own chin and said, "Nobody lectures a magician about cowering indoors—not even an ice princess. Of course we're going after Felix, you ninny. But I could hardly say that to Father, could I? He wouldn't have let me stay then; I'd have been dragged off to this other explorer's house."

"Oh." Stella blinked, momentarily taken aback. Then

she beamed at the magician. "Oh good. It'll be much easier with help."

"Of course it will," Ethan said. "You should send word to the others, too. They came in useful last time, even if the small one is a bit of an oddball."

"Shay and Beanie, you mean?" Stella asked. "Good idea. Yes."

A plan started to formulate in her mind. "I'll telegraph them to meet us at the Polar Bear Explorers' Club as soon as they can get there."

"The club?" Ethan said, surprised. "But the president has refused to help."

"Yes, he has, but I'm still going there to get my tiara. We also need to find a map of Witch Mountain. The map room must have one, even if it's incomplete."

"So you want to break into the Polar Bear Explorers' Club and steal their maps and magic tiara?" Ethan asked, raising an eyebrow.

"It's my tiara, which means I have every right to take it, and I'm only going to steal one map," Stella replied. "It'll be okay. We'll figure it out as we go."

Ethan sighed. "Oh, perfect—a figure-it-out-as-we-go kind of plan. My favorite. Nothing ever goes wrong with those."

CHAPTER SIX

As **IT WAS LATE** already, Stella and Ethan decided to sleep at the house and then leave for the Polar Bear Explorers' Club first thing in the morning.

Stella had sent telegrams to Shay and Beanie and then taken out her explorer's bag, which had the club's polar bear motif stamped on it, and a large backpack and packed everything that might come in handy for breaking into the club and then setting off on a dangerous and unauthorized expedition to Witch Mountain.

She kissed Gruff, who was snoozing by the fire in her bedroom, and was just about to go to bed when she heard a soft *tap-tap* at her window. She turned to see a fairy standing hesitantly on the ledge. Stella was surprised because fairies were famously reclusive creatures and usually very nervous around humans. It was only the very rare person—

like Felix—with whom they would have a conversation.

Stella went to the window and opened it slowly, so as not to startle the fairy, and watched, entranced, as she tiptoed in over the threshold. Fairies always had the prettiest clothes, and this one was no exception. Her gown was a deep cobalt blue, puffed up over layers and layers of lace petticoats. The hem and sleeves sparkled like starlight, and dozens of tiny blue flowers were woven into her coal-black hair. She had a pretty, acorn-colored face; small, pointed ears; and bright green eyes. Her wings, though, were the most dazzling thing about her. Like butterfly wings, they were patterned in green and black, with midnight-blue tips.

Stella could tell she was a messenger fairy because of the mailbag hanging from her shoulder and the peaked messenger cap balanced on her dark hair. Felix had told her that any letter written by a messenger fairy could be read only by the person it was addressed to. If anyone else were to see the letter, it wouldn't even look like a letter but would take the shape of a button, a glass bead, an old penny, or some other innocuous object that might easily have been found rolling around in a pocket.

"Hello," Stella whispered as the fairy set her bag down on the windowsill.

The fairy smiled, but she didn't say anything as she took some small sheets of paper from her bag, along with a rather handsome feathered quill. She sat herself down on the window ledge (Stella noticed that her boots had glittery golden wings at the ankles), picked up the quill, hovered it over the top of the paper, and then looked at Stella expectantly.

"Oh," she breathed. "Are you offering to take a message for me?"

The fairy nodded. Perhaps the fairies had seen Felix take off on the bone-eating vulture and wanted to help Stella rescue him.

"Could I send two messages?" Stella asked eagerly. These messages would arrive faster than any telegram!

Again the fairy nodded, so Stella proceeded to dictate a letter to both Shay and Beanie explaining what had happened, telling them about the poisonous rabbits, and asking them to meet her at the Polar Bear Explorers' Club as soon as they could. She thought briefly of trying to send a message to Felix to warn him about the rabbits, but she knew that the fairy would never be able to catch up with a giant vulture.

Once the letters were finished, the fairy folded them neatly, slipped them into tiny envelopes, and sealed them with a golden wax seal, which she stamped with a messenger stamp consisting of a pair of fairy wings. She wrote Shay's name on one, Beanie's on the other, and then, with a last wave at Stella, she fluttered out into the night and was gone, leaving only a smattering of sparkling fairy dust on the windowsill behind her.

The next morning, Stella slipped on her warmest dove-gray traveling dress and went downstairs to confront Mrs. Sap. The housekeeper tried to convince Stella and Ethan to stay at home rather than going off after Felix, but once she saw it was useless she went and made them a packed lunch to take on the train instead.

The junior explorers put on their cloaks—pale blue with a polar bear symbol embroidered on the front for Stella and black with a squid symbol for Ethan. Then Mr. Pash, the head groom, took them in the sleigh to catch the train. From the station they made their way to the harbor, where they were just in time to buy passage on the last ship of the day. They docked in Coldgate early the next morning. From there they had to make their way to the Polar Bear Explorers' Club on foot.

At last they arrived at the white gates with their gold-tipped spikes and majestic marble polar bear statues on each pillar. When Stella had been there with Felix, the gates had opened for them automatically, but this time they remained very firmly closed.

"Now what?" Ethan asked. "How do we get inside?"

Stella pushed hopefully at the gate, but of course, it was locked. She looked around until she located a golden button attached to some kind of intercom. She knew that Felix had visited the club many times: to consult the maps, to view the latest curiosities on display, or to exchange ideas with other explorers. Perhaps it was simply a question of asking to be admitted. She pressed the golden button, which buzzed loudly, and a moment later a voice came through the grate. "This is the Polar Bear Explorers' Club. How may I help you?"

"I'm Stella Starflake Pearl," Stella said. "I'm a junior member of the club, and I'd like to come in to consult the—"

"No visitors today," the voice interrupted. "The club is closed."

"Closed?" Stella had never heard of such a thing. "But why?"

"The president of the Jungle Cat Explorers' Club is here on important business," the voice informed her. "Come back next week."

And then the line went dead.

"Well," Ethan said, looking affronted. "No one would ever speak to a member of the Ocean Squid Explorers' Club like that. Never. By the way, did you know there's something wriggling around in your backpack?"

Frowning, Stella swung the pack off her back, put it on the floor, and unzipped it. Buster immediately poked his head out and looked back and forth between them, blinking in the sunlight.

Ethan groaned. "Why on earth did you bring your pet dinosaur with you?"

"I didn't mean to," Stella replied. "He must have climbed into my bag when I wasn't looking."

The T. rex had clearly had enough of being cooped up in a backpack because he squirmed his way out and landed in the snow with a *flump*. Stella reached out to grab him, but sensing that he was about to be imprisoned again, the dinosaur charged off—straight through the bars of the gate and into the grounds of the Polar Bear Explorers' Club.

"Oh no!" Stella cried. "Buster, come back!"

But the tiny dinosaur stubbornly ignored her as it ran into the ice garden, roaring excitedly, leaving tiny T. rex footprints in the snow, and was promptly lost from sight.

"Oh, that's just great!" Ethan complained. "Now we've got an escaped dinosaur to contend with on top of every-thing else."

"Maybe I should press the buzzer again and explain

that we need to come in to get Buster?" Stella suggested, already reaching for the button.

"I wouldn't," Ethan said, grabbing her hand seconds before she could press the button. "Any animals found on club property legally belong to the club. My brother had a fluffy wobbling penguin—"

"What's a fluffy wobbling penguin?" Stella asked eagerly.

"Exactly what it sounds like. Anyway, it wandered off in the Ocean Squid Explorers' Club once and ended up getting stuffed and put on display with the other animals."

Stella's hands flew to her mouth, and she stared at Ethan in dismay. "That's terrible! The Polar Bear Explorers' Club would never be so barbaric."

"Well, if you're completely sure of that, then why don't you go ahead and press the buzzer?" Ethan replied.

But Stella wasn't completely sure. After all, the club could be a bit barbaric sometimes. They'd had a display of pinned fairies in the front entrance before Felix had campaigned for their removal, they still had skinned polar bear rugs, and they had wanted to stuff Dora when Stella had brought her back from the Icelands.

"All right," Stella said. "We'll just have to think of another way to get inside."

CHAPTER SEVEN

ALMOST AN HOUR LATER Stella and Ethan finally reached the back of the Polar Bear Explorers' Club. The property was extremely big, and it had taken them quite some time to walk around the marble wall.

There they found a sleigh bearing the handyman coat of arms. Two men with gruff voices and beards had removed a grate from the floor and were standing on ladders inside, tinkering with something while complaining loudly about explorers.

". . . can always guarantee you'll get an emergency call from the explorers' club on what's supposed to be your day off," one of them was grumbling.

Stella and Ethan walked past them to the back gates, which were rather less impressive than the front ones, although still firmly locked. When they looked through the bars, they immediately saw the huge dirigible parked on the snow, tethered by several anchors to stop it from floating away.

"That must belong to the president of the Jungle Cat Explorers' Club," Ethan muttered.

Stella saw at once that he was right. The large gasbag was painted with images of green jungle foliage, through which you could glimpse the occasional tiger, alligator, or hippopotamus. The wooden passenger gondola underneath was also carved with images of snarling piranhas, jungle riverboats dodging ferocious-looking hippopotamuses, and various ruthless Jinnish gods baring their teeth. A magnificent jungle parrot served as a sort of figurehead at the prow, wings spread wide and head held high.

Ethan snorted. "All this adventurous, interesting stuff, but everyone knows their lot just sit around having expedition picnics all day."

"What is it this time, anyway?" the second handyman suddenly said behind them. "Penguin feathers blocking up the pipes again?"

"No. Get this—they said some tiny dinosaur got loose in the club and bit a hole in one of the pipes. Caused all kinds of havoc with the plumbing."

Stella gasped, and the two junior explorers spun around from the fence.

"Excuse me," Stella said, stepping toward the grate.

The two men looked up at her, taking in her blue explorers' club cloak. "Yes, miss?"

"I'm afraid that dinosaur is mine," she said. "He ran away from me earlier, and he just loves biting things, including pipes. As soon as you fix this problem, he'll only cause another one."

Both men sighed heavily. "We'll be here all day and night if that happens. And I promised the missus that we'd have a romantic dinner at the Ice Yeti tonight," he said. "I'll be in the dog house for sure."

"Does this pipe have access to the club?" Stella asked, pointing.

"Sure does," one of the men said. "Comes right up in the saltwater baths."

"You'd better let us through, then," Stella said. "Buster must be down there somewhere, and perhaps I can find him before he does any more damage."

"Do you think you could?" the man said eagerly.

"Well, it's worth a shot, isn't it?" Stella said. "Especially if it means you'll make your dinner date at the Ice Yeti."

The man looked a little unsure and said, "It's pretty wet down there. You wouldn't want to ruin your dress."

"Oh, I have plenty of spare clothes," Stella replied. Explorers could always be counted upon to be prepared, after all.

"Just how smelly and dirty is it down there?" Ethan

asked, peering at the grate dubiously. "I can't stand places that are smelly and dirty."

Stella elbowed him hard in the ribs, and he yelped in protest. "My dad had lunch at the Ice Yeti last time he was in Coldgate," she said a little desperately. "He told me that there are magic puddings in the shape of ice yetis that run around the table and sing you a song. And they wear little bow ties."

"Well, that settles it," the first man said, slapping his leg. "My wife would absolutely love that." He climbed out of the grate, closely followed by his partner. "You go ahead, miss. Anything's worth a try."

"I'll catch him," Stella promised. "Don't you worry."

And with that she ushered Ethan down the ladder before he could start complaining.

It was, unfortunately, very smelly inside the pipe, and Stella had to keep the hem of her gray dress lifted high to prevent it from trailing in the dirty water that rushed around at their feet. Ethan, of course, complained loudly and obnoxiously the entire time, but Stella had become used to mentally blocking out his whining during the last expedition and hardly even noticed. Instead, she concentrated on navigating the tunnel, while also keeping an eye out for Buster.

Eventually the pipe reached a dead end with a ladder attached to the wall. They climbed up, removed the grate at the top, and came right out into a drained pool in the club's saltwater baths. Another huge pool steamed beneath a glass-domed high ceiling; white marble pillars stretched down to the floor, and ornate wall tiles were decorated with polar bears and the club's official crest. Dozens of lit candles flickered away in glass jars and polar bear–shaped candleholders.

Since they'd been told that the club was closed to visitors, Stella had expected the room to be empty, but in fact, there were two explorers there, both wearing swimming trunks and sporting sideburns that had puffed up quite alarmingly in the steamy heat. Fortunately, they were too preoccupied with the gaggle of penguins stubbornly refusing to be budged from the Jacuzzi to pay much attention to Stella and Ethan.

"I can't believe someone let the penguins in here again!" one of them was complaining.

"It's an outrage," the other agreed. "You come in for a nice relaxing soak, and instead you're met with a highly stressful penguin situation. It's a wonder we're not all suffering from nervous breakdowns."

He poked at one of the penguins with a lifesaver hook he'd removed from the wall, but the penguin just honked at him indignantly and refused to budge.

"Not like that!" the second explorer said, snatching the stick from his colleague. "You have to poke them like this."

"No, no, no, that's all wrong, Maximillian," the other explorer complained. "Penguin poking requires more finesse than that. Look, here, allow me to demonstrate."

Ethan and Stella tiptoed past the squabbling pair and out into the corridor undetected.

"That's weird," Ethan said. "I thought the club was supposed to be closed."

Stella shook her head. "Let's just head for the map room. And keep an eye out for Buster."

As they made their way down the wide corridor, it became apparent that the club definitely wasn't closed. In the billiards room, several explorers were drinking brandy, smoking cigars, and arguing about the best way to escape a rampaging yeti. The murmur of voices clearly came from other rooms too, and Stella and Ethan had to scoot past doorways rather quickly to avoid being seen.

Fortunately, they soon found themselves at the entrance to the map room and quickly ducked inside. The huge place was full of dark wood, grand leather-inlaid desks, and green reading lamps. It reminded Stella of a library, even down to its papery smell. Massive globes stood between the tables, and ancient maps and charts lined the walls in impressive frames.

There were a couple of explorers there bickering over a place called Frogfoot Island.

"I tell you, it isn't there, Horatio," one of the men said.

"And I tell you that's balderdash! I saw it myself. I even set foot on it!"

"Well, I went to the exact coordinates and there was nothing there but ocean."

"That simply isn't possible!"

Stella and Ethan quietly crept past the quarreling pair. On any other occasion, Stella would have loved to explore the room properly, poring over the maps and sniffing the charts and spinning around in one of the spinning chairs, but there was no time for that today. She and Ethan lingered long enough only to locate the map to Witch Mountain. The maps were neatly stored on wooden shelves, in alphabetical order, so it didn't take long to find the correct one, rolled up in its own leather map tube. Stella slung this over her shoulder before they headed back out in search of the trophy room.

Unfortunately, neither of the junior explorers had been to the club enough times to get their bearings yet, and they weren't too sure where the trophy room that held Stella's tiara was. In their attempt to locate it, they eventually found themselves in the corridor outside President Fogg's office.

The sensible thing would have been to hurry away from there at once—since being spotted by President Fogg was really the last thing they needed—but as they crept past Stella clearly heard someone inside say her name. Ethan heard it too, and they both lingered to press their ears up against the door.

". . . if the girl's dinosaur is here, then surely she must be too," a male voice was saying. "The doorman said she tried to get into the club more than an hour ago."

"And was denied access, Wendell," President Fogg replied.

"Wendell! That's the name of the Jungle Cat president," Stella whispered to Ethan, remembering the letter she'd seen. "He's made an official complaint about me being a member of the club."

Ethan gave her a worried look. "We should press on," he said. "It sounds like they're already suspicious. President Fogg must have remembered Buster and put two and two together."

Stella nodded glumly. She needed to find her dinosaur before they could leave, and he could be causing havoc just about anywhere. She and Ethan hurried down the corridor, turned the corner, and immediately found themselves face-to-face with an enormous wolf. Far bigger than any ordinary creature, she had black fur and intelligent silver eyes that regarded them with obvious recognition.

"Koa!" Ethan and Stella both exclaimed.

Stella was so pleased to see the wolf that she would've loved to throw her arms around her neck, but Koa was a shadow wolf and therefore didn't have any physical substance.

"If she's here, then Shay must be here somewhere too,"

Ethan said. All whisperers had their own shadow animal, and Koa was never too far from Shay.

"Can you take us to him?" Stella asked the shadow wolf eagerly.

Koa immediately turned and padded off down the corridor, the two junior explorers close at her heels. She quickly led them to the trophy room, which was filled to bursting with glass cabinets displaying the many wonders and curiosities that the explorers had brought back from their adventures. A magnificent stuffed snow shark hung suspended above them from the ceiling, and all manner of objects filled the cabinets, from eternal snowballs to fossilized mammoth tusks to yeti teeth.

Stella didn't have much time to study the cabinets, though, because there in the center of the room, peering into a glass case, were their explorer friends Shay Silverton Kipling and Benjamin Sampson Smith (or Beanie to his friends—due to his great love of jelly beans).

"It's locked tight," Beanie was saying, scrutinizing the case. Beanie had a tendency to get attached to comfortable old things, and today he was wearing a knitted sweater that Stella recognized as one of his mother's creations, with a narwhal—Beanie's favorite animal—on the front. His uncle must have managed to bribe him with jelly beans to persuade him to get his hair cut because it was a little shorter than the last time Stella had seen him. This meant you could clearly see that Beanie's ears were slightly pointed at the tips. Beanie was part elf, as shown by his slender build and pointed ears.

"I wonder where they keep the keys for these things," Shay replied. The wolf whisperer wore his blue explorers' club cloak but had rolled up the sleeves, exposing the chocolate-colored leather bracelets adorned with silver wolf beads on one wrist.

Stella was delighted to see them both and ran over, Ethan and Koa close behind her. She threw her arms around Shay in a hug and then waved at Beanie because, although she would have loved to hug him, too, he wasn't a fan of physical contact.

"I'm so glad you're here," Stella said. "Thank you for coming!"

"We came as soon as we got your message," Shay told her.

"Here, I think this is yours," Beanie said.

Stella realized that Beanie was holding a struggling, squirming T. rex in his hand. "Oh, you found him!" she exclaimed.

"He was in the library," Beanie offered. "Ripping up Captain Filibuster's leather-bound travel almanacs. Luckily there were only two adult explorers in there and they were both asleep in their armchairs."

"Never run off like that again, you naughty beast," Stella scolded the dinosaur. "You caused me a huge amount of worry, you know."

The T. rex responded by rubbing his scaly head affectionately against her hand. Stella gave him a kiss and figured she couldn't really be too angry with him, since his biting of the pipes had allowed them to gain access to the club through the tunnels.

"Stella, did you know that they stuffed Pepe?" Beanie said indignantly, pointing to a nearby case.

Stella peered in and saw that the carnivorous cabbage that had attacked them on their last expedition had indeed been stuffed and put on display, its mouth open wide to reveal its hideous long teeth.

She couldn't help a shudder. "Well, at least it won't be biting anyone anymore," she said.

"It's not right," Beanie said. "I was fond of that cabbage. You wouldn't like it if they'd stuffed Dora, would you?"

Stella sighed. "It's hardly the same thing, Beanie. Look, now that we're all here, there's no time to lose. We've just got to snatch this tiara and then we'll be on our way."

"The case is locked," Shay said. "And we have no idea where they keep the keys."

"Ouch!" Stella exclaimed. Buster was squirming about and digging his claws into her hand. "Stop being such a fidget," she told him as she set him down on the glass case, where he proceeded to walk up and down looking grand and important.

"We can't mess around looking for keys," Stella said.

"Felix has probably arrived at Witch Mountain by now. We need to go after him, and quickly."

"Sir Rex Tiddlywinks Smith," Beanie said at once. "Murdered by black magic at Witch Mountain in—"

"I don't want any murderous witch facts!" Stella said, holding up her hand to stop him. "Please. Not until we've rescued Felix."

Unfortunately, Beanie had an excellent memory for the various ways that explorers had met sticky ends over the years and didn't always appreciate that there was a time and a place for sharing such information.

"Was his name really Rex Tiddlywinks Smith?" Ethan asked. "I bet he was a Jungle Cat explorer, wasn't he?"

"How did you know?" Beanie asked.

"They're buffoons," Ethan said. "Only a Jungle Cat explorer would have such a ridiculous name."

"Never mind that, now," Stella said. "We have to work out how we're going to get this out."

She pointed at the tiara, and everyone looked at it, including Buster. It sat sparkling in the glass case on a white velvet cushion decorated with purple woolly mammoths. Buster immediately began roaring at them through the case, and Stella had to tap him on the head to get him to stop.

"Shush, you," she said. "We're trying to think here."

The tiara itself was an incredibly beautiful object, sparkling with ice-white gems and frosted diamonds—although

Stella couldn't help finding its beauty slightly marred by the fact that it would freeze her heart if she used its magic too much.

"Dad says that all the locked cases in the trophy room are alarmed," Shay said. "And we can't risk setting it off or we'll never make it out of the club." He glanced at Stella. "I know it's frustrating, Sparky, but we're just going to have to find the key. We can't rescue Felix if we're locked up."

Stella sighed. He was right—setting off alarms and having guards and explorers bearing down on them was the last thing they needed.

"Okay," she said. "I think we should start with the secretary's office. That seems like the kind of place where they might keep—"

She didn't get any further, however, because Buster chose that exact moment to roar at the mammoths once again before suddenly lunging down toward the glass case. His teeth went straight through the glass, and dozens of cracks instantly spiderwebbed out from the points where his teeth made contact.

"Oh no." Stella gasped, plucking the dinosaur up in her hand.

But the damage was already done. The next second the entire case collapsed in on itself, shattering into a multitude of broken pieces.

The loud wail of an alarm instantly filled the room.

CHAPTER EIGHT

FOR A MOMENT THE junior explorers just stared at one another in dismay. Then Shay cried, "Stella, the door!"

They all turned to look and saw that an iron gate was rapidly coming down from the ceiling. As soon as it made it to the floor, it would cut off their only means of escape and they would be trapped in the room.

Stella snatched up the tiara in her free hand, thrust it onto her head, and shot a blast of ice magic at the gate, freezing it solid before it could come all the way down. Just like before, she felt an icy chill run down her back and couldn't help shivering.

"Guards will probably be here any minute!" She gasped. "We're going to have to be quick!"

There was just about enough room for them to roll under the gate and out into the corridor—only to find two large guards running straight toward them.

"Drat!" Stella exclaimed. She hadn't expected the Polar Bear Explorers' Club to be quite so efficient. She'd hoped for foolish, bumbling guards who were snoozing on the job somewhere comfortable, but these two looked alert, and cross, and ready to do damage with the heavy truncheons they were carrying.

"Stay right where you are!" one of them yelled.

Naturally, the junior explorers did no such thing; instead they turned and fled down the corridor as fast as they could. Stella had no idea where she was going—she just ran blindly, the guards close behind them, until they came to a door. Shay threw it open, and they all tumbled out into the snow, blinking in the sudden bright sunlight.

"They're going to catch us!" Ethan gasped.

Stella feared he was right. The guards were practically upon them; they didn't have enough of a head start. Even if they made it out of the club grounds, what then? They could hardly run all the way through Coldgate without getting caught. Their attempt to rescue Felix would be over before it had even begun. Stella could feel her heart beating so hard in her chest it was almost physically painful. Then her eyes landed on the massive dirigible they had spied from outside the gates, and a plan formed perfectly in her mind.

"The dirigible!" she cried. "It's our only chance!"

She set off at a run toward it, the others close behind her.

"You want to steal the dirigible belonging to the president of the Jungle Cat Explorers' Club?" Ethan gasped. "You've got to be kidding!'"

"Have you got a better idea?" she replied.

The explorers raced across the snow and reached the dirigible at the same moment that the guards caught up with them. One grabbed the back of Shay's cloak and the other grabbed Beanie. Stella's heart sank.

"Just go!" Shay yelled at her.

But then, all of a sudden, Koa appeared, charging toward the guards, hackles raised and snarling ferociously. The two men cried out in alarm, let go of the junior explorers, and fell back. Making the most of the momentary advantage, Shay and Beanie ran forward, and the four explorers shot up the ladder and tumbled into the dirigible.

"The ropes!" Stella cried. "We've got to release the anchors!"

The explorers raced toward each of the four ropes that held the dirigible down. They unhooked them and let them fall to the mooring blocks on the ground.

"Get back!" one of the guards yelled at Koa. "Get back, you devilish creature!"

He threw his truncheon at her, but of course, Koa had no physical substance, and the truncheon simply passed straight through her, landing in the snow with a *thud*.

The two guards stared for a moment. "It's a blasted shadow wolf!" the first guard exclaimed. "One of those dratted kids must be a wolf whisperer!"

Realizing that the wolf couldn't hurt them, both guards immediately started forward. Koa melted away like smoke and reappeared on the deck of the dirigible beside Shay.

"Good girl, Koa," he said as she wagged her tail at him.

One of the guards leapt for the ladder, but the dirigible had already risen too high and his fingers only just brushed the bottom rung before he fell back down into the snow.

The four young explorers raced to the wooden side, peering over as the guards—and the Polar Bear Explorers' Club itself—rapidly fell farther and farther away. Nobody could quite believe what had just happened.

They had managed to escape—but now, as the dirigible ascended higher and higher into the sky, an icy wind whipped around them, tugging at their explorers' cloaks and stirring their hair. Stella wondered whether any of them had any idea how to fly a dirigible. Frost showered down from the gasbag as it rippled in the wind, and frozen ropes creaked in the background. Then it started to snow—great white flurries that swirled and drifted all around them.

In all the panic and excitement and desperation of the escape, it hadn't really occurred to any of them that the dirigible might not be empty. So it came as rather a surprise when there was a sudden *thump* behind them and a shocked voice said, "Good gad, who are you people? What's going on here?"

The four explorers spun around to see a boy of about fifteen sprawled on the wooden deck. It looked as though he had just fallen out of the hammock swinging to and fro above him. He had glossy chestnut hair, hazel eyes, and a handsome, angular face. He was wearing the green robe with the Jungle Cat insignia that marked him unmistakably as a junior member of the Jungle Cat Explorers' Club.

"Oh, shoot!" Stella said, staring at him. "There wasn't supposed to be anyone else on board."

"Just toss him over the side," Ethan suggested.

The boy scrambled to his feet and started to back away, only to end up getting tangled in the hammock behind him.

"Too late," Shay said with a sigh, glancing back over the side. "We're too high, and he doesn't look like he'd bounce."

"Worth a try, though?" Ethan suggested hopefully.

"Nope." Shay shook his head. "Can't do it." He looked at the boy and said, "Sorry, mate, but it looks like you're coming with us."

"Who are you people?" the boy cried, finally managing to disentangle himself from the hammock. "What is this? Am I being kidnapped?"

"Settle down," Shay said, doing his best to sound friendly. "No one's being kidnapped. We're just—"

"I knew this would happen!" the boy said. "I knew it!" He pointed a finger at Stella and said, "Don't think I don't

77

know who you are, you awful witch! I told Father you'd come after us if he complained about you! I told him that—"

"Hey!" Shay said sharply, all trace of friendliness gone from his voice. "That's quite enough. Perhaps if you'd shut up for a moment you'd get a better handle on what's going on. First things first, no one calls Stella a witch. Not in front of me."

"Or me," Ethan said, glaring at the Jungle Cat explorer.

"She's not a witch anyway," Beanie said, looking rather confused by the whole exchange. "She's an ice princess."

"I know what she is," the boy spat. He looked at Stella again and said, "You're a villain. Dad says you're dangerous! And a disgrace to the clubs! And that you're probably going to end up killing us all besides!"

Normally Stella had no problem speaking up for herself, but the memory of those snow queen profiles she'd seen on Felix's desk came flooding back to her, and her tongue seemed to get all twisted up inside her mouth so that she couldn't say a word.

"Sounds like your dad's got his facts a bit mixed up," Beanie said, frowning. "Stella isn't any of those things. Maybe he's drunk too much fizzy tiger punch on those expedition picnics you're all so keen on? That can make you go a little bonkers, you know. In the last ten years, twenty-three Jungle Cat explorers have gone bonkers from overindulging in tiger punch."

"My dad is not bonkers!" the boy said. His nostrils flared alarmingly. "How dare you!"

"Or perhaps it was the jungle mosquitoes?" Beanie offered. "They can make you delusional. Captain Horatio Jordan Jones went completely delusional after suffering a mosquito bite in the Tikki Takki Jungle. He tried to make himself a suit and hat and matching parasol out of banana skins, but then his elephant got a bit confused, and unfortunately, he ended up getting—"

"My father is the president of the Jungle Cat Explorers' Club, as you must already know. I suppose that's why you decided to kidnap me," the boy said, looking at Stella. "But he will never give in to your demands, whatever they are."

"I haven't got any demands," Stella said, finding her tongue at last. "Really, I haven't."

"He'll never pay you a ransom," the boy went on.

"Why would anyone pay a ransom for you?" Ethan asked, curling his lip in distaste. "I'd pay to be rid of you, quite frankly."

"I knew it would be me who suffered if Dad stood up to the evil ice princess," the boy said, running a hand through his glossy hair. "I just knew it."

"This has got nothing whatsoever to do with you, you brat!" Shay exclaimed. "Stella isn't evil, and for the last time, this is not a kidnapping. This is a daring escape that you've unfortunately managed to get mixed up in simply because you were in the wrong place at the wrong time. Isn't there a magic carpet somewhere on board that you can just float away on?"

"Magic carpets belong to the Desert Jackal Explorers' Club! At Jungle Cat, we use elephants for getting about." The boy gave a sniff. "Far more reliable."

"And far less easy to transport." Ethan sighed. "Fat lot of good an elephant would be in this situation."

"Perhaps we can set him down someplace en route?" Shay said, glancing at Stella.

She sighed. "It'll mean a delay in getting to Felix, but I suppose it wouldn't be fair to take him with us to Witch Mountain." The snow had stopped, but a wisp of cloud floated past, and Stella glanced out over the side to see they'd floated up so high they were surrounded by clouds. "Speaking of which," she said. "Does anyone know how to steer this thing?"

"I want to be dropped off somewhere civilized," the boy said. "Not left for dead in the Icelands."

"If you don't want to be left for dead, then perhaps you'd better learn some manners, and quickly," Ethan snapped. "Do you have a name, or shall we just call you Snot?"

"Ethan, don't be rude," Stella said, even though she didn't particularly feel like defending the Jungle Cat boy. But perhaps they had just gotten off on the wrong foot. She hadn't liked Ethan all that much when she'd first met him, after all. Perhaps if she was really friendly and nice to him, he would realize she wasn't the evil villain some people seemed to think she was. Then he could report this back to his father, and he might drop his complaint against her.

The boy glared at Ethan and said, "My name is Gideon Galahad Smythe."

"Good heavens," Ethan said. "How awful for you. So what do you do?" He took in the boy's stylish haircut and said, "Expedition barber, I suppose?"

Gideon dusted snow from his jacket, stood a little straighter, and said, "That's quite enough sass from you. I'm a picnic master."

The other explorers all stared at him.

"I beg your pardon?" Ethan finally said. "What in the heck is a picnic master?"

"Someone trained in the proper rules and etiquette of expedition picnics, of course," Gideon replied.

"Good grief." Shay shook his head. "Is that all you know how to do? Doesn't sound like it would be much use on an expedition."

Gideon looked offended. "Picnics are the most important part of any expedition," he said. "Even kids like you ought to be aware of that."

"Well, you seem to know who I am already," Stella said. "I'm a navigator, by the way. And this is Shay Silverton Kipling, Beanie Sampson Smith, and Ethan Edward Rook.

Wolf whisperer, medic, and magician. And that's Buster," she said, pointing at the T. rex stomping around at their feet. "Watch out for your shoelaces when he's about."

But Gideon didn't seem to be paying much attention. Instead he was staring fixedly at the mooring block in front of him. "Where," he finally said, "is the anchor?"

"Oh, it's back at the club," Stella said. "We had to untie the ropes in order to escape."

To her surprise, Gideon gaped at her with an expression of horror. "You left all the anchors behind?" He gasped.

"Of course we did," Ethan said. "The dirigible wouldn't have been able to float away with them on board, would it?"

Gideon glared at the magician. "You idiots! Those were magical anchors. They would have become weightless the moment you brought them on board."

"Perhaps you were too busy snoozing in your hammock to notice, but we didn't have time to be messing about with anchors," Shay said.

The Jungle Cat explorer groaned. "You don't understand. Those anchors are the only safe way to land the dirigible. Without them our goose is cooked."

"Seems a strange time to be cooking a goose," Beanie said. "Especially if we're going to have to crash-land."

Gideon stared at him. "No, no," he said impatiently. "I mean we're sitting ducks."

Beanie gave him a worried look. "We're not ducks," he

said. "Maybe you hit your head when you fell out of that hammock? Perhaps you ought to have a lie-down."

Gideon glared at him. "Are you making fun of me, or is there something actually wrong with you?"

"Right, that's it." Ethan slapped Gideon on the back of the head, causing the older boy to cry out. "First you insult Stella and now Beanie. No one's allowed to insult or make fun of Beanie except for me. So, for heaven's sake, shut up."

"We're going to have to crash-land." Gideon groaned. "And probably all perish in the process."

"In that case I'm afraid we can't drop you off," Stella said apologetically. "We'll have to head straight for Witch Mountain and hope for the best."

Gideon buried his face in his hands once again. "Doomed," he said. "You've doomed us all."

"You'd better get out that map of Witch Mountain and start navigating," Ethan said to Stella. "Otherwise we're just going to float around at random."

Stella slung the map tube off her shoulder and was just drawing out the map when suddenly the unmistakable sound of drumming floated up somewhere nearby.

"What's that?" Shay asked, glancing around.

Gideon Galahad Smythe heaved a great sigh and then wordlessly pushed back his hammock, revealing what appeared to be four fairies underneath it. They were quite different from the fairies that inhabited Stella's yard back home. They had green skin and wore tunics fashioned from leaves, with slingshots tucked into the waistbands. In addition, they all had deadly looking snake fangs dangling from their ears, and their dark blue hair was arranged into ferocious-looking spikes. One of the fairies was energetically beating a tiny set of drums while the remaining three performed energetic somersaults and backflips while chanting the same thing over and over again: *"Fee-fi-fo-fo, fee-fi-fo-fo, fee-fi-fo-fo!"*

"Good heavens—who are they?" Ethan asked, peering at them suspiciously.

"Those are jungle fairies, of course!" Gideon snapped.

"Can't you see their jungle slingshots? They live on the diri-gible and accompany Father on all his expeditions."

"Well, do they say anything other than *'fee-fi-fo-fo'*?" Ethan asked.

"That's their chant of doom," Gideon said glumly. "They do that whenever doom approaches."

"Would you please stop saying 'doom'?" Shay asked. "It's not helping all that much, to be honest. Do the fairies have names?"

"Hermina, Harriet, Humphrey, and Mustafah." Gideon pointed them out individually before coming back to the one on the drums. "Mustafah is the leader on account of the fact that he has the most impressive hair."

On hearing this, Mustafah tilted his head and looked grand. The mention of hair seemed to remind Gideon of his own because he began running his hand through it again, and the next moment produced a mirror from his pocket, with which he proceeded to inspect his appearance.

"They are a great asset on expeditions, giving us fore-warning of danger," he said before tucking the mirror away. "Just don't upset them, whatever you do, or they'll get those slingshots out and start pelting us with stink-berries."

Stella sighed. She felt homesick for the pretty dancing fairies in her own backyard already.

"Oh dear," Ethan said. "I hope they won't be upset that we're going to Witch Mountain."

"I doubt it," Gideon replied. "Everyone says jungle fairies are the most intrepid explorers in the world. They'll probably be delighted to arrive somewhere fiendishly dangerous." The Jungle Cat explorer sighed and shook his head. "Nobody comes back alive from Witch Mountain," he said.

"So everyone keeps saying," Stella said. "But witch hunters go there, don't they? And if a witch hunter can survive, then I'm sure we can too."

CHAPTER NINE

NONE OF THE EXPLORERS had been on a dirigible before, and Gideon didn't appear to be in a helpful mood when it came to explaining how to fly it. The Jungle Cat explorer pointedly walked off and stood with his back to them on the other side of the deck. Fortunately, though, there was quite a lengthy section about airships in Shay's battered copy of *Captain Filibuster's Guide to Expeditions and Exploration.*

"It looks like it works similarly to a submarine," Ethan said, peering at the diagram; it was extremely detailed, with suspension cables, air scoops, nose-cone battens, and other interestingly named things, all clearly labeled. "The ballonets are like a sub's ballast tanks, I think."

"'When traveling by dirigible,'" Stella read aloud, "'the most vital thing of all is to ensure no gas valves are accidentally left open, as this can lead to sparks escaping. Sparks on board a dirigible most frequently result in fire, disaster, and catastrophic crash-landings.'"

The explorers looked at one another.

"We definitely don't want any catastrophic crash-landings," Shay said.

"One hundred and three Jungle Cat explorers have died in dirigible crashes since—" Beanie began, but was quickly shushed by the others. They were all feeling the pressure of trying to work out how to fly the dirigible with nothing but a few diagrams from Captain Filibuster. The last thing anyone needed was Beanie educating them about fatalities too.

Fortunately, after much passing around of *Filibuster's Guide* and squinting at diagrams, the four of them thought they had a pretty good handle on the mechanics of it and didn't think they were too likely to do anything that would result in fire and disaster.

"I'm glad I brought the guide after all," Shay said, tucking it back in his pocket. "It wasn't really all that helpful last time, was it?"

"Very lucky," Stella said, peering at the map. "So—we should be there by morning, if my calculations are correct. Then we'll just have to figure out how to land without blowing the whole thing up."

She wondered where Felix was at this moment and felt a flare of worry. What if they were already too late? Perhaps the witch had gotten to him and they would find him lying dead in the snow. She pushed the image away firmly. She could not afford to think such things.

The sun had set, and it quickly went dark as the dirigible sailed on through the silent night sky. As soon as the sun had gone down, a bunch of fire pixies had woken up and started zooming about inside their lanterns, causing them to glow a bright, fiery red. Stella was rather concerned that they might have been captured and put in the lanterns against their will, but when she went over to see if they needed to be freed, she saw that the pixies all wore little waistcoats with the Jungle Cat Explorers' Club crest stamped on the front.

"The Jungle Cat Explorers' Club is very progressive when it comes to fairies," Felix had told her once. "They're the only club never to have had a pinned fairy display. They've established a good relationship with the jungle fairies, and they even employ fire pixies, river sprites, tree goblins, and temple elves as expedition guides. Handsomely paid, they all are too. One month's service for the club can keep their family fed for an entire year."

So Stella said hello to the fire pixies and then left them to their own devices. It was extremely cold up on deck, especially since it had started snowing once again, and the dusky night sky was thick with falling flakes. Stella had assumed that there were cabins down below, but when Shay asked Gideon, he shook his head.

"Then where are passengers supposed to sleep?"

"The hammocks, of course." Gideon gestured behind him to his own hammock, and then realized that the jungle fairies were all busying about tying their tiny hammocks beside it. "Oh, do you have to tie them up there?" He groaned. "How am I ever supposed to sleep with you lot drumming away next to me all night?"

The fairy with the biggest hairdo—Mustafah—responded by producing a little red berry from the pocket of his leaf tunic and firing it straight at Gideon. It landed on the handsome boy's cheek with a quiet *splat*. The smell was immediate and terrible. It was even worse than polar-bear poo, moldy cheese, and hairy troll feet all wrapped up together.

Gideon shrieked, turned, and in his haste, ripped down the fairy hammocks with his foot. As he fled across the deck, Mustafah loaded up his slingshot to take a second shot.

"You can put your hammocks next to mine if you like," Stella said hurriedly to the fairies. Really, the last thing they needed was stink-berries flying around. Hermina was thrashing about trying to get out from under the hammock that had landed on her, so Stella plucked it from her head, folded it carefully, and gave it back to her. The fairy tucked it under her arm and gave Stella a big grin. "I'll help you put them up later," Stella offered. "I've never slept in a hammock before, but it sounds like marvelous fun."

"Oh sure," Ethan said with a sigh. "Marvelous. And cold. And uncomfortable."

They left the fairies to their hammocks and walked across the deck to join Gideon, who was wiping his cheek with a picnic napkin. His eyes were watering from the smell, and he'd gone quite red in the face.

"Perhaps you should have taken your own advice about not offending the jungle fairies," Ethan remarked pleasantly as Gideon took out his pocket mirror and started smoothing back his hair. "Oh, would you stop fussing over your appearance for five minutes?" Ethan said. He glanced at the others and said, "I'm famished. Have we got enough to cobble together a meal between us?"

"I brought some jelly beans," Beanie said. "And some cheese and bread."

"I've got a cold roast chicken," Shay said. "And a jar of barbecue sauce."

Ethan looked at Stella and said, "We've got some purple jellies and sugared marzipan left over from our journey, haven't we?"

"Not anymore, you don't." Gideon grunted.

They all turned to look at him. "What are you talking about?" Ethan asked. "If you've pinched the last of our sugared marzipan, then I'm really going to—"

"Not me." Gideon pointed over his shoulder. "Them."

Everyone stared at the four jungle fairies stretched out

on the deck beside their hammocks, licking their lips, their bellies enormous. A few crumbs and the odd smear of barbecue sauce was all that was left of their supplies.

"Jungle fairies will eat everything and anything that isn't nailed down or locked away," Gideon said as the explorers frantically checked their bags and pockets. "They'll even chew on stink-berries if there's nothing else available. And they're extremely sneaky thieves. Didn't you know?"

"I don't believe it!" Shay said, rooting through his bag. "There was an entire roast chicken in here! It was huge. Four little fairies couldn't possibly have eaten the whole thing."

"Never underestimate the appetite of a jungle fairy," Gideon said smugly.

"You know, it might have been helpful if you'd told us that before they gobbled up all our supplies," Shay said with a sigh.

Koa got up from where she'd been sitting by Shay's side and wandered over to inspect the fairies. One of them picked up a nearby slingshot and aimed it toward her in a lazy, half-hearted sort of way, then grunted and let the catapult fall to the ground, obviously deciding it was too much effort.

"Is there anything to eat on board?" the magician asked, peering toward the ladder that led belowdecks.

"Of course," Gideon replied, stuffing the mirror back into his pocket and then ticking the rooms off on his fingers. "Aside from a well-stocked larder, we've got a champagne ice-room, a scone bakery, a jams and preserves cupboard, and a clotted cream creamery."

Ethan snorted. "What is a creamery anyway?"

"It's where we make the cream, of course!" Gideon snapped. "For the scones. Why do you think Margaret is here?"

He waved over toward the other side of the deck, and the others noticed, for the first time, that a black-and-white spotted cow stood there, happily munching on some hay and gazing out at the passing clouds with a thoughtful expression on her face.

"You couldn't make it up, could you? You actually could not make it up," said Ethan incredulously.

"I think you'll find that our food supplies are extremely useful now that the jungle fairies have demolished the scraps you brought along," Gideon said. "I'll get the picnic stuff. Then you can see how civilized explorers go about things."

He disappeared down the ladder, and after a moment's hesitation Stella followed him. Fire-pixie lamps lit the inside of the dirigible too, and Stella saw that the walls of the corridor were painted with a variety of jungle animals, from spotted leopards and watchful baboons to flying panthers and fairy giraffes. There was even a river scene depicting an expedition boat under attack from an enraged hippopotamus, as well as a tiny jungle fairy boat that looked as if it were about to be swallowed whole by a particularly savage-looking piranha. It all appeared extremely danger-ous and thrilling, and Stella made a mental note to put the jungle on the list of places she wanted to explore one day.

She hurried off down the corridor and soon found Gideon in the kitchen—or the galley, as it was called on dirigibles.

"Can I do anything to help?" she asked.

The Jungle Cat explorer jumped at her voice and almost dropped the enormous picnic hamper he'd just lifted down from the top shelf of a cupboard. He gave her a quick, ner-vous look. "No," he said. "I don't need any help from an ice princess."

Stella sighed. "Look, I'm really quite a nice person," she said. "I know that snow queens have been pretty horrid in the past, but I'm not like them. I promise."

"Perhaps you aren't now," Gideon replied. "But Father says that all ice princesses turn into evil snow queens eventu-ally. It's just a matter of time."

Stella decided to try another approach. "It's jolly nice of you to put on a picnic for us," she said. "We really appreci-ate your—"

"I'm not doing it to be nice!" Gideon snapped. "I'm doing it because any Jungle Cat explorer worth his salt will produce a suitably excellent picnic for guests, even unwanted ones!"

And with that he locked the cupboard, picked up the wickerwork hamper, and barged past Stella so roughly that she was forced to jump back against the wall in order to avoid getting knocked down. She sighed and wished, more than ever, that she were just an ordinary explorer and not an ice princess. Felix wouldn't be in danger then, and an explorer she'd never met wouldn't have decided she was a dangerous villain before he'd even set eyes on her. She made her way back up on deck feeling rather low and wandered over to say hello to Margaret. The cow was extremely friendly, and her big brown eyes and soft nose made Stella feel a little better.

"Hey, Sparky," Shay said, joining her. "Everything okay?"

Stella shrugged and ran her hand along Margaret's smooth coat.

"You're not paying any mind to that idiot, are you?" Shay asked, jerking his thumb over his shoulder to where Gideon was clattering around with teacups and arranging napkins into rather complicated hippopotamus shapes.

"He's not the only one who thinks that way," Stella said in a quiet voice. "And the worst part of it is that he's right. You saw what happened on the last expedition. If I use the tiara too much, it does make me cruel. I *am* dangerous."

Shay reached up to scratch Margaret behind her ear. "Anyone can be dangerous, given the right circumstances," he said. "Sometimes ordinary people are the most danger-ous of all. Besides, people are always scared of what they don't understand. Why do you think we had to leave our village in the end? There was trouble with the wild wolves there and—because I could talk to them—some of the vil-lagers thought I must have had something to do with the wolves attacking the village, that perhaps I was encour-aging them to do it. I never did, of course—why on earth would I—but sometimes people can get so worked up and afraid that they just won't listen to reason. Don't let them get to you, Sparky." He reached out and pulled Stella into a tight hug, and she felt herself relax as she breathed in his familiar scent of wolves and earth and leather.

She felt grateful to Shay for believing in her more than she'd been able to believe in herself recently. They both jumped when the sound of a brass gong being rung broke through the frozen air. They turned and saw Gideon under an awning, the picnic laid out by his feet. "Dinner is served," he announced, striking the gong a second time.

They wandered over to join the others. Beneath the canopy roof, several wooden monkeys held fire-pixie lamps that glowed softly and gave off quite a lot of warmth as well. There was a fantastic spread laid out on the green-and-white-checked cloth. The plates and teacups were all stamped with the Jungle Cat Explorers' Club crest, and Gideon had finally succeeded in folding the napkins into hippos. Just the sight of the food was enough to make Stella's stomach rumble. There were great piles of crumbly scones, shiny fairy jellies, tiny sandwiches, sausage rolls, Scotch eggs, and most delightfully of all, little cakes perfectly shaped like elephants, right down to their white sugar tusks.

"This looks wonderful!" Stella exclaimed.

"Aren't you awful people going to change for dinner?" Gideon demanded.

For the first time, Stella noticed that the Jungle Cat explorer had changed into a green velvet waistcoat with a fancy brocade trim and silver buttons stamped with his explorers' club crest. He seemed very pleased with himself and kept checking his appearance in the glass of one of the nearby lanterns.

"We didn't bring any fancy clothes," Beanie said. "They're not exactly practical for an expedition."

"Even the jungle fairies have made an effort." Gideon gestured toward them, and the others saw that they had, indeed, all put on bow ties and even had one rather bent and battered top hat, which they kept swapping between them.

Stella turned to the fairies and said, "You all look lovely."

"Hermina!" Gideon exclaimed. "Get out of that teacup!"

The jungle fairy was reclining, quite majestically, in one of the teacups, but got out with some grumbling when

Gideon shooed her away. The four jungle fairies settled cross-legged in a line at the edge of the picnic blanket instead. They'd obtained little wooden plates from somewhere and held these up to Gideon hopefully.

But the explorer shook his head and said, "You know the rules. You can only join the picnic if you bring an offering."

The fairies put down their wooden plates with a clatter and fluttered off somewhere as the explorers settled themselves on the cushions. Stella put an elephant cake on her plate but thought it was so marvelous that she could hardly bear to eat it.

"Why do you lot want to go to Witch Mountain anyway?" Gideon asked. "It's a bit extreme, even for the Polar Bear Explorers' Club."

"My father is witch hunting there," Stella said. "We're going to help him."

"Oh dear. I was afraid it was going to be something like that."

The jungle fairies returned just then, carrying a plate between them. They set this down on the picnic blanket, and Stella saw that it was piled high with what appeared to be piranha cupcakes. They had pointed sugar teeth and dark-chocolate fins.

"Goodness!" she said, peering at them. "How extraordinary."

"I don't know where they're hiding that stash," Gideon grumbled. "I've been all over the ship, and I can't find it anywhere. All right, sit down," he said to the fairies, who were holding their plates up expectantly. The Jungle Cat explorer put some food on each of them, and the jungle fairies fell upon it happily.

They ate quietly, everyone busy with their own thoughts. As they were finishing, Mustafah marched right up to Stella and held out a cupcake decorated with a flower.

"Oh, goodness," Stella exclaimed. "Thank you very much! How lovely!"

The jungle fairy bowed once before flying back to join the others, who all blew noisy kisses at Stella.

"Traitors," Gideon muttered.

Stella ignored him and blew a kiss back to the fairies.

"Jungle punch?" Gideon asked, suddenly brandishing a large jug of fizzy orange liquid. Stella saw that hippo-shaped ice cubes floated on top, as well as one particularly large ice cube in the shape of an expedition boat. There were even little ice explorers standing on its deck, poised with their binoculars.

"Is that the same thing as tiger punch?" Beanie asked, peering at it suspiciously. "Because if it will make you go bonkers, then I'd rather not."

"It isn't the same thing," Gideon snapped. "Nothing in this picnic will make you go any more bonkers than you already are." He paused, then added, "Except, possibly, Captain Greystoke's Expedition-Flavor Smoked Caviar." He pointed at a little bowl of black stuff in the middle of the spread. "If you eat too much of that it can make you go a bit crazy."

Gideon proceeded to place a paper umbrella decorated with monkeys and bananas into each of their teacups. The jungle fairies had produced thimble-size wooden kegs of their own, and Mustafah held his up to Gideon hopefully.

"No!" Gideon snapped. "There isn't enough punch for you. You know the rules. Guests come first."

"I don't want any of that horrible stuff," Ethan said, wrinkling his nose at it. "The fairies can have my share."

"But you must all try the jungle punch," Gideon whined.

"You drink it if you love it so much," Ethan replied, narrowing his eyes at the Jungle Cat boy. "Why are you so desperate for us to have it, anyway?"

"I'm not," Gideon said quickly. "Just trying to be hospitable, that's all. Although why anyone would bother trying to be hospitable to members of the Polar Bear Explorers' Club, I have no idea."

"Don't call me a member of the Polar Bear Explorers' Club!" Ethan sniffed. "I'm from the Ocean Squid Explorers' Club, which is easily the best one of the bunch. In fact, it's superior to the rest of your clubs in every possible way."

While the explorers were squabbling about clubs, the

jungle fairies had produced a tiny ladder from somewhere and set this against the side of the punch jug. Mustafah had climbed to the top and dunked one of the wooden goblets in, filling it to the brim before passing it back down to Hermina, who greedily knocked it back in one gulp.

Suddenly noticing them, Gideon gave a cry of dismay and threw out a hand to shove Mustafah off the ladder. Unfortunately, he used a bit too much force and ended up knocking the entire jug over. The orange liquid fizzed out over the picnic blanket, soaking Mustafah in the process.

"Now look what you've done!" Gideon exclaimed. "You blasted things!"

He raised his arm, and for an awful moment Stella thought he was actually going to hit one of the little fairies. But Shay immediately grabbed his wrist and said, "If it's a fight you're looking for, how about picking on someone your own size?"

Gideon glared at Shay, who gazed back at him quite calmly. His shadow wolf, Koa, had appeared beside him, and she clearly didn't seem to think much of the Jungle Cat explorer either, for she bared her teeth in a way that was pretty menacing, despite the fact that she had no physical substance. Gideon snatched his arm away hastily.

Mustafah picked himself up, dripping wet, and limped to the edge of the picnic blanket looking rather bedraggled and sorry for himself.

"Oh dear, did you hurt yourself when you fell off the ladder?" Stella asked, noticing his limp. "Beanie, come here. I think this fairy is injured."

Not only was Beanie studying to be a medic, but he also had some healing magic thanks to his elf heritage. He came straight over and explained to Mustafah that he could make his leg feel better if he liked. The fairy stuck it out, and Beanie lifted his hand, holding it inches away. A soft green light glittered out from Beanie's fingertips, surrounding the fairy for a moment.

"There you go," Beanie said. "You should feel much better now."

The fairy carefully tested his leg and then, clearly delighted with the results, went running, stamping, and dancing off to rejoin the others. As the explorers cleared away the remains of the picnic, Beanie noticed that all four of the jungle fairies were practicing their headstands.

Gideon showed them where the hammocks and blankets were, and the four explorers strung theirs up under the awning, alongside Gideon's. It was not an ideal arrangement, and Stella found herself suddenly longing for her bed at home. The frosted deck of the dirigible was not a hospitable place, and it was impossible to feel excited about the upcoming expedition when she had so much worry building up about Felix. Besides which, they weren't on an expedition this time, but a rescue mission, straight to a place they knew to be dangerous. It did not feel exciting like it had before. It just felt scary in a hundred different ways.

To distract herself, Stella beckoned the jungle fairies over and helped them tie their hammocks alongside hers. There was a brief squabble between Hermina and Buster when the T. rex tried to steal her hammock, so Stella had to fashion the dinosaur a little hammock of his own from one of her handkerchiefs. Finally, everyone was quiet and settled and ready to sleep.

The fleecy blankets were actually fairly warm, and the hammock was extremely comfortable. Stella liked the slight rocking motion it made—and the soft creak of the ropes, combined with the rumbling snores from the jungle fairies, made a soothing background noise as the dirigible sailed on through the still, cold night.

She glanced over at Gideon, who had changed into a very fancy dressing gown and nightcap ensemble and was all tucked up in his hammock with his back to the rest of them. It was extremely bad luck that the Jungle Cat boy had happened to be on board. His presence made her uneasy. He clearly was not on their side, and she worried that he might sabotage them the first chance he got.

"Sparky," Shay whispered from the hammock next to her. Stella turned to look at him, and the wolf whisperer raised an eyebrow. "I'm just thinking that maybe we should take it in turns staying awake to keep an eye on old Jungle

Cat over there." He nodded toward Gideon. "He's likely to sabotage us the first chance he gets, I think."

Stella sighed. "I was just thinking the same thing," she whispered back. "We could do with some kind of guard to keep an eye on him. . . ."

As she spoke, a crackle of blue sparks leapt from her fingertips, just like they had back home when the snow unicorn had appeared. The sparks showered down to the carpet of frost beneath their hammocks, and Shay and Stella both looked down.

Before their eyes, a shape started to fashion itself out of snow. First it was just a lump. Then it developed chunky legs, arms, and finally, a head. The snow ruffled itself into the shaggy outline of fur that covered the thing from head to toe. Sharp canines extended over the creature's lips, and claws formed on its hands. It was, unmistakably, a yeti. A miniature yeti made entirely from snow. Whereas real yetis reached the towering height of sixty feet or more, this one would have come up to Stella's waist had she stood beside it.

"Did you just do that?" Shay asked, staring.

"I . . . I'm not sure," she replied.

The yeti blinked up at her, then slowly bent forward at the waist in what was very definitely a bow. It straightened and began walking up and down at the end of the hammocks, its big feet crunching on the frost.

"He's going to keep watch for us, I think," Stella said.

"Stella, how did you do that?" Shay asked. "I thought you could only do ice magic if you had your tiara on."

"I don't know," she replied. "Something like this happened at home. I was just thinking that it would be cool if there was a snow unicorn there and all of a sudden one appeared."

"Did you get that cold feeling?" Shay asked. "Like when you use the tiara?"

"No." Stella shook her head. "Actually, I didn't. Maybe it's because snow magic is softer than ice magic? It certainly feels that way if . . . if that's what this is."

"Perhaps." Shay looked toward the little yeti sentry. "I

guess there's a lot about snow queens and ice princesses we still don't really understand."

They left the yeti to his guarding and settled down in their hammocks. They'd need all their wits about them once they reached Witch Mountain, and a good night's sleep would definitely help.

"I'm coming, Felix," Stella whispered under her breath. "I'm coming to help, whether you like it or not."

Stella hadn't been asleep for very long when she was woken by the sounds of roaring. She jerked upright and saw that her yeti was responsible for the noise, standing at the end of her hammock and bellowing into the frozen night. The next moment Ethan scrambled from his hammock and charged over to the big navigational wheel where Gideon was standing. Ethan shouted something, and the two of them fell on each other. Stella jumped from her hammock and ran across the cold boards toward them. Shay arrived at the same time and pulled Ethan away from the Jungle Cat explorer.

"What the heck are you two scrapping about?" he asked. "Can't a chap get any sleep around here?"

"He's turned the dirigible around!" Ethan said, pointing a finger at Gideon. "I knew he was up to something. I just knew it! If that snow creature over there hadn't woken me up, he probably would have gotten away with it." Ethan gestured back toward where the snow yeti had been, but it had melted away.

"I made him," Stella said. "To be on guard."

Gideon turned visibly pale at this. "Snow magic." He groaned. "Father was right."

"Quiet!" Ethan snapped. He turned to the others and said, "That fairy who drank the jungle punch is out for the count, and do you know why? The punch was drugged. I'll bet my life on it! That's why he was so eager for us all to drink it."

"So what if it was?" Gideon gasped. "I can't go to Witch Mountain! It's crawling with witches! I'll be turned into a toadstool and boiled in some kind of awful soup for sure!"

Beanie clattered up to them, wearing his favorite pom-pom hat and looking confused. "What's that about soup? What's going on? Why is everyone shouting?"

"He's turned the dirigible around," Ethan said again. "We're sailing in the opposite direction to Witch Mountain." He shook off Shay's restraining hand and marched over to the wheel, spinning it so hard that the dirigible lurched sharply to the left and everyone staggered to stay upright. Stella distinctly heard a cascade of smashing teacups down below.

"You villains!" Gideon panted. "You'll pay for this, I promise you! My father will—"

Ethan threw out his hand, there was a flash of light, and the next second Gideon had vanished. In his place appeared a small spotted purple frog with bulging hazel eyes. Beanie immediately sneezed. He was, unfortunately, extremely allergic to frogs.

"Good heavens!" Stella gasped. "Did you mean to do that?"

Ethan drew himself up to his full height. "Certainly."

"You probably shouldn't have, you know," Shay said, scratching the back of his neck. "He's only going to be even more peeved with us all now."

"I don't care how peeved he is!" Ethan exclaimed. "I'm feeling pretty peeved myself!"

The frog blinked once and then began hopping around the deck, croaking loudly in a panic-stricken sort of way.

"Oh, settle down!" Ethan said. "There are far worse things I could have turned you into, believe me."

He reached down, scooped up the frog, and tried to shove him into his cloak pocket. It was a bit of a challenge, given that the frog seemed to be all legs that thrashed about most determinedly, but Ethan finally succeeded in wrestling him into the pocket, then firmly zipped it up.

"Oh dear," Stella said, staring at the wriggling frog-shaped lump. "Is he going to be all right in there?"

"He'll be fine," Ethan snapped. "At least this way we can all get some sleep without worrying that we'll wake up to find ourselves parked outside the Jungle Cat Explorers' Club tomorrow morning."

He turned and strode off across the deck. Shay shook his head. "He really does need to work on controlling his temper," he said. "I've honestly never met such an uppity prawn in all my life."

Beanie shrugged. "At least that was a wonky squish-squish frog he turned him into—they can smoosh up really small without being hurt, so he should be okay spending the night in Ethan's pocket."

Shay shuddered. "What a proposition," he said. "But it does kind of serve him right, I suppose."

The explorers returned to their hammocks, and Stella saw that Ethan had been quite right about the jungle fairy. Buster had knocked Hermina out of her hammock and onto the floor, and the fairy hadn't so much as woken up. Stella carefully picked her up, placed her in Buster's hammock, and tucked her in with a handkerchief before climbing into her own hammock and going back to sleep.

CHAPTER TEN

S TELLA WAS WOKEN SEVERAL hours later by the jungle fairies doing their chant of doom, which isn't really the most reassuring way to be woken up, especially on the very first day of a new expedition.

"Fee-fi-fo-fo, fee-fi-fo-fo, fee-fi-fo-fo, fee-fi-fo-fo—"

"Gods, isn't there an off switch for those things!" Ethan groaned from his hammock.

"We've arrived at Witch Mountain," Shay said from the railing. "If there was ever a time for the chant of doom, I guess it's now."

Stella jerked upright in her hammock so fast that she almost fell out of it. She scrambled off and hurried over to join Shay at the railing. The others were close behind her, and for a moment the four of them stood and stared in a kind of horrified silence. Hundreds of evil faces stared back at them. They had arrived just before dawn, and the mountain was covered in jack-o'-lanterns that were lit up orange against the dark sky, the candlelight flickering and shifting ominously. Some were grinning, some were snarling, and others had their carved mouths open wide in a gaping, ghoulish scream. It didn't exactly present itself as an ideal spot for an expedition.

The sky turned pink as the sun began to rise, and the glow of candlelight disappeared as daylight broke. Brooding and foreboding, Witch Mountain was enormous. Covered in snow and frosted pumpkins, the jagged peaks looked like teeth piercing the sky. Sinister dark clouds swirled at the top, and jagged forks of lightning flashed through them at regular intervals. It was not a welcoming sight at all. Everything about the mountain shouted at them to go away and leave it alone—including the giant sign hanging from a floating black hot-air balloon tethered at the top that actually read: BE GONE! WITCHES ONLY!

Now that it was daylight they could also see that Witch Mountain was, in fact, an island, surrounded on all sides by a dark, cold sea. A single galleon was anchored just offshore, bobbing on the choppy surface.

"Oh dear. I hope that isn't a pirate ship," Beanie said, peering down at it. "If it is, they'll probably start firing cannons at us any minute now and we'll be shot down for sure."

Stella took her telescope from her bag and trained it on the ship below. "It's not pirates," she said, causing everyone

to breathe a sigh of relief. "They're flying the hunters' flag. That's a hunter's ship."

"Well, good. We know we're definitely in the right place, then," Shay said.

"I suppose now all we have to do is crash-land the dirigible." Stella glanced at Ethan and said, "Where's Gideon?"

"In my pocket still," the magician replied.

"You should take him out," Stella said. "Make sure he's okay."

"He's fine," Ethan replied. "I can feel him squirming around."

Nonetheless, he unzipped his pocket and held the wriggling frog up for inspection. "See?" he said.

The frog rapidly blinked its enormous eyes at them. Stella didn't think she'd ever seen a more miserable-looking creature in her whole life.

"Okay, you've made your point," Shay said. "Now turn him back."

"But I prefer him this way," Ethan said.

"Turn him back, Prawn," Shay repeated through clenched teeth.

Ethan sighed but flicked his spare hand toward the frog. A burst of magic shot from his fingertip, but Gideon remained, very definitely, a frog. Everyone stared at him expectantly, hoping for some kind of delayed reaction.

"Ribbit!" Gideon croaked.

"Oh." Ethan frowned. "That's strange. That should have worked."

"Don't tell us you've forgotten the spell!" Stella exclaimed.

Ethan scratched his head. "Perhaps I wasn't concentrating enough."

He tried several more times, but nothing whatsoever happened. The others all started to berate him.

"Oh, settle down!" Ethan snapped. "You know, I've probably done him a favor anyway."

"Stop squeezing him so hard," Stella said. The way the frog's eyes were bulging was starting to make her rather anxious. "You're going to hurt him."

Ethan gave her a withering look. "Of course I'm not going to hurt him," he said. "Haven't you ever heard of a wonky squish-squish frog before? They're super squishy. Why do you think I chose this particular type? You can stretch and smoosh them as much as you like and they'll be absolutely fine." To Stella's horror, he proceeded to squish Gideon into a little frog-shaped lump. "In fact, they're like rubber," Ethan went on. "You can even bounce him like a ball. Look."

Before anyone could stop him, Ethan bounced the hapless frog on the wooden boards of the deck. Unfortunately, he somewhat underestimated just how bouncy a wonky squish-squish frog could be. The little round frog ball flew straight up in the air and went zooming toward the railing at startling speed. Stella had the terrible image of the little frog sailing right out of their sight and into the clouds, never to be seen or heard from again, but fortunately, Shay shot out his hand and the frog flew straight into his palm with a *smack*.

"That's quite enough," the wolf whisperer said. He pointed at Ethan with his free hand. "Stop showing off. There'll be no more bouncing the president of the Jungle Cat Explorers' Club's son up and down on the deck. It's impolite. And undignified. Plus, we all know that the only reason you chose this particular type of frog is most likely because it's the only one you know how to do, not because of some clever strategy."

Stella took the frog from Shay and began carefully unsquishing him back into a frog shape as best she could.

"He ought to be thanking me," Ethan insisted stubbornly. "My spell has probably saved his life. When we crash-land this dirigible and all go up in flames, he's likely to be the only one crawling from the wreckage and hopping away to freedom. Wonky squish-squish frogs are pretty much indestructible."

"And you're talking absolute nonsense," Shay replied.

Ethan pointed a righteous finger at Gideon. "You could set that frog on fire," he said. "And it would be absolutely fine."

Shay clutched his head with both hands. "Do not set the

frog on fire!" he said. "We will have a very terrible argument if you do." He dropped his hands. "And stop saying things like that out loud. You're giving the jungle fairies ideas."

Stella looked down and saw that Mustafah had produced a match from somewhere and was holding it up to her. Perhaps he was still miffed about getting knocked from his ladder the day before. He looked up at her hopefully.

"No, Mustafah," Stella said, tightening her grip on the squirming frog. "No one is setting anyone else on fire. Even if they are mean and horrible."

Shay took Gideon from her hand and zipped him up in his own cloak pocket. "I'll take care of him for now," he said. "We could continue arguing about this for hours and, meanwhile, Felix could be with the witch already. We need to work out how we're going to crash this dirigible."

"We could puncture the gas balloon," Ethan suggested. "It'll sink fast enough then."

"I've got a better idea," Beanie said. "One that doesn't involve crashing."

A short while later, the four junior explorers had dug out every single picnic blanket they could find on board the dirigible and had finally succeeded in tying them all together in one long coil.

"Do you think it'll be long enough?" Stella asked, gazing down at the blankets winding their way all over the deck. "And hold our weight?"

"There's one way to find out," Shay said, and with that he gathered up the blankets in a big pile and threw them over the side of the dirigible. The explorers peered over. As far as they could tell, the blanket rope went almost all the way down.

"Close enough," Shay said. "It's worth a try, at least. If we crash-land, then we'll have no way of making our escape once we have Felix."

The jungle fairies had collected all the napkins and tied these together in imitation of the junior explorers. Stella had tried explaining to them that they really didn't need to bother since, having wings, they could flutter down easily enough under their own steam, but they seemed eager to join in, so the explorers decided to leave them to it. When the fairies threw their own rope over the side, it barely reached a fraction of the length, but they were very excited to climb down it anyway.

Stella stuffed Buster into the inside pocket of her cloak. She didn't trust him not to squirm his way out of it, so she zipped him in up to the neck, leaving only his indignant face peering over the top.

"It's for your own good," she said, tapping him on the snout. "T. rexes don't bounce either."

The four junior explorers hoisted their bags onto their backs, and then Ethan insisted on taking charge of Aubrey, Beanie's wooden narwhal. His father had carved it for him before he went missing on his final expedition across the Black Ice Bridge, and Beanie was extremely attached to it. Unfortunately, the last time they had climbed something high, he'd nearly dropped Aubrey and had dragged Ethan right off the ladder in his attempts to save him.

Beanie handed the narwhal over reluctantly, and then the four of them began the treacherous descent. Climbing down a rope was not as easy as it looked, and the muscles in Stella's arms burned with the effort. It seemed to go on and on forever, not helped by the fact that the rope blew about in the wind, and every time it moved, they feared one of the knots would give out and the whole thing would unravel.

Soon enough, the jungle fairies ran out of napkins and fluttered free of the rope. They decided to perch on Stella's shoulders, casually swinging their heels and reaching up to give her an encouraging pat on the head from time to time.

A moment later there was the sound of a long, low, plaintive moo from above. When Stella looked up she saw that Margaret had wandered to the railing and was staring at them over the side with a heartbroken expression in her big brown eyes.

"We forgot about Margaret!" Stella called down to the boys.

"Who's Margaret?" Ethan replied.

"The cow."

"Oh, who cares about a cow?" the magician replied.

"This is hard enough as it is. We can't exactly climb down a rope with a cow strapped to our backs, can we? And it's not as if any of us intend to stay on Witch Mountain for longer than we need to. She'll be fine."

"Uh-oh," Shay suddenly said. He had finally reached the end of the rope.

"What?" Stella called.

"We've run out of rope and, um, we're still a bit high," he called back.

The others looked down. Stella's breath caught in her throat, Ethan made a strangled sort of noise, and Beanie groaned. "A bit high" was an understatement. The end of the rope dangled some fifty feet from the snowy ground below, far too high for any of them to let go without injuring themselves, except for Gideon, who would no doubt bounce harmlessly in his wonky squish-squish frog form.

"Whose stupid idea was this anyway?" Ethan demanded.

"It was worth a try," Beanie said glumly.

"Now what?" Shay said.

"We're going to have to climb back up," Beanie replied.

Stella felt a cold feeling of dread. It had taken all her strength to climb down, and she was already exhausted. Climbing back up would be even more difficult, and she worried she might not have the strength to physically do it. Besides which, the blankets were starting to strain under their weight. More than once she had felt something slip.

The knots had held out up until now, but it would take only one to unravel and they would all drop to the ground like stones.

Going back to the dirigible seemed to be the only option available. Stella remembered the explorer's pledge she'd taken when she'd first been initiated back at the Polar Bear Explorers' Club: I shall keep a stiff upper lip, keep calm, and carry on regardless . . . even when experiencing those narrow escapes and close shaves that are the unavoidable experience of intrepid gentlemen explorers across the globe.

She gritted her teeth against the icy air. Explorers didn't dangle helplessly from ropes and admit defeat—they continued on and did what needed to be done. So, slowly but surely, hand over hand, Stella began the long, hard climb back up to the dirigible. Her arms felt like they were on fire, and it took all her willpower not to groan aloud. When she looked up, hoping she was almost there, she saw that she wasn't even halfway, especially when another blanket's knot loosened beneath her grip and lengthened the rope. Margaret's face gazed patiently back at her from a significant distance away.

A particularly savage gust of air blew the rope around wildly, and Stella heard Ethan's sharp intake of breath below her as they all held on for dear life.

"It's no good," the magician called. "We're never going to make it. The rope is unraveling. I say our best bet is if I turn us all into wonky squish-squish frogs and we take our chances."

This suggestion was met with a chorus of loud protests.

"Well, it's better than dying, isn't it?" Ethan demanded.

"Is it?" Beanie asked. "Our lives as people would be over because there'd be no one to turn us back into humans again."

"Perhaps we could find a witch to do it," Ethan said. "We are at Witch Mountain, after all."

"If five frogs go hopping into a witch's cave, I don't think her first thought will be about how she can help them," Shay said. "More likely she'd chuck the lot of us straight into a bubbling cauldron."

"Wonky squish-squish frogs can actually be set on fire without getting hurt, you know," Beanie said. "Ethan was right about that. So they can probably survive boiling water too. If she threw us into a cauldron we'd be able to hop right back out again quite unharmed."

"But still frogs," Shay pointed out.

Another gust of wind blew the rope, and Stella tightened her grip desperately. Her hands were going so numb in the cold that she could barely feel her fingers. Between her frozen hands and all this talk of turning themselves into frogs, she was starting to feel a little panicked. But then, quite suddenly, out of nowhere, something incredible appeared before her—something so marvelous that for a moment she thought she must be imagining it.

It was a magic carpet, floating serenely, so close that she could have reached out and touched it with her fingers had she taken her hand off the rope. It was woven in a hundred different shades of purple, from lilac to indigo to plum, along with jewel-bright teal and turquoise. Intricate drawings of camels and genie lamps were stitched across its surface, and there was a shiny gold trim at the edges, along with tassels in each of the four corners. It jiggled these at her now in a way that was somehow unmistakably friendly.

Below her the boys were still squabbling about the pros and cons of the wonky squish-squish frog plan, so Stella called down to get their attention.

"Hey!" she shouted. "Look what's just appeared. Right when we needed it!"

The other explorers stopped their argument and looked up. Shay and Beanie were immediately delighted, but Ethan narrowed his eyes suspiciously. "Nothing just turns up right when you need it," he said. "Expeditions don't work like that. This could be a trap."

"Well, we haven't got much choice," Stella said, making up her mind. "We can't stay dangling from the end of this rope forever."

She was just about to release one hand and reach out for the carpet when the jungle fairies all fluttered from her shoulders and settled themselves on the edge of it. Unfortunately, one of the fairies had unzipped Buster's pocket, and the little dinosaur lunged after them. T. rex legs aren't really made for jumping, though, and he certainly would have plunged to his death if Mustafah hadn't fluttered forward to grab him.

He set the dinosaur down on the rug and then, before anyone could stop them, Harriet and Humphrey each grabbed a corner of the magic carpet, turned it upward, and shot away back to the dirigible.

"Hey!" Ethan shouted after them. "Come back here! Blasted things—what are they doing now?"

The explorers watched, dismayed, as the flying carpet sailed right over the side of the dirigible and disappeared from sight, along with Margaret.

"I'm going to wring their scrawny necks!" Ethan exclaimed.

"Stella, why don't you try calling them?" Shay suggested. "They seem to listen to you."

Stella was just about to do so when the magic carpet burst straight through the side of the dirigible with such force that splinters of wood came raining down on the four explorers. The carpet went sailing past them carrying Buster, the four jungle fairies, and rather precariously, Margaret. The cow only just managed to fit on the carpet and didn't seem too happy about the arrangement. Her panic-stricken *moo*s carried back to them all the way down to the ground.

"I don't believe it!" Ethan exclaimed. "This is turning out to be the most ill-fated expedition in the history of exploration. A wonderful, miraculous magic carpet appears, only to rescue a cow and a bunch of fairies!"

"Five seconds ago you were saying that the carpet was probably a trap," Stella replied.

It was hard not to feel frustrated as the magic carpet flew down and out of their sight on the other side of the dirigible, though. Less than a minute later, however, it was back, minus the cow, fairies, and dinosaur.

"They've probably been gobbled up by whatever awful monster is lurking below," Ethan said. "Is there blood on the carpet? Blood is a sure sign of treachery."

Stella ignored him and grabbed the magic carpet with both hands, dragging herself onto it in one smooth motion. Her gray skirt puffed out around her as she sat down, and she felt the magic carpet shift a little under her weight, but it seemed able to carry her perfectly easily. It moved down so they could pick up the others—Stella noticed that Ethan climbed onto it quickly enough, despite his complaints and suspicions. Shay was next, and finally, Beanie. He stepped on not a moment too soon. Seconds later one of the knots in the rope finally gave out and the entire thing fluttered to the ground in one long coil.

Once they were all aboard, the magic carpet swooped down so fast that Stella's long white hair was lifted right off

her neck, and they all had to grab on to one of the edges for support. Soon enough the magic carpet deposited them on solid ground, right beside the rest of their party. Margaret, the jungle fairies, and Buster all stood in a row, waiting for them patiently.

"Oh good," Stella said. "We're all still here." She glanced at Ethan and said, "See? I told you it wasn't a trap."

At that exact moment, a shadow suddenly fell across them. "Well, well, well," a deep voice said from behind. "I'm glad to see that my magic carpet found you all right."

CHAPTER ELEVEN

THE FOUR EXPLORERS SLOWLY turned to find themselves looking up at the most enormous man any of them had ever seen. Stella's first thought was that he must be a pirate. He had a black bushy beard, huge arms covered in tattoos of mermaids, and what looked very much like a pirate's hat perched on top of his wild head of hair.

"Welcome," he boomed, "to Weenus's Trading Post—a fantastical emporium designed to meet all your needs in the field of expedition and exploration. I am Munch Mendelsson, at your service."

He swept his arm back to gesture behind him, and the four explorers peered past to see a wooden stall set up on the snow. A striped awning had been erected above it, and the words "Weenus's Trading Post" were carved into a crooked sign hanging there. The little wooden tables were filled with all manner of things, including what looked like a selection of antique rifles, a crate of Captain Ishmael's Expedition-Strength Salted Rum, several genie lamps, and a rather shabby camel that gazed at them with a haughty expression before flaring its nostrils and spitting loudly.

Stella had heard of Weenus's Trading Post before, many times, from Felix. He'd told her that an entrepreneur named Wilfred Weenus had set up these trading posts all over the globe, no matter how remote the location, anywhere he thought explorers, hunters, and adventurers were likely to pass through and find themselves in need of supplies. A Weenus's Trading Post could be a lifesaver. But Wilfred Weenus was a twitchy little man, by all accounts, and a mongoose whisperer to boot, which Felix said was always a sign of bad character. A Weenus's Trading Post might well provide you with just what you needed, right when you needed it, but there was always a price, and Mr. Weenus would have the shirt off your back if he could.

"Don't usually get explorers around here," Munch Mendelsson said. "Witch hunters mostly. Or prisoners—some chap crash-landed a witch's vulture nearby just yesterday, so no doubt he's a prisoner, destined for the cauldrons."

"Oh, that must have been Felix!" Stella said eagerly. "What did he look like?"

Munch shrugged. "Landed too far away to tell. Set off straight up the mountain, though, so there's another one who'll never be seen or heard from again, you mark my words. Witches send their vultures to bring back prisoners from time to time, but it's a long journey across the sea, and the birds are often plum worn out by the time they get here, so they make their way up the mountain on foot. Of course, their prisoners usually run away if that happens. This one must have had a death wish."

Stella was delighted. She'd feared that Felix may have simply flown straight to the top and could be confronting the witch at this very moment, but it appeared he was only a day ahead of them.

"We had a lost Desert Jackal expedition passing through just the other day too," Munch went on. "That's where the flying carpet came from, as a matter of fact. And the camel. You kids don't want a camel, do you? Bad-tempered thing, constantly spitting at me and any customer that comes near."

"We could do with some supplies," Stella said. "But I guess it depends how much everything costs."

Munch gazed down at her and said, "Well, now, that's just details, me hearties, just details. I'm sure we can reach an agreement easily enough." He glanced over at Margaret and said, "Fresh out of magic beans, though, which I guess is what you was hoping for when you brought the cow along. Plenty more to tempt you with, even so."

He hustled them over to the stall, which was an absolute

treasure trove of supplies, knickknacks, curiosities, and equipment.

"We have a fine selection of magic suitcases." Munch gestured to one corner where there was, indeed, a little cluster of magic cases. You could tell they were magic because they were all shuffling around and moving about on their own. Some had wings, others had legs, and some even had fins.

"You'll never have to carry your own equipment again with these beauties," Munch said, patting the nearest one affectionately. They were rather beaten-up and battered, with an extremely interesting array of stickers on their leather surfaces. Other cases, rather alarmingly, had warning stickers on them announcing that the luggage trunks would bite porters if not handled with care and respect.

"Great for carrying valuables and breakables, these ones," Munch said, seeing Stella looking. "If you've got any fancy delicates you want to transport up the mountain, then this is the luggage for you. It'll take the hand clean off anyone who tries to ignore any 'Fragile' labels and just chucks it onto a trolley."

"Where did they come from?" Ethan asked, narrowing his eyes suspiciously.

"Traded 'em," Munch said promptly. "From passing travelers."

"Not scavenged from dead bodies and doomed expeditions?"

Munch laughed. "'Course not," he said. "No one goes

on expeditions up Witch Mountain. Far too dangerous. Even before all them poisonous bunnies arrived."

Stella realized that Munch must be the trader who'd sent the report about the rabbits.

"Are they roaming the mountain?" she asked.

"Not likely," Munch replied. "Even witches would kick up a fuss about that. That batty old witch just keeps 'em as pets, I reckon."

"Was it a witch with burned feet?" Stella asked quickly.

"Don't know. Never seen her. But I chatted with the pirate what delivered 'em, and he told me the witch's name was Jezzybella and that she was mad as a hare. But never mind about her. How about some bath bubbles? I imagine you probably like to stay clean on the road."

"A bubble bath would be lovely," Stella said. "But not much use if there are no bathtubs around."

Munch shook his head. "Not bubble bath," he said. "Magic bath bubbles." He leaned over to a nearby helmet that was resting upside down and scooped up a handful of shiny purple bubbles. They were fat, round, and smelled faintly of gooseberries. "Burst one of these against your head and you'll be clean as a whistle and smelling of roses for goodness knows how long," he said. "Look here."

He proceeded to walk over to the camel, which immediately curled back its lips and bared its teeth in a menacing sort of way.

"Now, now, Nigel," Munch said. "Don't make a fuss in front of our guests." He reached up and pressed the bubble against Nigel's bony head. It popped, and the camel was transformed. His shabby fur became glossy, his eyelashes were long and curled, his teeth gleamed white, his gold anklets shone, and his tasseled headdress and leather saddle looked polished and new. Around the ears, his fur even puffed out into fetching ringlets. Nigel responded by shaking his head and spitting at Munch in an outraged fashion.

Stella looked longingly at the bath bubbles. They certainly would come in handy during an expedition, especially if they cleaned your clothes as well. Her explorer's cloak had quickly gotten incredibly grubby last time, and boots tended to become caked with snow and mud. She was rather fond of her gray traveling dress and would have preferred to keep it nice.

"If you're going up the mountain, you might like one of these." Munch thrust what appeared to be a moldy old blanket at her.

"Ew." Stella wrinkled her nose. "What would I want with this?"

"Ain't you never heard of a magic fort blanket, girl?" Munch exclaimed. He shook his shaggy head. "Good grief. Dead eager on 'em in the Desert Jackal Explorers' Club, they are. Crawling with jumping cactuses, it was, when I first got hold of it, but I think I got 'em all cleared out now. Best not go sticking your hands into any dark corners, though. Better safe than sorry when it comes to cactuses, my brother always said." He scratched the back of his neck, gave a hearty sigh, and said, "Got ate by a whale in the end, did Crunch."

"I've never heard such a load of tall tales in my life," Ethan scoffed. His own older brother, Julian, had been killed by a screeching red devil squid in the Poison Tentacle Sea, and Ethan was a little touchy about deep-sea-monster stories. "You can't honestly expect us to believe you had a brother called Crunch, let alone that he was eaten by a whale."

"What's wrong with the name Crunch?" Munch asked, looked genuinely puzzled.

"There are twenty-nine types of man-eating whale in the world, you know," Beanie said. "Including the fat-man-gobbler whale from the Frozen North Sea, the head-crunching terror whale from the Voltic, and the one-gulp giant blue whale from the—"

"Don't try to tell me about whales!" Ethan snapped. "I'm from the Ocean Squid Explorers' Club—I know all about the dangerous things in the sea that can kill you."

"It were a fat-man-gobbler what done for Crunch," Munch said. "Ironic, really, considering he was the skinni-est beanpole you ever saw. Could've used Crunch to fence with, if you had half a mind."

"You must have half a mind if you think we're going to be taken in by this lunacy," Ethan said. He snatched the blanket from Stella's fingers, dangled it at Munch, and said, "Did you honestly think you could pass off this bit of old rag as a magic fort blanket?"

Munch gave him a withering look and took the blanket from him. "The password," he said, "is 'rattlesnake ragtime.'"

The moment the words were out of his mouth, the blanket magically transformed itself into a magnificent fort, which sprang up around them. It was big enough to encompass the five people and the entire trading post. There was even room for Margaret and the camel, which seemed most put out by the sudden appearance of the tent and spat at the wall in an offended manner.

Stella could hardly contain her delight. The huge tent was full of overstuffed cushions, velvet beanbags, gilded ottomans, and billowing silk curtains. There was even a fire pit in the middle of the tent, crackling away warmly. You could tell it was an explorers' tent from the maps that lined the walls, the rifles slung over the backs of chairs, and the pith helmets and safari hats hanging from pegs in the corner.

"Outsider alert," Munch said, and the whole thing collapsed back into an old blanket in his hand. He gave Ethan a self-satisfied look. "Well?" he said. "Not so full of smart comments now, are you?"

"This would be incredibly useful," Shay said. "And so would that magic carpet. How much would you like for them?"

"One hundred pieces of gold for the magic fort blanket," Munch said promptly. "And five hundred pieces for the magic carpet."

"We've got nowhere near that!" Stella said.

"Well, what have you got?" Munch demanded.

The four explorers did a quick check of their bags and pockets. Then Stella turned back around and said, "We've got five pieces of gold."

"And a wonky squish-squish frog," Ethan said, pulling Gideon from his pocket and dangling him by his foot.

"We're not trading Gideon," Stella hissed. "Put him back."

"Five pieces of gold!" Munch exclaimed, looking horrified. "Why, that's not enough to even buy this rusty old compass, and that's broken besides. I thought explorers were supposed to be loaded. You kids already owe me eighty gold pieces."

"But we haven't bought anything from you!" Shay protested.

"You've had two magic carpet trips," Munch said, holding up two fingers. "That ain't for free, you know. And somebody owes me for an entire crate of Captain Ishmael's Premium-Grade, Expedition-Strength Salted Rum."

"We haven't had any rum, you scoundrel!" Ethan said indignantly.

"No, but they have." Munch pointed at the jungle

fairies, who had passed out in a heap on Margaret's back, snoring loudly and reeking of booze. "And they're your fairies, ain't they?"

"Those fairies do not belong to us," Ethan said firmly.

"Well, they're part of your gang, and no one short-changes Munch," he said. "No one. Mr. Weenus would have my guts for garters."

Shay sighed. "We could give you the cow?" he offered.

"If you promise to take care of her," Stella hastened to add.

Munch eyed Margaret dubiously. "Is she a milking cow?" he asked.

"The best," Ethan said. "There's a whole creamery on that dirigible that she's filled with all kinds of delicious cheeses and—"

Munch snapped his fingers. "That'll do it," he said. "I'll take the dirigible and we'll call it quits. I'll even throw in Nigel."

He gestured at the camel behind him. "We don't want a camel—" Shay began.

"Neither do I," Munch said, unlooping the reins and passing them to Stella. "Camels and cows don't get on—everyone knows that. So if I'm taking the cow, then you've got to take Nigel. He's been nothing but trouble for me since the moment he arrived."

Nigel seemed to sense he was being talked about,

because he peered down his nostrils at Munch with an offended look. Still, at least it meant they'd have something to carry their bags.

"If you're going to take the entire dirigible, then you'll have to give us the magic fort blanket too," Shay said, folding his arms. "It's not a fair trade otherwise."

"Naturally, matey, naturally," Munch said. "Weenus's Trading Post only deals in fair bargains. Besides which, if you're heading up the mountain, then all this stuff is guaranteed to come back to me pretty quick anyway." He thrust the blanket at the wolf whisperer and gave the explorers a toothy grin. "Nice doing business with you kids."

CHAPTER TWELVE

S TELLA CAREFULLY SCOOPED UP the snoring
jungle fairies and draped them over one of Nigel's
humps, before tying some of the bags to the camel
and putting Buster back in her pocket. They examined the
map, but it wasn't really any help in working out where Jezzybella lived. In fact, it didn't have much detail on it at all.
As President Fogg had said, there was only one expedition
that had ever gone to Witch Mountain and almost everyone
on it had perished. There were just a few things on the map
that the surviving jungle fairy had filled in, but the expedition had taken place more than twenty years ago and things
could have moved around since then for all they knew.

But there was only one path winding its way up the
mountain, and so the explorers followed it, their boots
crunching in the deep snow. When they'd put a decent
amount of distance between themselves and Weenus's

Trading Post, they stopped to take stock of their provisions.

They had Stella's magic tiara, a small selection of food, a pixie lamp, a telescope, a camel, a magic fort blanket, and four drunk jungle fairies. Beanie had brought a bag full of jelly beans, which he'd managed to keep hidden from the fairies, and also a medical kit. Ethan said he had packed all manner of useful supplies in his bag, from weapons to binoculars, but unfortunately, he had somehow picked up Gideon's bag instead of his own, and this seemed to be filled with napkin rings, hairbrushes, a few pocket mirrors, and some silver tins of Captain Greystoke's Expedition-Flavor Smoked Caviar.

"Well, there's no use worrying about that now," Shay said. "We're just going to have to make do with what we've got."

"I suppose this witch is bound to live right at the top of the mountain," Ethan grumbled as they set off. "That would be just our luck."

"We're going to have to be extremely careful," Shay said. His shadow wolf, Koa, was padding along at his side, her pointed ears flat against her head as she sniffed at the air. "This isn't like before. This time we know exactly what lies ahead, and it's not good."

Stella shuddered. Up until now some small part of her hadn't quite believed that she was really going to come face-to-face with the witch who had murdered her parents and tried to kill her, too. The thought was too big and horrible and wrong. She should be running away from the witch, not toward her. Jezzybella must be extremely powerful to have been able to kill both of Stella's parents in their own castle, surrounded by an army of stone trolls. But that was exactly why Stella couldn't leave Felix to face her alone. And while the witch roamed free, she knew she could never feel safe herself either.

She gazed up at the jagged peaks of Witch Mountain, which reached straight up into the stormy sky, and she couldn't help thinking that they were just four junior explorers, a camel, and a wonky squish-squish frog. What could they possibly do?

"Don't think about the entire task," Felix told her whenever something seemed too difficult or overwhelming to even make a start. "Just think about the first thing you have to do to begin, and go from there. That's all there is to it. That's the secret to achieving unachievable things. Just take it one tiny, little, manageable piece at a time."

Stella knew that the first thing she had to do was take one step up Witch Mountain, then one more, and another one after that, until she found the witch's lair. And if she was scared at the thought, well, it didn't matter. She was going to do it anyway.

"Smells like magic," Ethan said, tilting his pointed nose into the air. "That can't be a good sign."

He was quite right. A smell of burned sugar hung about the place, thick as treacle in the air around them.

"It was only to be expected," Shay said calmly. "We all knew what we were going to find here."

Stella looked at her friends and felt a burst of gratitude and gladness that they had come with her—had rushed straight to her aid the moment she needed them, in fact. Difficult things were always easier to face when you had good friends at your side.

They trudged on through the snow, pulling their cloaks closer to keep out the cold. Sometimes the path wound around the edge of the mountain—and they very quickly had to turn their eyes away from the sheer drop below—and at other times the path cut right into the black rock, which soared above them steeply.

They were in one of these rocky chasms when Ethan suddenly stopped and said, "Does anyone else have the feeling that we're being followed?"

The others paused, gazing back at the empty path behind them.

"You're imagining it," Shay finally said. "It's the mountain playing tricks on you."

Ethan frowned. "I thought I heard footsteps behind us a moment ago. And felt eyes on the back of my neck. Magicians are extremely sensitive to eyes on the back of the neck, you know. We can sense when we're being watched."

"It might be bats, rats, or cats," Beanie said. "Witch Mountain is bound to be crawling with those."

"Perhaps," Ethan said doubtfully.

They continued on their way, and almost at once Stella knew what Ethan meant. She could sense it too—a prickly feeling right on the back of her neck. Several times she glanced sharply behind her, but the path was always completely empty.

"Would you two stop doing that?" Shay said. "This is going to be a very long journey if we're all jumping at shadows every moment."

They turned around a corner in the path just then and found themselves face-to-face with a cave entrance—two cave entrances, in fact, side by side.

Beanie groaned. "Caves are never good," he said. "There are so many ways you can perish in a cave." And to everyone's dismay, he started counting them off on his fingers. "Ravaged by bats, drowned in rock pools, crushed by a rockslide, suffocated by moths, eaten by hairy-leg spiders, sliced in half by—"

"Beanie, stop it," Stella said. "No one wants to hear these things."

"There's no other path," Shay said. "And no way around." He glanced at the others and said, "If we want to continue, then we're going to have to go through one of these caves."

Ethan sighed. "A pitch-black cave in Witch Mountain," he said. "I'm sure it will be fine. Absolutely fine."

Stella dug out the map from her bag, and they all gathered around it. The map did indeed show two caves. One of them was marked as the CAVE OF HYPNOTIZING WHITE CATS. The other was marked as UNKNOWN.

"Hypnotizing white cats don't sound good," Shay said, chewing his lower lip. "I mean, I like cats normally, but these will be witches' cats, won't they?"

"Witches' cats can be extremely dangerous," Beanie agreed. "You've got hypnotizing cats, levitating cats, eye-clawing cats, fury-spitting cats." He frowned and added, "There were reports that Captain Unwin Marjory Banks decided to buy a hypnotizing white cat when he retired to the Karzak Jungle. One day he didn't get up to feed the cat its breakfast, so it hypnotized him into walking straight into the piranha-infested river outside."

"Why would anyone want a hypnotizing cat as a pet in the first place?" Ethan demanded. "Seems like a terrible idea."

"Too much tiger punch, perhaps?" Beanie suggested. "He was a Jungle Cat explorer, after all."

"Well, let's go with this other cave," Shay said, pointing at the unnamed one. "For all we know, there might not be anything dangerous in that one at all, whereas we know the other one is going to be tricky for a fact."

"Koa seems to prefer it, though," Stella said.

They all looked to see that Shay's shadow wolf was,

indeed, standing right outside the Cave of Hypnotizing White Cats, gazing back at them hopefully and wagging her tail.

"Oh, Koa loves cats," Shay said. "She can probably smell them in there and doesn't realize that they're hypnotizing ones. I say we go through the other cave. It hasn't been explored yet anyway, so we ought to go that way to help complete the map."

There was no arguing with that. They were explorers, after all, so when faced with a choice of this kind, they should always choose the unknown. Stella took the pixie lamp from her bag and gently prodded the fire pixie awake. The pixie uncurled from the floor of her lantern, shook out her fiery long hair, and immediately began flitting to and fro, emitting a bright golden light. Stella whispered her thanks, lifting the lantern up high, and the four explorers and the camel stepped into the mouth of the cave, Koa padding after them reluctantly.

The fire-pixie lamp blazed bright enough to illuminate a good portion of their surroundings, and they saw that the cave was huge, reaching high up into the rocks and stretching away from them into the darkness. Frozen stalactites and icicles reached down from the ceiling, and blue rock pools gleamed below. The place smelled of cold water and frosty dampness.

"I don't like the look of those," Ethan said, gesturing

toward the icicles and stalactites above them. "They look like hanging swords that could pierce you right through if they were to fall off."

"Captain Leroy Livingstone Pritchard," Beanie said promptly. "Impaled by a falling stalactite in the bat caves of Eastern Vampira. It was so huge and sharp that it drove right through his pith helmet and straight into his brain."

"Thank you, Beanie," Ethan said with a sigh. "Very helpful."

"You're welcome," Beanie said, looking pleased.

The four explorers moved cautiously forward. The sense of being watched was stronger than ever, and Stella felt like there were hundreds of unseen eyes peering at them out of the darkness, just beyond the light from the lantern. There was no snow inside the cave, and their boots crunched over frozen pebbles. After a little while, Ethan tapped Stella on the shoulder, and when she glanced at him, he jerked his head back toward the path behind them. Stella could hear it too—the unmistakable crunch of footsteps. It was almost lost under the sound of their own, and Stella supposed the faint sound could just be an echo. But it could also be someone, or something, following them.

They continued down the path, which soon reached a vast stony bridge. Savage-looking stalagmites reached up from the chasm below, interspersed with blue rock pools. Every now and then a big, fat bubble would rise to the surface of a pool and pop in a suspicious manner, as if there were some large creature breathing beneath the surface.

"I guess we'll have to cross," Stella said. "The bridge looks solid enough, at least."

Still, there were no handrails, and the explorers stepped carefully onto the damp stone. They made their way step by careful step.

At first Stella thought it was the flickering, shifting light of the pixie lamp that made it seem as if there were dark shapes gliding above them, but more and more she felt like she could see something moving up there, out of the corner of her eye. She tried lifting the pixie lantern a little higher and squinting upward, but the ceiling was too far away for her to see, and she could only make out shadows of movement.

"I think there's something up there," she said eventually.

"Bats, probably," Beanie said. "There are ninety-three types of bat in the known world, ninety-one of which will attack humans if they're provoked—"

"Fortunately, we're not provoking anyone," Ethan said. He had Nigel's reins in his hand and gave a bit of a tug to keep the reluctant camel moving. Stella expected him to spit in response, but strangely, the camel seemed to have taken rather a shine to Ethan and leaned its head down to nibble at his hair in an affectionate manner.

"Get off!" Ethan batted him away. "Ew! Camel breath stinks! It's a good thing I snatched some of those bath bubbles from Weenus's Trading Post. I'm not going to walk around smelling like camel breath the entire time."

"You stole from him?" Beanie exclaimed, looking upset. "Stealing's wrong. And Munch was very nice to us."

Ethan waved his concern away. "He was cheating us for all we were worth."

The explorers were about halfway across when suddenly the rock pools below began to bubble, as if the water were boiling. The four children glanced down at the rock pools, and instinct told them that this was not a good development. All the fur on Koa's back was standing on end. And as if any further proof were needed, the jungle fairies suddenly woke up and immediately started doing their chant of doom.

Stella turned and saw Mustafah banging away at his drums on Nigel's back, while Hermina, Harriet, and Humphrey showed off their handstands and backflips. The camel's ears twitched in irritation, and he shook himself in an attempt to dislodge the fairies, but they were staying firmly put.

"Guys," Stella said, "I think we should—"

Before she could finish, one of the rock pools below them seemed to explode in a great sea of sparkling white spray and freezing foam. A six-foot-long shark burst from the water—mouth open, monstrous teeth gleaming. But rather than flopping onto the rocks and beaching itself there, like a normal shark would have done, this one soared right up into the air as if it were water. Its sleek gray body seemed to ripple with muscle as it swam through the air up toward the bridge, snapping its teeth at them on its way past their heads. The explorers all ducked in alarm and then looked up only to be met with a terrifying sight.

The air above them was suddenly filled with sharks. Stella was sure they must have been the shapes she'd noticed earlier, only now they'd come lower and glided menacingly between the stalactites, staring down at the explorers with cold, dead eyes. There must have been twenty of them at least. Some were huge, others were slightly smaller—but they all had rows of gleaming, razor-sharp teeth, and they were all heading their way.

"—run!" Stella gasped.

The four of them scrambled back to their feet and sprinted the rest of the way across the bridge as more sharks came bursting out of the rock pools below. The camel's hooves kicked up showers of stone as Nigel bleated indignantly, and the jungle fairies kept up their *fee-fi-fo-fo* chant. The sharks came at them all at once, from both above and below, moving with a terrifying speed as they charged through the air.

Even though they were all racing, the breath burning in their lungs, they couldn't go fast enough. One of the larger sharks was almost upon them—teeth gnashing, tail thrashing, mere inches from taking a giant bite out of poor Nigel's behind—when Ethan twisted and threw magic back over his shoulder. The spell hit the shark full in the face, and it instantly turned into a wonky squish-squish frog, hopping along the bridge and looking bemused. It was hard to tell whether Nigel stamped on the frog accidentally or

deliberately, but either way Ethan was clearly right about them being practically indestructible—it was flattened into the ground one moment, then popping back into frog shape and hopping off to the nearest rock pool the next.

The spell bought the explorers the time they needed to reach the end of the bridge, but to everyone's dismay, the cave didn't continue as they'd expected it to. Instead, the bridge led to a dead end—nothing but a sheer rock face reaching up to the spiked ceiling. The chasm was too deep to jump down, even if it hadn't been full of shark-infested rock pools and fatally sharp stalagmites. The only escape was to go back the way they'd come—over the bridge—and that was now impossible. The entire structure was crowded with sharks, their huge bodies rippling first one way and then the other as they glided back and forth.

Shay had his boomerang in his hand but seemed reluctant to throw it. Stella guessed it was because a boomerang hit to the nose was probably more likely to enrage a shark even further than do any real damage to it. "Can you turn them all into frogs?" the wolf whisperer asked, looking at Ethan.

"As long as they come one at a time," the magician replied. "And not too quickly."

"I can freeze some of them," Stella said, already reaching for her tiara and placing it on her white hair.

The moment she spoke, a shape darted at them from the

side, and Stella threw up her arm, freezing the shark solid. It hung in the air for a moment before falling to the ground, splintering into pieces on the rock below. Stella couldn't help feeling bad, as it wasn't really the shark's fault it wanted to eat them, it was just its natural sharkish nature. But as more sharks followed and she froze a second and then a third, she felt her guilt slipping away as an icy feeling ran down her back and the tiara did its job of chilling her heart.

Koa stood before them on the bridge, snarling and growling at the sharks, but she wasn't as effective a distraction with them as she'd been with the guards back at the Polar Bear Explorers' Club. The sharks seemed to be able to sense that she had no physical substance and simply glided straight through her on their way to the explorers.

Beside her, Stella was aware of Ethan turning two more sharks into frogs, one after the other. Unfortunately, with potentially catastrophic timing, Gideon chose that moment to wriggle free from Shay's pocket. He landed with an ungainly splat on the bridge and immediately hopped off toward the other frogs. Perhaps he had been a frog for too long and mistook the others for his own kind. Whatever the reason, there were soon three wonky squish-squish frogs on the bridge, and they all looked identical, which was not good news at all. Beanie lunged at the frogs and stuffed them in his own pocket, sneezing violently, while Ethan and Stella battled with the incoming sharks. But there were so many of them and they were coming too quickly now, diving at them one after another.

"It's no good," Stella gasped. "There are too many!"

She pressed herself right back up against the wall seconds before a particularly long shark snapped at the space where she had been. The explorers looked around desperately for a means of escape, but they were trapped and it really seemed as if this was it. They were going to be swallowed up by magic sharks before they'd been on Witch Mountain for five minutes.

But then a clear voice rang out across the cave. "Stay right where you are!"

Stella looked up in time to see a figure dressed in boots, a tattered cloak, and a wide-brimmed hat crouched at the top of a rocky outcrop. Just as a shark passed by below, the person leapt from the rock straight onto the shark's back. The creature bucked and thrashed in an attempt to throw him off, but the rider had spurs on his boots and pressed these into the shark's side while leaning down low over its back, grabbing its fins, and pointing them in the direction of the explorers. When they drew level, the figure leapt from the shark, cloak flying out behind him, and threw a bottle of bright red liquid on the ground at his feet. The moment it smashed, the sharks all tumbled from the air—some to fall back into the rock pools with a splash, while others fell, thrashing angrily, among the stalagmites.

"Not a moment to lose," the newcomer said, and Stella was astonished to see that the rider was female, no older than Stella, with dark brown skin, a cheerful smile, and large brown eyes.

"Who are you—" Ethan began.

"The red bottle has a gravity spell in it, but it won't last long," the girl said, cutting him off. "Those sharks are about to come bursting back up out of the rock pools, and they'll be mad as all hell when they do. There'll be a witch hole around here someplace. They've got to get in to feed the sharks somehow. Aha! Here it is, by gum!"

She'd dragged a boulder away from the wall, and to their astonishment, a gaping hole led down into the rock behind it, stretching away like a slide into the darkness.

"But who are you?" Ethan demanded. "Where does that hole go? How do we know this isn't some kind of death trap?"

The girl glanced back at them. "Oh. Haven't you heard of me? I'm Cadi Sarah Salt, witch hunter extraordinaire." She paused for a moment, then added, "Or, at least, witch hunter in training." She pointed at the hole behind her. "And this is your one and only chance of escape."

At that moment, with a roar of awful fury, fifty sharks burst from the rock pools below. Whatever effect the red liquid had had was now clearly gone—the sharks soared straight up into the air, teeth gnashing in hungry anticipation as they made straight for the explorers. Cadi turned back around, gripped the brim of her hat, gave them a wide grin, and said, "Best come with me if you want to live."

And with that she leapt feetfirst into the hole, leaving the others to scramble after her, dragging the camel behind them.

CHAPTER THIRTEEN

N IGEL WAS MOST PUT out about the witch hole. It slid straight down into the rock for quite a long way, and the problem was that camels just weren't designed for slides.

"Twelve Desert Jackal explorers have been killed by accidental camel crushing in the last ten years!" Beanie squeaked as they all did their best to avoid Nigel's flailing hooves.

The statistic didn't comfort anyone very much, but fortunately they soon came flying out the end of the tunnel, whereupon they landed in a gigantic pumpkin patch. The pumpkins broke apart under the impact, orange pieces flying everywhere.

"How do witches manage to crawl up that thing?" Ethan groaned, flat on his back in the middle of the patch.

"Witches slide up rather than down," Cadi said as she

stood up and dusted herself off. "They're tricky like that."

With a rather ungainly sprawling of long legs and hooves and humps, Nigel managed to get himself back on his feet and immediately began spitting at everyone in general outrage. Quick as a whip, Cadi pulled off her hat and used it as a shield against the camel spit. A great tumble of brown dreadlocks went cascading down her back as soon as they were free.

"Gosh, your camel is a bit on the haughty side, isn't it?"

"I think most camels are quite haughty," Stella said, picking herself up and brushing pieces of pumpkin from her explorer's cloak. She checked her pockets to make sure Buster was still there and then said, "Felix says they can be quite conceited, too. Well, wasn't that fun? I've never slid down a witch hole before. Or seen a flying shark, for that matter . . ."

She trailed off as she became aware that Cadi Sarah Salt was staring at her.

"What is it?" Stella asked nervously. She hoped Cadi was just staring the way most people did when they saw her white hair and skin for the first time—or perhaps it was because she had a piece of pumpkin sticking out of her ear, or something like that—but after Gideon's reaction to her on the dirigible, she was worried it was more likely to be because she'd been recognized as an ice princess. Even witch hunters read the papers, after all.

"You're her, aren't you?" Cadi asked, confirming Stella's fears. "You're the ice princess."

Stella stiffened, and she felt her explorer friends all suddenly go still beside her.

"What gave me away?" she asked, trying to smile, while snatching the tiara from her hair and stuffing it back in her pocket.

She'd braced herself for Cadi to snarl some insult at her, or recoil, or at least take a step back. So she was astonished when the other girl hopped straight over the broken pumpkins and threw her arms around her in a tight hug.

"Oh, thank you!" she said. "Thank you, thank you, thank you!"

"For what?" Stella asked.

Cadi drew back, beaming. She was quite a bit taller than Stella, who had to tilt her head back to meet her eyes. "For showing all those stuffy old clubs that girls can be just as good at exploring as boys, of course!" she said. "Witch hunting's okay—you get to travel a bit and meet interesting people and the like—but all I've ever really wanted to be is an explorer." She clapped Stella on the back. "And you're the reason I finally can! I've applied to all the clubs. Well, all the clubs that will now accept applications from girls." She glanced at Ethan's black Ocean Squid explorer robe and said, "Your group is a strange bunch, aren't they? I visited the Ocean Squid Explorers' Club in person last month to see if I could apply to be an explorer there, and some awful chap at the door brandished a tentacle at me and told me to get lost. He wasn't at all civil."

"The Ocean Squid Explorers' Club is the best explorers' club in the world!" Ethan said, pushing away Nigel, who'd startled nibbling at his hair again. He sighed, then added, "But they're wrong about the girl members thing."

"This doorman told me that the day the Ocean Squid Explorers' Club started admitting girls was the day that starfish would all float away into space—ooh, space exploration. Now, wouldn't that be something? Isn't it a shame that there's no Space Alien Explorers' Club? One day, I suppose."

"You talk rather a lot, don't you?" Beanie said. He tended to point out such things to people, which could sometimes cause offense, but Cadi didn't seem fazed.

"Witch hunters work alone," she said. "So you have to make the best of company when you find it."

"But surely you're not here on Witch Mountain alone?" Shay said. "Isn't it a little dangerous?"

"Oh, yes, witch hunting is terribly dangerous," Cadi replied. "But I've been through years and years of training, and this is my chance to qualify as a fully fledged witch hunter—by capturing a witch by myself."

"You can help us capture a witch if you like," Stella said. "That's what we're here for."

"You're after the witch who murdered your parents, I suppose?" Cadi said. She took a penknife from her pocket and began cleaning her fingernails with it. "The newspaper stories were full of it."

"Yes, that's right. My father, Felix, has gone after her by himself."

Cadi shook her head. "Silly thing to do. Only a trained witch hunter should ever go hunting alone. There are lots of dangerous things on the mountain." She nodded back toward the flying-shark cave. "As you've just discovered."

"Can you help us?" Shay asked.

She gave him another of her big grins. "Sure can, my friend. Say, I like your wolf bracelets!" She gestured at the cords of leather wrapped around Shay's wrist, studded with wolf beads.

"I'm a wolf whisperer," Shay said. "Shay Silverton Kipling, at your service. Thanks a lot for your help back there, by the way. We'd have been sitting ducks without you."

Beanie scratched his head. "We wouldn't have been sitting ducks," he said. "We'd have been dead. Gobbled up by sharks. Thirty-three explorers have been gobbled up by sharks in the last twenty years, but they were all snow sharks or sea sharks. I've never heard of flying sharks before."

"That's Benjamin Sampson Smith," Shay said, pointing at him. "He prefers to be called Beanie. He's a junior medic, so he'll patch you up if you get any scrapes and bumps." He turned to Ethan and said, "That's Ethan Edward Rook, magician. Nigel, the camel, and those four acrobats chanting on his back are Mustafah, Humphrey, Hermina, and Harriet, the jungle fairies, and a great early-warning signal of doom."

Mustafah stood up and began pointing at himself energetically, so Stella said, "Mustafah is the leader—on account of having the most impressive hair."

Mustafah gave her a pleased look and then joined the others.

"And this is Gideon Galahad Smythe," Beanie said with a sneeze, producing a frog from his pocket. "He's a Jungle Cat explorer and a picnic master."

"Is that frog actually Gideon?" Shay asked with a sigh. "There seemed to be a bit of frog confusion for a while in there."

Beanie held the frog up, dangling him by one of his back legs, and peered at it. The frog blinked back at him with bulging eyes.

"You know, it's really quite difficult to tell," Beanie finally said. He produced the other two frogs from his pocket and said, "One of them's got to be Gideon."

"Here, give them to me," Ethan said, holding out his hands. "I'll take care of them until I remember that spell."

Beanie sneezed again and passed over the frogs.

"We've no time to lose," said Stella. "We need to press on after Felix." She glanced at Cadi. "I don't suppose you know where Jezzybella lives?"

"I don't, but if she's one of the criminal witches, then she'll probably be at the top of the mountain somewhere. The wanted witches have higher bounties, you see, so they put themselves right at the top. Witch Mountain is littered with traps and pitfalls and monsters and hazards, and the more you have to travel through, the greater your chances of coming to a sticky end."

"What a cheerful thought," Ethan said darkly.

"Where's your shadow wolf?" Cadi asked Shay. "All whisperers have them, don't they?"

As if hearing herself mentioned, Koa suddenly materialized at Shay's feet. Even sitting back on her haunches, she was so large that her head was level with Shay's waist.

"Here she is," Shay said.

"Gracious," Cadi said softly. "How absolutely marvelous. Well, while we're making introductions, I have someone I need to introduce you to as well." She put two fingers to her mouth and gave a loud, piercing whistle. Stella was very impressed and made a mental note to get Cadi to teach her if they traveled together for a while. "Gus!" Cadi called cheerfully. "Here, boy!"

There wasn't much to see from where they stood except for the ruins of the pumpkin patch, but the mountain path curved around the corner and Cadi was gazing in that direction. Stella wasn't too sure what exactly she expected to come in response to the hunter's call and was ready for practically anything—from an elephant to a magic carpet. She rather hoped it might be an arctic fox, or a penguin, or even a unicorn. Unicorns were Stella's absolute favorite, along with polar bears, of course. But, in fact, Gus turned out to be none of these things.

Instead, a gigantic, eleven-foot-long walrus came lolloping around the corner, propelling itself forward with two flat flippers, sliding along the ice on its belly. Its huge, blubbery body was covered in short, bristly cinnamon-brown fur, and it looked somewhat like an enormous seal, only with a much more whiskery face that had something of a mustache look about it and reminded Stella quite forcibly of the president of the Polar Bear Explorers' Club. It also had two great white tusks protruding from its mouth. There were several bags tied to its back, along with an odd-looking saddle, and strangely, a long stick that stretched out over the walrus's head and dangled a sorry-looking fish just out of its reach.

Stella had seen drawings of walruses in Felix's books back home, but she'd never seen one in real life before and hadn't expected it to be so big. It was even larger than Gruff. There was something a little different about this walrus, though, and that was that his eyes both pointed in slightly different directions rather than looking straight ahead.

"This is Gus," Cadi said proudly.

"He's wonderful!" Stella exclaimed, delighted.

"Why is there a fish dangling from a string over his head like that?" Shay asked.

"Oh, I tied that there before I came down the mountain to see you," Cadi said. "I was a little farther up when I saw your airship arrive. I wanted to come and have a look at you without Gus following me." She glanced at the walrus. "It's a little mean, really, as he can't actually reach the fish, but he'll bat around at it with his flippers for hours and it keeps him entertained enough that he won't go wandering off and get himself into mischief."

As if sensing he was being talked about, Gus gave a loud bellow before sliding forward across the ice toward them. He obviously did have poor eyesight, because the walrus almost collided with Ethan. When he realized there was a person there, the walrus became very interested and immediately raised himself up to snuffle all around Ethan's hair, pressing his soft, whiskery face right up close to the side of the magician's head.

"Great Scott, this is even worse than the polar bear!" Ethan exclaimed. "He'll have my eye out with one of those tusks!"

"No, he won't!" Cadi said indignantly. "His whiskers are just his way of seeing you properly."

Gus insisted on inspecting every one of the explorers this way. When he got to Stella, she couldn't resist flinging her arms around him in a big hug, causing him to snort appreciatively. When he tried to greet Nigel, though, the camel spat at him in outrage, although Gus didn't seem to mind particularly. He just sloped off back to Cadi, who kissed him on the neck.

"Why do you have a walrus, anyway?" asked Ethan.

"Why do you have a camel?" Cadi shot back.

"He was foisted upon us," Ethan said. "Although, actually, he's not half bad. I rather like him."

"Well, Gus wasn't foisted on me," Cadi said. "I chose him. Apprentice hunters all get to pick their own walrus when they go off to hunt witches in the Icelands. They're terribly useful for carrying all your supplies and things. Plus they help keep you warm in a blizzard. Walruses are supposed to be good for hunters because they make hardly any sound as they glide along the ice. Nobody wanted Gus on account of his being a little odd, but I liked him more than the stuck-up, noble walruses."

"Seems to me that a noble walrus is just what you ought to be picking rather than an odd one like this," Ethan said.

"Don't be rude," Stella said. "And don't call him odd. You'll hurt his feelings."

"Oh, Gus doesn't mind," Cadi replied. "He's been called far worse. Anyway, you'll certainly be safer with us. I know a bit about what to expect from the mountain. I've been here a few times before. For example, I could have told you to travel through the Cave of Hypnotizing White Cats rather than the Cave of Flying Sharks. That would have been much simpler."

Cadi set her hat back on her head and adjusted it to a jaunty angle. "I would like to offer my services as a guide."

"And what is it you want in return?" Ethan asked, because he always thought that everyone had an agenda.

"References," Cadi said promptly. "And testimonials. Dad says the clubs are still a bit twitchy about accepting girls, and they might not think a hunter has the right skills to be an explorer. Well, if I prove myself useful to you here, then you'll all provide references for me, won't you?"

"Seems fair," Shay agreed.

"Then we have a deal."

"You can take the witch we capture as your bounty too, if you like," Stella said. "Before we take her to the Court of Magical Justice."

"Oh, that won't be necessary. I already have a witch," Cadi said. "Captured her before you arrived. But then I saw your dirigible, and all that business with the cow and the flying carpet, and I thought you just had to be explorers. No one else would be loopy enough to send a cow flying down on a magic carpet. Don't worry. We will pass my witch on the way."

"Won't two witch prisoners be a bit difficult to handle?" Stella asked.

Cadi waved a hand. "I don't need to take the witch back," she said. "Just one of her hairs as proof. You know, like how woodcutters have to bring the princess's heart back to the evil queen?" She glanced at Stella then and said, "Oh, sorry, no offense."

"None taken," Stella replied.

A *boom* in the sky made everyone jump, and they looked up in time to see what appeared to be an enormous vulture hovering in the air over the mountain. It flapped its wings several times, and then its image started to break up. Stella realized that it was actually made from hundreds of little pieces of paper, which dispersed as they fluttered to the ground in the distance.

"What was that?" Ethan demanded.

"It's probably the witch looking for her vulture," Cadi replied. "One crash-landed here yesterday, you know. That's a location spell that shows the witch where the vulture is. It'll be making its way up on foot, I expect."

"That's where Felix is, then," Stella said. "So he's not that far ahead of us, at least."

Cadi hoisted her bag on her shoulder and pointed to the path winding its way through the pumpkin patches. "We should press on," she said. "It's best that we're out of the pumpkin patches by sunset. They bite, you know. Once they light up, they sort of come alive and gnash at you. They'll take a chunk out of your leg if you're not careful."

Since nobody wanted to have a chunk taken out of their leg by a gnashing pumpkin, the explorers quickly gathered up their things and set off on their way, Gus bellowing happily and Nigel giving the occasional bleat of protest as he trudged along behind them, looking pretty disgusted by the whole affair.

CHAPTER FOURTEEN

THE MOUNTAIN PATH WASN'T the easiest to climb, and they found themselves slipping and sliding on the snow every time it got too steep. At one point they passed a little cloud of magical vulture confetti, each tiny vulture flapping its wings as it flew along.

"They're following in the path of the real vulture," Cadi said, pointing them out. "The spell will start to wear off eventually, and they'll hop along on the ground for a bit before finally turning back into ordinary paper. You might see some on the floor as we go."

They all automatically glanced down at the path around them, and then Beanie said, "Oh, look, that screaming pumpkin doesn't have any teeth!" He turned to Stella and said, "Do you think I should take it back as a present for Moira? Perhaps then she'll come to my party."

Moira was Beanie's cousin, and at Beanie's last birthday she had announced that she was never coming to one of his parties again because he was weird and she didn't like him.

"Forget Moira," Stella said with a sigh. "She's always so horrible to you. I don't know why you try so hard to be friends with her." She noticed, however, that Beanie picked the pumpkin up anyway and strapped it to the back of Nigel's saddle with a great deal of care.

Eventually, they were out of the pumpkin patches and the path leveled out, turning away from the mountain edge and leading them into the crags of the mountain itself.

"Can't you shut him up?" Ethan asked, jerking his thumb toward Gus. The walrus had kept up an almost constant stream of bellowing since they set out.

"He talks to himself when he's happy," Cadi replied.

"Well, he's giving our position away to any witch who might happen to pass by," Ethan grumbled. "Between that and the jungle fairies' chant of doom, we're making quite a racket. We might as well all start blowing trumpets to announce our location."

"We didn't bring any trumpets," Beanie said, giving him a puzzled look. "And I don't think that would be a very good idea, at any rate."

They continued on in this manner for most of the day, climbing farther and farther up the mountain, as the air became increasingly colder and sharper around them.

They were some way into the afternoon when Shay suddenly lifted his head and said, "What was that?"

"I didn't hear anything," Stella replied, but the words were barely out of her mouth when a faint howling filled the air.

"Oh no," Cadi said, stopping on the path. "It's the witch wolves. They don't normally come out until nightfall."

"What are witch wolves?" Ethan demanded. "They sound bad."

Cadi turned to look at them, her face suddenly pale. "They are," she said. The fact that the hunter was worried was a little unnerving to the others, especially given that she'd jumped onto a flying shark's back with no sign of fear at all. "They're soul eaters," she said. "But we've got another problem to deal with right now. Look over there."

The others followed her pointing finger and immediately saw the witches. There were six of them lined up on a distant crag far above. Their dark silhouettes were motionless, all long skirts and pointed hats, but Stella felt sure they were staring directly at them. A large sign on the mountain beside them read: TRESPASSERS WILL BE EATEN BY SCARECROWS.

"Those witches are always there," Cadi said. "Day and night. Hail or thunder. I think they must be guardians of some kind. The legend goes that once they've laid eyes on you, you're doomed."

Beanie gave a little squeak of alarm, but Ethan snorted. "Rot," he said. "They've seen you before, haven't they? And you've lived to tell the tale."

Cadi grinned and adjusted her hat. "Yes, but I'm a hunter," she said, leaping onto a nearby rock just as the snow beneath the explorers started to shift and warp into long-fingered hands that wrapped themselves tight around the children's ankles.

They were, unmistakably, witch's hands. Even though they were made of snow, the explorers could see that the fingers were crooked, the nails were dirty, and the knuckles had warts on them. The cold seemed to seep right into their bones as the frozen hands tightened their grip.

"It's the witches," Cadi said, pointing up at the guardians on the crag. One of them had lifted her broomstick and was pointing it straight at the explorers.

Turn back! A disembodied voice seemed to float across the air to them. *Turn back!*

"Never!" Stella gasped. "Not without Felix."

Before Cadi could offer any advice about how to escape, Stella had pulled a box of matches from her bag, lit one, and dropped it on the snow hand. The match burned straight through the wrist, leaving a smoking hole in its path. The hand jerked back at once. Following Stella's example, the other explorers quickly produced matches of their own to ward back the hands—all except Ethan, who threw magic fire instead. The jungle fairies came to their aid too, taking aim with their slingshots from the safety of Nigel's humps. The terrible smell from the stink-berries was so potent that they melted the snow where they landed every bit as much as the matches. Soon the hands had lost their shape entirely and were just twitching lumps of snow on the ground.

"You might have warned us!" Ethan exclaimed, glaring at Cadi.

"I just wanted to be sure you could look after yourselves," the hunter replied. "If not, I would have sent you home. Witch Mountain is no place to be if you can't think on your feet. But come on, we'd better hurry. They'll regrow quickly enough, and it's harder to escape them once they're bigger and stronger. We need to get out of sight of the witches."

The explorers didn't need telling twice. They quickened their pace and soon passed around a bend in the path, glad to leave the watching witches on the crag behind them.

"Thank you for your help," Stella said to the jungle fairies, who were shaking one another's hands in a congratulatory fashion. Mustafah gave her a bow so low that the top of his spiky hair brushed against Nigel's hump.

A soft noise made them glance back, and they saw that the snow hands had already re-formed and were stretched out toward them, long fingers grasping and clutching at empty space.

Stella felt a cold all over that had nothing to do with the weather. In an effort to push it away, she said, as scornfully as she could, "It'll take more than that hocus pocus to frighten us."

"I thought the hocus pocus was pretty scary, actually," Beanie said in a quiet voice.

Stella dropped the bravado. If Beanie could be brave enough to admit being frightened, then so could she. "You're right," she said with a sigh, patting her friend gently on the back. "It was."

To make things even worse, the witch wolves started howling again, somewhere in the distance.

Shay clamped both hands over his ears, his eyes screwed shut. "They're so loud." He gasped. "They must know I'm here. They're all trying to speak to me at once."

The wolves were still nowhere to be seen, but the group could hear their howls in the distance.

"Witch wolves used to be people," Cadi said. "They were cursed by witches, and now they're trapped in wolf shape, forced to roam the mountain for all time, looking for other souls to devour. They're drawn to water. Probably because they have ice in their veins and frozen hearts." She glanced at Stella and added, almost apologetically, "Like snow queens. Just one bite and you'll turn into a witch wolf yourself."

Stella shivered. What if that happened to Felix? What

if it had already happened? His might be one of the howls they could hear out there. A low whimpering caused Stella to look down at Koa. The witch wolves were obviously affecting her, too, for she was cowering on the ground at Shay's feet. Stella had never seen the shadow wolf cower before, and it was unnerving. Normally Koa was so cool and calm. It wasn't as if anything could harm her, anyway, given that she had no physical body, and yet she looked terrified. Stella was dismayed to see that Shay's hands were shaking too.

"Come on," Ethan said, taking the wolf whisperer by the arm. "We should get going. Put some distance between us and the wolves. We just have to keep away from them, that's all."

They continued on up the mountain. Soon enough they had left the sound of the wolves behind, but Stella noticed that Shay stumbled a couple of times in the snow, which wasn't like him at all—he was usually so sure-footed.

"Are you all right?" she asked, noticing that his hands were still trembling.

Shay glanced at her, a confused expression in his dark eyes. "I don't know," he said. "I don't think so. As soon as those wolves started speaking to me I got the most awful headache."

"Healing magic can help with that," Beanie said. They paused while the medic took off his glove and raised his hand to one side of Shay's head. A fizz of green sparks filled the air, and Shay breathed a sigh of relief. "Thanks," he said. "That helps." He frowned and added, "Koa isn't right, though. I can feel it."

The shadow wolf was nowhere to be seen, but Stella knew that Shay still felt a connection to her even when she wasn't visible.

"Could you make out what the wolves were saying?" she asked.

"Not properly," Shay replied. "Only that they're trapped and tormented."

"We should press on," Cadi said. "The sooner we get to this witch of yours, the sooner we can leave Witch Mountain."

Stella took out her explorer's compass, which didn't give directions of north, east, south, and west, but more interesting headings like yetis, ravines, food, and danger. She set hers for "witches," and the group continued on their way in a rather subdued state for the rest of the afternoon. Everyone was worried about the odd effect the witch wolves had had on Shay and Koa, and they all found themselves straining their ears for the sound of wolf howls and wondering what might happen if the wolves came back.

CHAPTER FIFTEEN

I T WAS EARLY EVENING and they had traveled some way before Stella nudged Cadi and said, "What's that?" She pointed toward the horizon, where, rising from behind a rocky outcrop, were several columns of white, twisting steam.

Cadi grinned. "Come and see," she said.

The explorers, camel, jungle fairies, and walrus made their way through a rocky chasm that led out into a sudden clearing filled with dozens and dozens of smoking ice towers. Most of them started wide at the base and then became thinner and thinner, leaning over at crooked angles until they tapered off into points. They rather reminded Stella of giant wizard hats.

"They're called ice fumaroles," Cadi told them. "Ice dragons live inside them. They're what cause the smoke."

Stella gasped. "How extraordinary! I've never seen

a dragon. Even Felix has never seen one. He says they're incredibly rare. Are they dangerous?"

Cadi shrugged. "I don't think so."

"I can't recall any explorers who've been killed by a dragon," Beanie said. "Plenty have perished due to rampaging elephants, hippos, polar bears, yetis, squids, jellyfish, and jungle cats, but never a dragon so far as I know. Although Sergeant Jameson Kirby Smith did get trapped in a dragon's lair while exploring the Black Pepper Caves of Aragba, and a search party had to be sent to dig him out. There was no sign of any dragon, though."

"Well, you won't see one here either," Cadi said. "I've been to this place several times with my father, and he says he's never seen so much as a dragon's claw. Ice dragons are very reclusive, you see. Some people even think they no longer exist—that it's just the smoldering remains of their dragon nests that cause the towers to smoke like that. But I like to think that the dragons are in there."

"Oh, I would so love to see one," Stella said, gazing at the smoking towers wistfully.

"Good heavens," Shay said under his breath. He gave her a nudge with his elbow and said, "Stella, look."

He pointed at the nearest ice tower, and everyone stared in astonishment at the sight of a small scaly snout poking over the top of it. This was quickly followed by a lizardy head, front legs, wings, and a long tail, as the ice dragon

clambered out from the fumarole, steam still billowing from its snout as it gazed down at them.

It was made of ice, from nose to tail, with glorious bright blue eyes that fixed on them with interest. Its every movement caused it to sparkle in the setting sun as it scrabbled down the tower toward them.

All around, more dragons were emerging from the ice towers, and the explorers stepped closer to one another warily, half fearing an ambush. But in fact, the dragons seemed more playful than aggressive as they slipped and slid down the ice towers, claws scrabbling in the snow, or else spread their wings and wheeled down from overhead. They were quite small dragons—about the size of foxes—

and they all seemed particularly interested in Stella.

At first they grouped together on the snow, peering at the explorers. Then, finally, one of the dragons broke away from the others and came right up to Stella, rubbing itself around her legs and poking its steaming snout into her hands like an affectionate dog.

"Perhaps they can sense you're an ice princess?" Shay said.

The dragons were too cold for the others to touch. When Cadi tried to stroke one, the ice burned her hand, and Beanie had to heal it for her. Stella, though, found she was able to handle them with no difficulty at all. They crawled into her arms, nosed at her face, settled on her shoulders, and poked their snouts into her pockets, getting rather a surprise when they found Buster in one of them.

The sun was rapidly setting, so the explorers decided to make camp there for the night. The ice fumaroles provided a little shelter from the wind, and Cadi said that the presence of the dragons would help keep the witch wolves at bay.

As it went dark, they saw that the ice dragons had tiny glittering specks of light deep within their bodies, lit up like tiny stars. They put on quite a show for the explorers as they unloaded the bags from Nigel and Gus, wheeling and turning overhead like a display of fireworks. An orangey haze hung over the mountain from all the many jack-o'-lanterns lighting up its surface, giving a fiery glow to the darkness, and the pumpkin on Nigel's back glowed brightly too. Stella was glad to see that Koa had returned and sat close to Shay's side, gazing up at the dragons with her usual calm expression, seeming back to her normal self.

Finally, the dragons disappeared back to their ice towers for the night, and Shay produced the magic fort blanket from his bag. "Right," he said. "Time for us to turn in as well. I don't know about you, but I'm looking forward to snuggling up in those cushions."

Stella thought of the gilded ottomans, the velvet beanbags, and the crackling fire and couldn't wait to settle into the magic fort for the night. They'd glimpsed it for only a minute before, and she was looking forward to having a poke around. Perhaps she might even be lucky enough to discover a jumping cactus if Munch had overlooked one in a corner somewhere.

"Rattlesnake ragtime," Shay said loudly.

Everyone stared at the blanket in his hand, but it stubbornly remained a manky old, boring blanket.

Shay frowned. "That was right, wasn't it?" he said. "Those were the words Munch said?"

"Yes, they were," Beanie replied. "Perhaps you have to say it with more enthusiasm?"

"It doesn't matter how you say it," Cadi said. "As long as you say the correct words, the magic fort should appear."

"That's not a magic fort blanket!" Ethan said with a sneer. "That's just a ratty old piece of rag! Munch swapped them and passed you a fake one. I told you he was a good-for-nothing scoundrel who was cheating us."

"Well, if you know so much, why did you let him cheat us in the first place?" Shay demanded, stuffing the blanket back in his bag in frustration. "You could have spoken up at the time, when it might actually have done some good. Normally there's no shutting you up."

"I didn't say anything because there was no need to," Ethan said coolly. He reached into his cloak and produced an old blanket with a flourish. "This is the real magic fort blanket. I swiped it from Munch's pocket when he was fussing around untying Nigel. Rattlesnake ragtime!"

Instantly, the blanket transformed and the magic fort popped up around them. It really was extremely big—easily large enough to encompass the explorers as well as all their animals, Gus included. It was clear that the fort had once belonged to someone from the Desert Jackal Explorers' Club, because the walls were covered with maps of various deserts, including the Scorpion Desert, Tarantula Desert, and Scorching Sands Desert. There were also sand capes slung over chair backs, pith helmets on tables, and safari hats hanging from hooks. Whoever had owned the fort before must have left in a terrible hurry. Stella remembered Munch telling them that a Desert Jackal Explorers' Club expedition had passed by Witch Mountain recently, and that was how he'd come by the magic carpet and the camel. The magic fort must have been traded at the same time too. At least, Stella hoped it had been traded. She couldn't help remembering what Ethan had said about scavenging from dead bodies and doomed expeditions.

One thing was different from the last time they'd seen the fort, however, and that was that there was an enormous pot of meaty stew bubbling away on a hook above the fire. Shay frowned at it and said, "That wasn't there before, was it? Could there be someone living here?"

"Impossible," Beanie said at once. "When a magic fort blanket reverts back to its blanket shape, it's too small to contain people. Usually, any explorers or animals are automatically forced out, but there was one recorded incident of a fort blanket's magic malfunctioning and failing to eject the explorers before it collapsed back down."

"What happened to them?" Cadi asked.

"Oh, they were pulverized," Beanie said. "Completely. There was nothing left of them. When the blanket was finally recovered, all anybody found was blobs of stuff—"

"That's very rare, though, right?" Stella said, cutting him off with a shudder.

"Extremely," Beanie reassured her. "In fact, you're more likely to be killed by a spitting camel or a rampaging walrus than by a magic fort blanket."

Everyone turned their heads to stare at Nigel and Gus, who both gazed back innocently.

"That's all very well," Shay said, shaking his head. "But if there's no one here, then how do you explain this?" He pointed at the pot of cooking food.

"I don't know," Beanie said. "Perhaps it's just part of the fort's magic?"

"But look here," Stella said, pointing to the table. "It's been set out for us, almost as if someone knew we were coming."

She was right. Part of the long table was covered in a jumble of maps and helmets, but the rest of it had been cleared away to make room for five bowls and five spoons.

"There's even a table set for the fairies. Look."

Stella pointed at the tiny table that was perched on their big one. It had four chairs around it, along with four tiny bowls.

"Speaking of the fairies, if we're going to eat some of this stew, then we better get a move on before they gobble it all," Shay said.

The explorers turned around only to find that the jungle fairies were already attacking the pot with spoons they'd produced from somewhere. The four of them were sitting on the edge of the pot with their legs dangling over the side, leaning forward to dip their spoons into the stew and slurp at the contents.

"For heaven's sake!" Ethan exclaimed, ushering them away. "Come on! Shoo! This food belongs to everyone—not just you!" The magician batted them away with an exclamation of disgust. "Oh, gross. One of them had her feet dangling in the stew! I think it was Hermina! Hermina, don't be so repugnant! None of us wants to eat food that's had hairy fairy feet in it!"

The fairies ran guiltily back to their own table—one of them leaving stew footprints across the floor behind her—and immediately began putting on their bow ties and squabbling over their one top hat.

"Oh, don't make such a fuss," Cadi said, reaching for the ladle cheerfully. "Jungle fairy feet never hurt anyone. Bring the bowls over and I'll serve it up."

They ate their stew quickly, before the fairies could get back into the pot. It was one of the most delicious things Stella had ever tasted, and just the thing after a long day of exploring.

After the stew, the jungle fairies honored their side of the deal by producing a plate of piranha cupcakes from somewhere (although the explorers would have allowed them to share the meal even without this). Hermina obviously felt bad about the feet-in-stew incident because she made a special point of personally taking a cupcake to Ethan.

The magician sighed. "I hope you haven't wiped your nose or anything horrid on this," he said.

"Sometimes it's worth just accepting kindness where you find it, Prawn," Shay remarked from the end of the table.

It seemed to Stella that the wolf whisperer had been a little quieter than normal, and while the others were enjoying the cupcakes, she took the opportunity to quietly ask him if he was okay.

"I'm just worried about the witch wolves," he told her. "Somehow I feel like . . . like they might be able to hurt Koa." He glanced down at the shadow wolf, who lay quietly at his feet.

"But how?" Stella asked. "I mean, she's a shadow wolf, isn't she? So she doesn't have any substance."

"No, but witch wolves are different too. Cadi said they were soul eaters, didn't she? Well, some people think that a whisperer's shadow animal is part of the whisperer's soul given shape. I've never seen Koa cower before, ever. She's afraid of the witch wolves, and that terrifies me."

"Oh dear. I'm sorry," Stella said miserably. She reached her hand down to Koa, who sniffed at her fingers. "If it weren't for me, then you wouldn't be here and Koa wouldn't be anywhere near the witch wolves."

Shay immediately gripped her hand and squeezed it tight. "Don't be sorry, Sparky. I'm not. I wouldn't be anywhere other than here with you. Witch Mountain is far too dangerous to face without friends by your side. This witch needs to be dealt with so that you don't have to live in fear anymore, and we can't allow anything to happen to Felix either."

Stella felt tears suddenly fill her eyes, and she wasn't sure whether it was because of Shay's loyal words, her fear and worry over Felix, or a combination of the two.

"What would happen to you, though?" she asked, blinking them away. "If Koa got hurt, I mean."

Shay shook his head and brushed his long dark hair back with one hand. "To be completely honest, I don't know. Koa's just always been there. The two of us are linked. I know that if I'm in pain she feels it too, so I guess it would work the other way around as well." He gave Stella a quick smile and said, "Hopefully we won't have to find out."

Having finished their food, Mustafah immediately fetched his drums and the others started up their chant of doom in the middle of the table.

"They're peculiar little things, aren't they?" Cadi said, sweeping back her mass of dreadlocks. "Do you think they get bored doing all that chanting and drumming all the time? Looks a bit repetitive." She snapped her fingers suddenly and said, "I wonder if they'd like some flags. They look like flag wavers to me. Does anyone have any paper and coloring pencils by any chance?"

Beanie had brought some pencils in case they were able to fill in any of the blank spaces on the Witch Mountain map. He also had a sketchbook to draw any interesting things they might discover along the way and had already filled several pages with the flying sharks and ice dragons. He tore a couple of sheets out for Cadi, who set about making four little flags. When she was finished, she cut them out and stuck each one to a twig.

"Let's see what happens with this," she said, handing the first flag to Mustafah.

The jungle fairy took it from her cautiously, stared at it for a bit, then scratched at his head, looking puzzled.

"You're supposed to wave it," Cadi told him. "Like this, look." She took the flag from him and waved it back and forth. Mustafah's eyes immediately lit up, and he practically snatched the flag from her and started waving it energetically, clearly delighted.

"There. I knew they'd like them," Cadi said, looking pleased as the other fairies eagerly rushed forward for their flags.

"Oh, you've drawn the explorer club crests on them," Stella said, peering closer and seeing that the flag Hermina was waving over her head was illustrated with the Polar Bear Explorers' Club crest.

"I thought they could help me decide which club to join," Cadi replied. "Assuming any of them accept my application, of course."

Ethan squinted at the fairies and then said, "There's

no such thing as a Space Alien Explorers' Club."

"No, but there's no point making an Ocean Squid Explorers' Club flag, is there?" Cadi asked. "Seeing as they don't accept girl members."

Ethan seemed rather put out about this and fairly snatched the sketchbook from Beanie so that he could make a flag of his own.

"Is that supposed to be the Ocean Squid Explorers' Club crest?" Shay asked, peering at it once he was done.

"Of course it is," Ethan snapped.

Shay grinned and said, "Well, that squid looks more like a banana peel, if you ask me."

"Nobody is asking you," Ethan said, and then gave the flag to Mustafah, who seemed even more thrilled with two flags than he had been with one, bounding around with them in quite a frenzy.

"Let's have a poke around and explore," Ethan announced, pushing the sketchbook away. "I need to find some food for Nigel, and we ought to take stock of what's here."

The others were only too willing to explore the magic fort. The table was set in a sort of kitchen area, with lots of cupboards, and they found these well stocked with tins of food and dried supplies. There was a brief commotion when Ethan stuck his hand into a drawer and was immediately attacked by a jumping cactus, which was basically a ball of vicious barbs that stuck themselves firmly into his skin. Eventually they were able to remove it, and Beanie provided a bit of healing magic and then offered Ethan a polar bear bandage from his pack. On the plus side, though, it turned out that jumping cactuses were food to camels. Nigel quickly ate the one that had jumped on Ethan, before wandering around the fort, poking his snout into corners, and picking up the other cactuses that Munch had failed to remove.

As well as a kitchen and living-room area, the fort had its own sleeping quarters, containing a neat row of narrow beds, all hung with mosquito nets.

"All right, there's definitely someone here," Ethan said, staring. "Look, there's exactly five beds made up, and they've even put four matchboxes out with hankies for the jungle fairies to sleep in."

As well as the made-up beds, there were five pairs of slippers neatly set out, all bearing the crest of the Desert Jackal Explorers' Club. It certainly looked as if there was someone in the fort with them, but they had seen no sign of anyone, and the fort consisted of only the two rooms.

"Hello?" Stella called, gazing around. "Is there anyone here?"

Nobody answered her.

"Maybe they're hiding?" Cadi suggested. "Perhaps they're shy?"

"Well, we're going to have to root them out, whoever

they are," Ethan said. "I'm not sleeping here if there's some unknown person lurking about. We might all be murdered in our beds. Garroted, most likely."

"I don't think that's their plan," Stella said. "So far all they've done is cook us dinner and make us up somewhere to sleep."

They traipsed back into the living area, where five steaming mugs of hot chocolate stood on the table.

"This is ridiculous!" Ethan exclaimed. "It's like we keep just missing them, but where are they scooting off to?"

"Aha!" Beanie exclaimed from the corner. "I think I've found them!" He turned around with a genie bottle clutched in his hands. "There's bound to be a genie in this," he said. "They're extremely popular at the Desert Jackal Explorers' Club, aren't they?"

The others came over and peered at the bottle, which was dark gold in color and had a variety of jewels and gems studded around the base.

"Well, give it a rub," Shay suggested. "Isn't that what you're supposed to do?"

Since none of them had had any contact with a genie before, no one was quite sure how to proceed. Beanie tried rubbing the bottle, as suggested, but this had no effect, so he removed the lid and peered inside instead.

"He's in there!" he exclaimed. "The genie's in there! I can see him!"

The others all squeezed against one another in their attempt to catch a glimpse. Stella gasped in delight at the sight of a tiny marbled bathroom contained within the genie bottle, complete with a claw-footed bathtub, in which a genie was soaking himself while a bright yellow rubber duck bobbed on the surface.

"Um . . . hello?" Beanie said. "Mr. Genie?"

At the sound of Beanie's voice, the genie gave a great start, splashing around and slopping soapy water onto his marble floor. The next moment, pale blue smoke poured from the top of the genie bottle, and a full-size genie stood dripping wet before them. He had blue skin and an incredibly twisty black mustache, which the president of the Polar Bear Explorers' Club would certainly approve of. He wore a bathrobe emblazoned with the crest of the Desert Jackal Explorers' Club. Stella could clearly see the rubber duck sticking out of one pocket.

"Oh," she said. "Hello. We didn't mean to—"

"No, no, don't tell me." The genie held up one hand. "It's the little marshmallows. I knew I'd forgotten something that you explorers absolutely must have. I knew it would be something terribly important that couldn't wait even a single instant. I knew I wouldn't be able to have my bath in peace. Really, I don't know how I could ever have been so optimistic as to run a bath in the first place. I ought to have just gone outside and rolled around in the sand."

"We're on Witch Mountain," Beanie said. "There's no sand outside. Only snow."

"Rolled around in the snow, then," the genie snapped. "If we're in the Icelands, then no wonder it's so miserably cold all the time. That's why I wanted to have a bath—to warm myself up." He marched over to the kitchen and started banging around in the cupboards.

"We're terribly sorry to have disturbed you," Stella said, going after him. "We were just curious about who was doing the cooking and things, that's all. We didn't mean to interrupt your bath."

"Would you like rattlesnake marshmallows or scorpion ones?" the genie asked.

"Oh dear, are those the only choices?" Stella replied. She tried to peer over the genie's shoulder into the cupboard. "You don't have any unicorn ones, I suppose?"

"Scorpion marshmallows it is," the genie said, and set about dropping a few into each mug.

"Thank you very much," Stella said, trying to salvage the situation. "My name's Stella Starflake Pearl. And you are . . . ?"

"Ruprekt," the genie replied. He turned around to face the group of explorers, seeming to take them in for the first time. "Good heavens, you explorers seem to get younger and younger all the time! But no matter. I'll tell you the same thing I told Lord Rupert Benedict Arnold, and that is that I am a fort genie only. My role is to look after the place and your comfort. I can grant minor wishes involving particular requests." He snapped his fingers and a fat bag of unicorn-shaped marshmallows appeared in his hand. He handed these to Stella without a word, and she couldn't help wishing that he'd produced these before he'd filled her mug up with scorpion-shaped ones. "I'm happy to fulfill requests for particular types of marshmallows, or duck-shaped hot-water bottles, or exotically flavored breakfast dishes, or extra-fleecy blankets; I can provide knitted nose warmers, or foot massages, or scorching-hot baths. But I cannot grant any premium wishes. So if somebody gets themselves bitten by a poisonous snake, I can't magic away the venom. I cannot extract a jumping cactus from any part of your body without leaving scratch marks and scars. And I certainly can't snap my fingers and magic away an infestation of tarantulas from anyone's underwear."

"Great Scott!" Ethan exclaimed. "Being in the Desert Jackal Explorers' Club sounds like a nasty business!"

"Furthermore," the genie went on, "if you get yourselves trapped in a ravine, or buried in a sandstorm, or stuck in a gorge of some kind, then put up the fort for shelter, by all means, but do not expect me to be able to magic the expedition to safety on some kind of magic carpet. Now, here are your breakfast menus." The genie produced five cards from the pocket of his robe. "Please tick your choices and leave them on the table no later than midnight. If you require anything else from me tonight, kindly ring the genie bell rather than sticking your overlarge noses into my private, personal space." He waved a hand in the direction of a blue and gold bell set on a table in one corner of the tent, and then—before anyone could say another word—smoked back inside his genie bottle.

Stella would have liked to continue speaking with the genie, but since he seemed to be in quite a bad mood, they left him to his bubble bath and set about turning in for the night.

Stella noticed that Beanie had brought his father's journal with him again. It had been found among his things at the deserted expedition camp part of the way across the Black Ice Bridge, and Beanie was always poring over it, hoping for some clue to explain his father's disappearance.

He was still set on being the first explorer to cross the infamous bridge one day, but Stella wasn't convinced it was a good idea. The bridge was said to be cursed, and countless expeditions had vanished trying to cross it, never to be seen or heard from again. Perhaps, after all, there were some places in the world that were so cursed and forsaken that no person should venture into them, even if they were an explorer.

Stella left Beanie to his bedtime reading and then fetched a pith helmet that she and Cadi proceeded to fit to

Gus's big head. He'd crashed into things a few times, and the girls were concerned that he might hurt himself.

"I think this helmet makes him look rather dashing," Stella said, giving the walrus a pat on the back.

"You know, I rather agree with you," Cadi said. She glanced at Stella then and said, "So, what's it like being a princess? Is it absolutely marvelous?"

Stella sighed. "Not really. Being an explorer is absolutely marvelous, but being an ice princess isn't that great most of the time."

"Gosh, I'd give anything to have magic powers," Cadi said. "It sounds like glorious fun."

"It would be," Stella said. "But if I use my powers too much, my heart will freeze solid and I'll turn into a villainous snow queen. That kind of takes the fun out of it. Even if I just use a little bit of tiara magic I can feel myself becoming colder. And crueler." She shivered. "I stop caring about the people I love. And that's a terrible, lonely, awful feeling."

As if sensing she was feeling sad, Gus leaned forward and gave her a big sloppy kiss all the way up the side of her cheek. Stella laughed and scratched the walrus behind his ear. They left him preening at himself in front of the mirror, admiring his helmet from various angles, and settled into their sleeping quarters.

Stella felt bad about how they had disturbed Ruprekt during his bath, though. So a few minutes later, she tiptoed back out to the living area, where the fire still crackled cheerfully away to itself. She wanted to do something to make it up to the genie, so she took her scarf from her pocket and wound it carefully around the genie bottle. Felix had given her the scarf a few years ago, and it was a beautiful thing made from white yeti wool and stitched with pale blue polar bears and unicorns. Ruprekt had mentioned being cold, after all, so perhaps wrapping up the genie bottle would help keep him warm in there.

Stella still felt like this wasn't quite enough, though. She recalled the snow unicorn and the snow yeti she had somehow managed to create and the magic that had fizzed through her fingers. She thought for a moment, and then walked over to the genie bell on the other side of the room. She lifted her hand and concentrated hard on what she wanted to do.

Sure enough, sparkly strands of blue magic fizzed from her fingertips, and moments later an entire troll family—no larger than the jungle fairies—stood on the table before her, all made from snow. They had big feet and tufts of hair that stuck out in all directions, and they each held a sign that read: GENIE SLEEPING: DO NOT DISTURB.

"There," Stella said, pleased. "That ought to do it. Don't let anyone ring the bell," she said to the trolls, who were all gazing up at her expectantly. "Poor Ruprekt deserves to get a good night's sleep just the same as the rest of us."

The trolls nodded at her and then began marching up and down, clutching their signs. It proved to be a good precaution because, just as Stella was making her way back to bed, Ethan came out and headed straight for the bell. He'd decided he wanted a duck-shaped hot-water bottle, but when he tried to reach for the bell, one of the trolls bit him rather hard on the finger, before waving his sign at him energetically. The magician probably could have done something to the trolls if he'd really wanted to—turned them all into wonky squish-squish frogs, for example—but he could see Stella watching him from the bedroom doorway, so he shrugged bad-temperedly and stomped back over to her.

"You're not wearing your tiara," he remarked. "So how did you manage to make those trolls?"

"I don't know," Stella replied. "It seems like I don't need to be wearing the tiara to do snow magic."

"What does that mean?" Ethan asked.

Stella shook her head. "I have no idea."

CHAPTER SIXTEEN

WHEN THE JUNIOR EXPLORERS woke the next morning, they each found a rubber duck at the end of their beds. They were all bright yellow and each wearing a different hat. Stella's duck had a tiara, Cadi's had a wide-brimmed cowboy-style hat, Beanie's had a knitted pom-pom hat, Ethan's had a pointed magician's hat, and Shay's had a cap with a wolf's head printed on it.

"I wonder what these are supposed to be for," Cadi said, picking up her rubber duck. The second her fingers touched it, a curtain sprang up around her bed, which disappeared to be replaced by a claw-footed bathtub filled with steaming-hot water.

"Gosh, this is what I call service!" she exclaimed. "It even has my favorite bubble bath in it! Raspberry-scented!"

The others lost no time picking up their own ducks and

all found themselves with baths of their own. Stella was particularly excited about hers because the bubbles smelled like marzipan, the soap was in the shape of a polar bear, and there were even little toy penguins floating about in the water, as well as little icebergs.

Once the explorers were all washed and dressed, they made their way to the table, which Ruprekt had already set out with their breakfast choices. Stella had requested pancakes, and on approaching, she was delighted to see that the genie had produced unicorn-shaped ones for her.

"Good morning, Miss Stella," Ruprekt said, materializing beside her. "Allow me to pull out your chair. I hope the breakfast will be to your satisfaction."

"Thank you very much," Stella said, beaming at him.

The genie was wearing a robe stitched in an elaborate pattern of gold and blue, with emerald-green braid trim. He was also wearing Stella's scarf in a jaunty fashion around his neck.

"No one has ever given me a gift before," the genie said.

Stella had meant for the scarf to be more of a loan than a gift, but faced with the genie's obvious delight, there was no way she could ask for it back. And she knew Felix would understand why she had given it away.

"Gosh, never?" she asked. It seemed to her that it must be a very sad thing to have never ever received a gift from anyone. "But that's terrible!"

"Genies are servants, miss," Ruprekt said quietly. "That's how they see us in the Desert Jackal Explorers' Club, at least. And nobody gives gifts to servants."

"Well, you're not a servant to us," Stella hurried to reassure him. An awful thought occurred to her, and she said, "You're not a prisoner here, are you?"

"Oh no," Ruprekt replied. "Genies are paid well enough for their services, and I was freed from my lamp long ago. You don't get many captive genies these days." He gave a haughty sniff. "But that doesn't mean you necessarily get treated well either."

"Well, we don't expect you to be at our beck and call all the time," Stella said. She gestured over toward the snow trolls beside the genie lamp, who all seemed to have grouped together in one big ball of troll and gone to sleep in a tangle of hairy feet and big nostrils. "Just ask the trolls to pick up their signs any time you don't want to be disturbed."

"You're most kind," the genie replied, giving her a bow. "A true lady."

"Stella's a princess, in fact," Beanie said. "An ice princess."

"How glorious!" Ruprekt said. "I'm delighted to serve you, Your Majesty."

"Oh, there's really no need to call me that," Stella replied. "Please, just call me Stella."

"As you wish," the genie replied.

He snapped his fingers, and a little bubbling cauldron of hot chocolate appeared beside each of the explorers' plates. A little toy witch perched on the side of each cauldron, stirring the hot brew with a sugar broomstick.

They took their seats and ate their breakfast quickly. Stella was eager to head off as soon as possible. They absolutely had to catch up with Felix. The little toy witches stirring their drinks made Stella feel even more desperate to be away, especially when one of them hopped onto her broomstick and started flying around the room on it.

Noticing Stella's expression, Cadi said, "What's wrong?"

"Just the witch," Stella said, gesturing toward it and trying not to shudder. "They're such horrid, evil things."

Cadi looked a little surprised, and even Stella was taken aback by the force with which she'd spoken. But a witch had killed her parents and now threatened Felix, too, so she really felt that she had every reason to hate them.

Without any further ado, they packed up their stuff, collapsed the magic fort back down to a blanket, said goodbye to the ice dragons smoking away in their fumaroles, and set off, heading farther up Witch Mountain. The air felt bitingly cold after the snug warmth of the fort, and they were all glad of their snow boots and thick cloaks.

Stella noticed that she wasn't as cold as she should have been, however. On the last expedition she'd worn layers and layers of sweaters and thermal trousers, just like everyone else, and she'd still been cold most of the time. It was no less icy on Witch Mountain, and yet Stella wasn't wearing explorer's garb like before, only her gray dress beneath her cloak. As it was a traveling dress, it was made from wool, and Stella had thick, sparkly snowflake tights on underneath, but this shouldn't have been enough to keep her warm in the Icelands. The others shivered, rubbed their hands, and stamped their feet far more than Stella did. She hadn't even so much as needed to put on her gloves. And that worried her. It had to be something to do with the fact that she was an ice princess, and—if her new magic powers were anything to go by— becoming more and more of one all the time.

"Just up ahead is the Forest of Enchanted Broomsticks," Cadi said, glancing around at the others. "That's where I need to find the witch I captured earlier and take one of her hairs."

"And after the forest?" Shay asked. "What comes next?"

Cadi shrugged. "Your guess is as good as mine," she said. "I've never ventured farther than that before."

"Is the forest safe?" Beanie asked.

"Not particularly," Cadi replied. "It's an enchanted broomstick forest in Witch Mountain, after all. It's full of all kinds of dangerous things."

"Oh good," Ethan said. "That sounds like fun."

"I don't think it sounds like fun at all," Beanie said, looking concerned.

"It *is* fun, actually," Cadi said with a grin. "It wouldn't be so interesting if it were safe in there." She clambered up onto the saddle on Gus's back.

"That walrus looks even more absurd wearing a pith helmet," Ethan remarked, shaking his head. "It's no wonder you were turned away from the Ocean Squid Explorers' Club if you turned up with that thing in tow."

Cadi stuck her tongue out at the magician. "At least Gus doesn't spit at people," she said.

Nigel immediately spat at a nearby jack-o'-lantern, whose expression clearly offended him.

They hadn't been traveling long before they reached the Forest of Enchanted Broomsticks. There was no missing it. The trees loomed large on the mountain before them, looking rather like an ordinary forest at first glance. But when they got closer, they saw that the long brown trunks weren't trees at all, but giant broomsticks. And instead of leaves or branches, they had bristly brushes that stuck up into the sky like dead twigs, creating a thick canopy that made the forest itself dark and full of shadows, despite the sunlight. There was a strange, still feeling about the place—an absence of the rustling and scurrying and chirping that you might usually expect to find in a normal forest. They were all aware of it. Koa stood close to Shay's side with her ears back, which was always a bad sign. Stella couldn't help thinking that this was definitely not the type of woods where teddy bears went to have their picnics.

Cadi didn't seem to mind, however, and looked back over her shoulder to give the others a wide grin. "Here we go, folks," she said with a wink. "Best keep your wits about you."

At that moment an explosion in the sky alerted them to another confetti vulture marking Felix's position on the mountain ahead of them. It was on the other side of the Forest of Enchanted Broomsticks, confirming that they were going in the right direction.

The explorers, the witch hunter, the camel, the shadow wolf, and the walrus entered the forest quietly and cautiously. Even Gus seemed to understand that he mustn't make any noise, refraining from his usual bellows. There were four members of the expedition, however, who failed to appreciate the need for stealth. The jungle fairies' chant of doom started up within seconds. . . .

"*Fee-fi-fo-fo, fee-fi-fo-fo, fee-fi-fo-fo!*"

"Oh dear." Cadi looked around to stare at the fairies, who were chanting in the dip between Nigel's humps. "I wouldn't let them carry on like that, you know. There's all kinds of things in this forest that are better off not knowing we're here."

Ethan reached up and snatched the drums from Mustafah, who shook his fist at him in an agitated manner. The magician shook his fist right back. "You stupid fairies are going to get us all turned into toadstools!" he hissed.

"Here, let's give them the flags," Stella said before the fairies started shooting them all with stink-berries.

Cadi dug the tiny explorer flags from her pocket and handed them over. Mustafah threw the Ocean Squid Explorers' Club flag away rather pointedly, but they kept hold of the other four flags and waved them about a bit, although it was more of a sullen movement than an excited one this time.

They continued deeper into the forest. The broomsticks around them were extremely tall and thin, reaching up three hundred feet or more into the sky. The canopy of bristles was so thick that it kept out the snow as well as the light, and they found their boots crunching on crisp bristles that had come loose and fallen down. The place smelled of damp wood and stale air and, unfortunately, camel breath—all those jumping cactuses seemed to have given Nigel a bad case of indigestion.

It was so dark in the forest that Stella had to retrieve the fire-pixie lamp from her bag and poke the pixie awake to light their path. They couldn't see all the way up to the bristles clearly, but every now and then they heard the rustle of something moving.

"What's up there?" Shay whispered to Cadi, peering into the gloom.

"Bats probably," the hunter replied. "Maybe some owls. There's lots of bats and owls on Witch Mountain. Don't worry. They won't hurt you."

"What about rabbits?" Stella asked. "We were told that Jezzybella has been bringing poisonous rabbits onto the mountain."

"Really? I've never seen a rabbit here," Cadi replied.

"Magic forests are never good news for explorers, even when they're not on Witch Mountain," Beanie said. "I expect there are all kinds of terribly dangerous things to be found in here, from rock monsters to gobble-grogs to—"

"My witch should be just through here," Cadi said, guiding Gus through the bristles.

They came out in a little clearing, where they found the narrowest, most crooked-looking gingerbread house Stella could have imagined. It was leaning at such an angle that it was a wonder it managed to stay up at all. With chocolate roof tiles, barley-sugar windows, gingerbread walls, and a candy-cane fence, it looked like something straight out of a fairy tale.

"Come on," Cadi said. "She ought to be waiting around the back."

The explorers followed the witch hunter to the other side of the house, where there was a stone garden, a little rock pool full of fat toads, and what appeared to be a wishing well.

"Don't throw any pennies into the wishing well," Cadi warned as they went past.

"Why not?" Ethan asked.

"A troll lives there," she replied. "And he gets ever so cross if people chuck dirty old pennies at him." She glanced back and said, "Oh, and I wouldn't let the jungle fairies feast on the house like that. It's got a magic spell on it that will make anyone who eats it terribly ill."

While the four explorers hurried to drag the jungle fairies away from the house, Cadi slipped off Gus's back and walked, spurs jangling, over to a broomstick tree. There was a tree house perched, rather precariously, between its bristles, and Cadi picked up one of the pebbles at her feet and threw it, with expert aim, up to the house. The tree house was obviously made of gingerbread too, because the pebble caused a cascade of gingery crumbs to come showering down on the hunter, making her sneeze.

The jungle fairies loved the taste of the big house, and it took all four explorers to prize them away. Stella caught hold of Mustafah just as he succeeded in breaking a massive slab of gingerbread from the windowsill. She had to admit that it did smell incredibly good, like it had just been freshly baked.

"Don't do it," she warned, and tried to pluck it from Mustafah's hands.

The fairy was too quick for her, however, and shoved the entire brick of gingerbread into his mouth in one piece.

"Oh, Mustafah." Stella sighed. "Cadi says this will make you ill. You should never trust witches' gingerbread, you know."

The jungle fairy clearly didn't share her concern, however, because he swallowed the gingerbread down in one self-satisfied gulp.

"I think Harriet's eaten some too," Shay said, peering at the fairy in his hand.

"Let's just hope that jungle fairies have stronger stomachs than humans," Stella said. "Best keep a tight grip on them for now." She peered down at Mustafah. "I'm sorry, but it's no use squirming like that," she told him. "This is for your own good."

The explorers joined Cadi at the base of the tree house. The witch hunter had a fine collection of gingerbread crumbs amassed in the brim of her hat from the pebbles she'd thrown.

"Drusilla!" she hissed. "Where are you?" She glanced at the others and said, "Drat, I think she must have wandered off."

"You didn't just leave her free, did you?" Stella asked, surprised. "Surely you at least tied her up?"

"No, but she promised she'd wait here," Cadi replied.

"You can't trust a witch's promise."

Cadi shrugged. "Never mind. She can't have gone far. We'll probably come across her if we push on."

The explorers continued on their way. Almost as soon as they left the house they came across a foul-smelling swamp. The thick green liquid oozed and bubbled, emitting a horrid smell of rotten eggs and dirty old feet. There must have been hot springs underground, because the surface steamed. The stench was so strong that it even seemed to have affected the broomstick trees, which weren't tall and straight here, but curled and leaned at odd angles. Even the bristles had been affected, growing longer and stragglier, hanging down toward the swamp in thick coils of hairy rope.

"Don't stick your hand in the swamp," Cadi whispered to the others. "There are trolls living in there and they'll drag you right in if they can."

"You must think we're utterly brainless," Ethan said, one hand covering his nose. "Who in their right mind would stick their hand into that foul thing? I would rather die than dip so much as a toe in it."

After a little while the path led steeply up a very high bank before running out completely, and they found themselves facing the most rickety-looking bridge Stella had ever seen. Felix had told her before that rickety bridges were all part of exploring, and it was some kind of rule that bridges in unknown lands were never strong and new and sturdy, but always wobbly and shaky and unsound.

"That's what makes them such fun," he'd said.

Stella really wasn't too sure about this bridge, however. It consisted of rotten-looking wooden planks tied to two lengths of rope that seemed like they might unravel at any moment. Each end was tied to one of the bent broomstick trees, and the bridge stretched right over a vast expanse of bubbling green swamp.

"This has got to be some kind of cruel joke!" Ethan groaned.

"Looks like it's the only way across," Cadi said cheerfully, rolling up her sleeves, throwing her mass of dreadlocks back over her shoulder, and seeming pretty delighted with the whole affair.

She nudged Gus forward, but Ethan hurried around to plant himself in the walrus's path. "No, no, no," he said.

"You are not going first on that thing. I mean, look at it! It's as big as an elephant! There's no way the bridge will bear his weight."

"Well, there's only one way to find out," Cadi replied. "If worst comes to worst and he crashes through, then we can all climb onto his back and he'll swim across. Gus is an excellent swimmer, even in swampy water like this."

"Nigel can hardly climb on his back, can he?" Ethan said, pointing at the camel, who had curled his lip in disgust at the smell of the swamp. "And didn't you say there were trolls?"

"Well, what would you suggest, then?" Cadi replied. "Since you're so smart?"

"I'm going first," Ethan said in a firm voice. He held up a hand and said, "I know I'm being selfish, and I'm sorry. But every time someone puts weight on that bridge they're weakening it further, making it even more likely that the whole thing will just collapse. Since I'm the one who can't stand being dirty, it seems only fair that I go first."

"I don't like being dirty either," Stella protested indignantly.

"No, but you don't mind being covered in polar bear slobber," Ethan shot back. "We should go one at a time, and I'm first."

Before anyone else could protest or argue with him further, Ethan stepped onto the bridge. The moment his boot touched the first plank, it swayed, groaned, and creaked beneath his feet in a most alarming manner, and the magician had to stick both arms out to keep his balance. Looking at the great length of the bridge stretching out before him, Stella couldn't help wondering whether he'd manage to make it to the end, especially as there were no handrails to hold on to.

"Ethan, I'm not sure about this," she called. "Perhaps we should look for another way across."

"It's too late now. I'm doing it," Ethan replied.

He'd managed to walk several feet out onto the bridge and was about halfway over when Beanie suddenly said below them, "I've found another way. There's a tunnel that goes under the swamp. We don't need to cross the bridge."

The others all turned around and saw that Beanie had scrambled off the bank to the marshy grass below and had, indeed, unearthed the entrance to a tunnel. It had been hidden by a thick hanging curtain of bristles from one of the broomstick trees, but now they saw that it led straight underneath the swamp. It was too dark to tell whether it reached the other side or not, but everyone agreed it was worth a shot. No one wanted to navigate an uppity camel or a witless walrus across the bridge.

Stella called Ethan's name, meaning to tell him that they'd found another way, but he waved his arm at her irritably without looking back.

"Would you stop distracting me?" he snapped. "Anyone would think you want me to fall in!"

"Just leave him," Shay told her. "He's more than halfway across now. And we don't know how safe this tunnel is, or whether it'll get us across."

They scrabbled down the bank to join Beanie, who looked at Cadi and asked, "Do trolls live in the tunnel, too?" He tugged at his pom-pom hat anxiously. "Trolls are very dangerous to explorers, you know. There have been troll-related deaths and maimings and injuries linked to all four of the explorers' clubs. The desert-dwelling sand troll torments the Desert Jackal Explorers' Club, while the salty ridge web-footed water troll has been known to attack submarines belonging to the Ocean Squid Explorers' Club. Ice trolls are second only to yetis in the destruction they've wreaked on the Polar Bear Explorers' Club, while the jungle-dwelling, nose-picking, bogey-eating trolls of Monkey Jungle have spoiled many a picnic of the Jungle Cat Explorers' Club." He peered at the tunnel and said, "So, are there likely to be trolls in there, do you think?"

The hunter shrugged. "I couldn't say. I've never been in any tunnels on Witch Mountain before."

"I suppose it's likely to have all the same hazards as the caves," Beanie said glumly, before ticking them off on his fingers. "Biting bats, nibbling rats, poisonous snakes, poisonous spiders, poisonous—"

"Oh, no, no," Cadi said cheerfully. "You might find those things in normal caves, but in Witch Mountain caves you're far more likely to come across flying sharks, hypnotizing white cats, crazed bug-eyed gremlins, suffocating dancing mushrooms, or—"

"All right." Shay held up his hand. "We get the picture." He glanced at Beanie, who was shuddering from head to toe and tugging at his pom-pom hat again in agitation. "You never know. Perhaps there'll be nothing dangerous or horrible in there at all." He went to clap Beanie on the back, but then remembered at the last moment that the medic wouldn't like that, so instead, he said, "Just think about narwhals and jelly beans and we'll be out the other end in no time."

At the mention of narwhals, Beanie remembered the wooden carving his father had given him and took it from his pocket to clutch for comfort. Stella reached up for Nigel's reins and lifted the glowing pixie lamp a little higher, and the four children stepped forward into the gaping dark tunnel.

It smelled of damp and cold stone, with green lichen creeping up the walls and slippery moss sparkling in a coat of frost underfoot.

"Well, gremlins have definitely been in here at some point," Cadi said. She pointed at the wall. "These are gremlin holes, for sure."

Stella lifted the fire-pixie lamp and they all contemplated the multitude of holes burrowed into the rock.

"Looks like they haven't been here for some time, though," Cadi said, gazing around. "There'd be more little bones scattered about if gremlins lived here."

Gus slid easily over the slippery moss and seemed delighted to be in the tunnel. It was a good thing they'd fashioned him with a pith helmet, though, because he raced happily ahead of them and instantly smashed into a wall in the bend up ahead. He shook his head, looking a little confused but otherwise unharmed.

The tunnel curved around to the right, and as soon as they turned the bend, they found they no longer required the fire-pixie lamp because light flooded in through the walls, which weren't made from solid rock but from a clear material.

"What is this?" Stella asked, peering at it. "Glass?"

"Witchstone," Cadi replied.

The witchstone windows took up most of the tunnel, including the roof, allowing them to see that they were surrounded by swamp on all sides.

"How come the swamp is so bright?" Stella asked as they all pressed their noses up against the witchstone window for a better view. "It looked solid green from above."

"Strange," Cadi said. "There must be something glowing in there." She turned to Beanie and said, "You seem to be the troll expert. What do you think? Is there such a thing as a glow-in-the-dark troll?"

Beanie frowned. "I'm not a troll expert," he said. "There are more than three hundred types of troll in the discovered world, and so far I've only memorized the habits and habitats of sixty-two. Perhaps I should ask Uncle Benedict for a troll book for Christmas."

"Come on," Shay said. "Whatever's in there, it's probably nothing nice. We should push on. Ethan will think we've been snatched away by goblins."

They continued down the tunnel. Every now and then a shape would glide past the window, but it came and went so quickly that Stella wasn't able to make it out properly. She was sure that Shay was right, though, and nothing good was likely to dwell in a swamp on Witch Mountain.

"There's Ethan. Look," Beanie said, pointing through a witchstone window in the roof of the tunnel.

They peered up and saw that the magician was, indeed, directly above them. From their position they could see his boots on the bridge above. It looked like he had almost reached the other side of the swamp.

"The light seems brighter here," Beanie said.

Stella realized he was right. The water was extremely bright right underneath where Ethan was standing.

"Uh-oh," Cadi said.

"What?" Shay looked at her sharply.

"I think I know what's creating that light," the hunter said. She pointed out the window and said, "Glow-piranhas."

Stella followed the direction of her finger and gasped. There was indeed an entire hoard of devilish fish directly underneath Ethan. They appeared to be mostly teeth— rows upon rows of them—sticking straight out of the fishes' mouths, curving over their lips, and giving them a ferocious look. Their fins emitted a silvery light that glowed bright enough to cut straight through the murky swamp. Their attention was fixed on Ethan, and they were all gnashing their teeth in an expectant manner.

"Great Scott!" Shay exclaimed. "If he falls in the swamp, he's toast."

"He won't be toast," Beanie said, frowning. "He'll be a dead magician if he falls in the swamp, that's what he'll be. A shoal of glow-piranhas can strip the flesh off a fully grown man in under a minute."

Just when they thought things couldn't get any worse, a large white shape suddenly slapped down onto the roof of the tunnel, making the explorers jump back in alarm. They found themselves staring up into the eyes of a pale troll with gangly limbs, narrow eyes, wild seaweedy hair, and webbed fingers that suckered down onto the witchstone like an octopus's tentacles as the awful thing hissed through the water at them, displaying rows of needle-sharp teeth.

"And that's a web-fingered vampire troll," Beanie said. "They feed off blood and are often found living in close proximity to glow-piranhas."

"Cripes!" Stella exclaimed. "The swamp is crawling with monsters! Quick! We've got to warn Ethan!"

They set off at a run, the camel's hooves clattering noisily on the stone floor as Nigel bleated indignantly at being forced to move above a sedate trot. As they raced along they saw more and more of the pale vampire trolls flitting about in the water, which was bright with piranhas.

They tumbled out of the end of the tunnel in a panic just as Ethan stepped off the bridge. He looked astonished to see them. "How the heck did you—"

"Tunnel!" Stella gasped. "Beanie found it."

"Well, you might have told me," Ethan huffed.

"Perhaps if you'd waited a moment rather than racing to be the first person to cross the bridge then you could have traveled safely with us instead," Shay replied. He reached his hand down to Koa, who nuzzled the air around his fingers. "It doesn't always pay to be selfish, you know, Prawn."

Stella pointed at the swamp and said, "The water down there is absolutely crawling with monsters. You were very lucky!"

The magician gave her a withering look. "It's got nothing to do with luck and everything to do with my excellent balance and sure-footedness." He glared at Shay. "And don't call me selfish! If anything, I was doing you lot a favor. If the bridge was unsafe, then I would have been the first to find out."

"Well, it doesn't matter now, so let's not argue about it," Shay said with a sigh. He reached out for Ethan's elbow and said, "Let's just concentrate on getting away from this monster-filled swamp."

Rather than accepting the steadying hand, Ethan snapped, "Don't touch me! I don't need your help!"

He batted Shay's hand away, but unfortunately, the movement caused his heel to slip in the soft mud at the edge of the swamp. Shay lunged forward but managed only to snatch at Ethan's fingertips, which immediately slipped from his grasp as the magician fell backward, straight into the green slime.

CHAPTER SEVENTEEN

ONE MOMENT THE MAGICIAN was there, the next he had been sucked down beneath the surface of the water with a glugging noise. Stella heard Beanie's words from the tunnel: *He'll be a dead magician if he falls in the swamp, that's what he'll be. A shoal of glow-piranhas can strip the flesh off a fully grown man in under a minute. . . .*

She had the terrible image of plucking a skeleton from the green waters and that being all that was left of Ethan. Zachary Vincent Rook would not be at all happy if they presented him with a bag of bones when they got home. But there was no time for panic or running around in a flap. Felix always said that the first rule of exploring was not to lose your head in a crisis.

"After all, if explorers panicked every time a member of their expedition got washed over a waterfall, snatched away by a yeti, or buried in an avalanche, then we'd be in a state of mayhem all the time, wouldn't we?" he'd said.

However, it was a little difficult to stay calm when one of your expedition had just fallen into a glow-piranha- and vampire-troll-infested, noxious-smelling swamp. Beanie, unfortunately, completely lost his head and started reciting piranha-related explorer deaths while tugging at his pom-pom hat, and Cadi put both hands to her mouth and stared in horror at the surface of the water, but Shay and Stella sprang into action at once.

Together they grabbed one of the overhanging hairy branches and started to pull it down. The tree groaned in protest, and they had to tug hard to get the branch beneath the surface, but the plan worked, because Ethan grabbed hold of it at once, and when they let the branch go, it flew back with a snap that yanked the magician from the water in an explosion of green slime. He landed on the bank covered in the horrible stuff, as well as, oddly, dozens of wonky squish-squish frogs, which were hopping and crawling all over him. Once they realized they were on land, however, they jumped off the magician and headed straight back toward the swamp.

"I didn't know there were wonky-squish-squish frogs in there!" Cadi said.

"Those aren't frogs!" Beanie gasped. He pointed at the nearest one. "That one's got teeth sticking out of its mouth.

And that one over there has a dorsal fin on its back. I think they're piranhas. Ethan must have used a spell on them."

"Didn't Ethan have Gideon in his pocket?" Shay asked.

A panic followed as everyone scrabbled to collect the frogs before they could disappear. Some of them did have a sort of piranha look about them still—whether this was teeth, fins, a glow, or just a general savageness—but others looked like perfectly ordinary frogs, and any one of those could easily be Gideon.

Stella collected some up in her skirt, wrinkling her nose against the smell—for the frogs were, of course, all covered in swamp water as well. Cadi whipped off her hat to deposit some in; Shay stuffed some into his bag, and Beanie used his pom-pom hat. By the time they tipped their amassed frogs into Shay's backpack, they were all pretty covered in slimy swamp goo. But not as much as Ethan. He was drenched with the stuff and still lying in a gasping heap on the mossy grass.

As Shay zipped up the bag of frogs, the magician staggered to his feet, looking rather like a swamp monster himself, and tried to wipe the green goop from his eyes. It was in his hair, dripping from his fingers, and sliding down the back of his neck.

"Oh my gods, that is the worst thing that's ever happened to me!" he gasped, almost crying in outrage. "I can't believe you're messing around with frogs at a time like this!"

"If you hadn't been such a stubborn idiot, then you wouldn't have fallen in the swamp in the first place!" Shay said. "I've never met anyone who's their own worst enemy as much as you are!"

"I was going to share them, but just for that you can find your own magic bath bubbles!" Ethan snapped.

He scooped the purple bubbles he'd stolen from Munch out of his pocket.

"Oh, are those bath bubbles?" Cadi said, peering at them.

"They're mine!" Ethan snarled.

"Okay, but I wouldn't use ten of them together like that if I were—"

"They're mine!" Ethan said again. "If you lot wanted some, then you should have stolen them from Weenus's Trading Post back when you had the chance." He glared at Shay fiercely and said, "You can accuse me of being my own worst enemy all you like, but it seems to me that I'm the only one of us who's got any foresight."

"The thing is, though, that if you use more than one at a time, then the results can be a bit—" Cadi began, but Ethan cut her off again.

"You're not tricking me into sharing! How stupid do you think I am?"

And with that he lifted his hand and slapped all ten of the bubbles against his forehead at once.

Stella remembered how Munch had used one of the bubbles on Nigel and the camel had been transformed into a sleek, glossy, immaculately groomed version of himself. But that had been one little bubble for an entire camel. The result of ten bubbles used on a boy was rather different. Stella expected Ethan to be himself, except cleaner, but in fact, he disappeared altogether. They thought he had actually vanished at first, but then Beanie spotted the purple object lying on the grass, and they all hurried over to inspect it.

It was a soap—about the size of Stella's palm—and it was fashioned in the shape of a magician, complete with pointed wizard's hat, flowing robes, and even a wand and an impressively bushy beard. For a moment they all stared at it in silence. Then Shay said, "He's actually turned himself into a soap, hasn't he? Using nothing more than his own stupidity."

"You can only be so clean without being soap, I guess," Cadi said. "I've never seen someone use ten bubbles together before. That was a daring move, for sure. A friend of mine used three of them once and he blew soap bubbles every time he spoke for an hour afterward."

"It's not permanent, though, is it?" Beanie asked anxiously. "I mean, is he still alive in there?" He reached out and prodded the magician soap cautiously. There must have been a bit of magic fizzing around it still, because the act of touching it instantly caused Beanie to become spotlessly clean—all traces of swamp gone from his clothes and skin.

The others hurried to touch the magician soap too, and Stella was pleased to find that the yucky swamp disappeared from her cloak, leaving her coated in a pleasant gooseberry smell.

"Hopefully it'll wear off," Shay said, squinting at the magician soap. He reached up and put it on Nigel's saddle, securing it there with one of the tassels. The jungle fairies all grouped around the soap in interest, but they backed away pretty hurriedly when Humphrey touched it and found his blue hair instantly in ringlets, his nails free from dirt, and his feet newly pedicured.

"We'll just have to keep our fingers crossed that he turns back eventually," Shay said. He glanced at the others. "For now we really need to concentrate on getting out of this enchanted forest."

After the swamp incident, everyone was in agreement about this. Shay picked up the bag of frogs, and they continued on their way, eager to put as much distance between themselves and the swamp as possible.

They followed the path, and soon enough the swamp was behind them and the broomstick trees had gone back to being tall and straight once again. They continued on through the forest, and after a little while Cadi said, "I think we might be coming toward the edge. I can see light up ahead. Goodness knows what's become of my witch! I hope you're keeping an eye out for her."

Cadi was right about there being flickers of light on the path, but as they traveled farther they saw that this wasn't daylight, as they had hoped, but more jack-o'-lanterns. The pumpkins lined the edge of the path on both sides, gazing at them with their grinning, gaping faces.

"It's almost like they're leading the way to something," Beanie whispered to Stella.

"The way out, perhaps?" she replied hopefully.

It turned out, however, that the pumpkins weren't leading the way out of the forest, but straight into another clearing. The explorers turned a corner and came upon it quite suddenly. It was full of red and white spotted toadstools, moss, dozens of flickering jack-o'-lanterns, and . . . teddy bears.

There must have been a dozen teddy bears before them, all different shapes and sizes. Stella saw an enormous pink bear with long whiskers, a tiny white teddy with delicate jointed limbs, a black bear with bright blue eyes, and even a fuzzy green bear with enormous paws. Every single teddy was wearing a pointed witch's hat. They all were sitting around an orange blanket decorated with black cats. And on this blanket was spread one of the most lavish picnics Stella had ever seen.

There were chocolate broomsticks, toffee cauldrons

overflowing with hard candies, marzipan cats, licorice bats, candy-floss frogs, and sugar mice. Hollowed-out pumpkins served as cups filled with hot chocolate, finished off with broomstick-shaped marshmallows.

Stella remembered what she had thought on first entering the forest—about this not being the sort of place where teddy bears would come to have their picnics—but, of course, these were no ordinary bears. Normal teddy bears couldn't move on their own, for a start, or blink, or stand up. But suddenly all the bears were on their feet, all had little wands in their paws, and all were pointing these toward the explorers in a distinctly threatening manner.

"Sorry." Stella held up her hands. "Don't mind us. We didn't mean to disturb you. We're just passing through. Please do go back to your picnic."

The bears said nothing, but there was something quite sinister in the way the light from the jack-o'-lanterns flickered in their staring glass eyes. And the fact that they all wore witch's hats wasn't very comforting either.

"We're just going to leave, okay?" Stella said. "No need to hex us or anything."

She began to walk slowly around the edge of the clearing, and the others followed her lead. The bears kept their eyes trained on them, turning their heads to stare but not making any move to stop them.

Stella was just starting to think that it might be okay

when, with a loud soapy pop, Ethan turned back into a real-life magician. He looked almost entirely like his usual self, except for the fact that his hair—which was usually brushed straight back and immaculately gelled—fell around his ears in tight little ringlets that did, unfortunately, make him look rather like a girl.

The sudden transformation startled Nigel, who reared back in alarm, bleating loudly. This panicked one of the teddy bears, who threw a fire spell from the tip of its wand. Fortunately, it missed the camel, but the spell went sailing past him and hit a nearby tree, which smoked and smoldered.

The next thing they knew, all the teddies were firing magic spells at them, lighting up the clearing like fireworks and filling the air with the smell of explosives. The explorers were forced to duck behind the broomstick trees for cover.

"Great Scott!" Ethan cried, pushing his hair out of his eyes. "What in the blazes is going on here? Why the devil is my hair curled up into ringlets? And are those teddy bears that are attacking us?"

"Ferocious little things, aren't they?" Cadi replied. "I remember Drusilla told me once that they can get terribly upset if you interrupt one of their picnics."

The teddy bears were advancing toward them, so Beanie reached into his bag and grabbed the first thing he found, which happened to be the rubber duck from the

genie. He hurled it on the ground, and a bathtub immediately appeared, steaming with jelly-bean-scented bubbles
and a collection of floating narwhals.

The teddy bears stopped and stared at this for a moment
before hurling so many magic spells at it that the bath
exploded into pieces, water and narwhals sloshing out onto
the ground before them.

"I'm going to have to freeze them," Stella said, reaching
past Buster to dig her tiara out of her pocket. "We're all
going to get blown up otherwise."

She shoved the sparkling tiara on her head and stepped
out from behind the tree to face the teddy bears, blue magic
already sparking and glittering at her fingertips. Just as she
was about to throw ice magic at the teddies, a girl came
crashing into the clearing.

"Sorry I'm late!" she cried. "Sorry! But I brought gingerbread!"

Everyone turned to stare at her. She was, quite obviously, a witch. Stella thought she must have been about ten
years old. She wore a black dress edged with lace, a pointed
witch's hat, black-and-orange-striped stockings, and black
shoes with little block heels and shiny gold buckles. She had
a broomstick in one hand and a tray of gingerbread men
balanced in the other.

All the teddy bears turned and fled from the explorers, rushing over to the girl and crowding around her feet,

tugging at her skirt with their paws, and finally speaking. At least, Stella thought they were speaking, but really it just sounded like gibberish—a strange mixture of growls and squeaks and snorts.

"Drusilla!" Cadi exclaimed.

"Oh," the witch said, staring at the scene before her. "Hi, Cadi. Who are all these people?" She hefted the tray and said, "Would they like some gingerbread? I made enough for guests."

"Are you friends with a witch?" Stella looked at Cadi, aghast.

The witch hunter shrugged. "Sure, we're friends," she said. "How about I introduce you? Drusilla, this is Stella Starflake Pearl. She's an ice princess and—"

"But witches are evil!" Stella exclaimed, cutting her off. "How can you possibly be friends with one?"

"I say, that's rather mean," Drusilla said. She marched across the clearing and stared up at Stella with a fierce look. The top of her pointed hat barely came up to Stella's shoulder. "And rude, too. Princesses aren't meant to be rude. They're meant to be lovely." She jabbed at Stella with her broomstick. "Why aren't you lovely?"

"Stella is extremely lovely," Beanie said loyally. "She's the loveliest person I know."

"Well, it doesn't sound much like it to me," Drusilla said. She gestured behind her. "The teddies say you interrupted their picnic and then threatened them with ice magic. Totally unprovoked too."

The tiara glittered in Stella's hair and her hand was still outstretched, blue sparks of magic fizzing around her fingertips.

"I wouldn't exactly call it unprovoked," Shay said reasonably.

"They attacked us," Stella said. She jerked her head over her shoulder and said, "Look at the trees."

Drusilla glanced at the broomstick trees, which were singed and still smoking a little.

"Well, you can't blame them for that," she said. "You frightened them."

"We didn't mean to," Shay said. "Look, I think this is all a bit of a misunderstanding." He reached up, gently took hold of Stella's wrist, and drew her hand back down to her side. "But there's no real harm done, is there? And I'm sure no one wants to magically attack anyone else without good reason."

"Why are your fairies being sick?" Drusilla asked, narrowing her eyes suspiciously. "Have they been eating my house? They better not have been eating my house."

Stella turned and saw that the jungle fairies were, indeed, being frightfully ill—clutching onto Nigel's humps and vomiting over his side.

"Oh dear," she said. "Well, at least it means they'll leave the picnic alone."

Drusilla set the tray of gingerbread men down on the floor, and the little man-shaped biscuits instantly got up from the baking sheet and started running around. The teddies raced after them, scooping them up before they could escape into the forest (although one or two of them did manage to climb up into the safety of a broomstick tree) and taking them back to the picnic spread.

"Everyone, this is Drusilla," Cadi said in a firm voice. "She's a witch, but she's also a friend, and I'm sure you'll all like her very much if you give her half a chance."

"But if she's your friend, then how come you're capturing her to prove yourself as a hunter?" Stella asked.

"Dru's just doing me a favor," Cadi said. "Besides, I already told you I'd rather be an explorer than a hunter."

"I've just remembered—don't ice princesses have frozen hearts?" Drusilla asked, looking at Stella warily.

"This one doesn't," Cadi said. She glanced at Stella and said, "Not all ice princesses are villains, are they? Well, guess what? Not all witches are evil either." She patted Drusilla on the shoulder and said, "Most witches are just people who like cats and magic. This one can be a bit of a cheeky monkey sometimes, but she's definitely not evil."

Stella looked down at the little witch in front of her. She had to admit that she certainly didn't look evil. Her eyes were bright green and shining with curiosity—there was a smattering of freckles over her nose, which turned up just a little at the end, and her hair was a bright, bold red and frizzed out in all directions beneath her pointed hat.

Stella reached up and removed the tiara from her hair, tucking it back into her cloak. She could practically hear Felix's voice in her head, chastising her for believing that all witches were evil. Hadn't she herself suffered the exact same prejudice from people who thought all ice princesses were wicked and who had judged her before they had even laid eyes on her?

Suddenly Stella felt rather ashamed of herself. "Oh dear, I am sorry," she said. "I had a bad experience with a witch when I was little, but that doesn't excuse being beastly to every witch I meet. I hope you can forgive me."

Drusilla beamed up at her. "Think nothing of it," she said. "I've forgotten it already. The bears say you can stay and share the picnic with them if you like."

"They were trying to blow our heads off five seconds ago!" Ethan exclaimed.

"Bears don't hold grudges," the witch replied.

"Magicians do," Ethan grunted.

"Thank you," Stella said. "Normally we'd be delighted, but I'm afraid we can't stop. My father has gone after a very dangerous witch who lives here, and we've got to catch up with him before he reaches her."

"That's terribly brave of you," Drusilla replied. "We may not all be evil, but there's still plenty of fiendishly dangerous witches living on Witch Mountain. Not to mention the witch wolves."

Stella noticed that at the mention of the witch wolves Shay shuddered beside her. She reached over and gave his hand a squeeze.

"It's a shame you can't come too, Dru," Cadi said.

"Why can't she?" Beanie asked.

"Infant witches aren't allowed past the Forest of Enchanted Broomsticks," Cadi said. "We think it's because the witches who live at the top of the mountain are all pretty dangerous, so they don't want kids wandering around up there."

"That's right. Except I'm not an infant witch anymore," Drusilla said, beaming. "Haven't you noticed anything different about me?"

Cadi looked at her for a moment, then gasped, her hands flying to her mouth. "You've got your witch's hat!"

Drusilla nodded. "The spells goblin visited me last night. I'm a witch in training now!"

"How marvelous!" Cadi replied. She glanced at the others and said, "When infant witches become witches in training they get a visit from the spells goblin, who bestows them with several gifts." She counted them off on her fingers. "One pointy witch's hat, one pair of magic shoes, one flying broomstick, and a familiar egg."

"What's a familiar egg?" Shay asked.

Drusilla rummaged in her pocket and produced a small, smooth egg that looked like it was made of black marble. Swirling veins of white shot through it.

"The spells goblin left it in my shoe," Drusilla said. "Isn't it absolutely marvelous? It's jolly wonderful being a witch, you know."

"It's just a lump of rock." Ethan grunted. "What's so marvelous about that?"

Drusilla rolled her eyes. "It's not a rock," she said. "It's an egg. I have to take care of it until it hatches."

"Hatches?" Stella exclaimed. "But what's in there?"

"I don't know," Drusilla said. "That's the best part! A witch's familiar could be a cat, a bat, a raven, a fox, a frog, a newt, an owl, or a monkey, but you don't know what until the egg hatches."

"You can't seriously expect a monkey to hatch out of that thing?" Ethan said, peering at the little egg dubiously. "Monkeys don't come from eggs."

"Neither do bats, or frogs, or newts, or foxes, or cats," Beanie said. "Unless it's the hissing, egg-hatching spotted cat from the Floating Island of Munga Munga, and they're meant to be extremely dangerous. They go straight for the eyes, you know."

"Witches' familiars aren't like normal animals," Drusilla explained. "They're magical animals to assist the witch with their spell-making. The spells goblin decides what would be the best fit for you when they give you the egg. I hope I don't get a newt. My sister, Cordelia, got a newt familiar last year, and he's ever so grouchy. Sometimes he sticks his tongue in your cereal just for the sake of it. Although I suppose that makes sense, because Cordelia is the same."

"She sometimes sticks her tongue in your cereal just for the sake of it?" Beanie asked, staring.

"No, I mean she's grouchy like Herbert. That's the newt's name." She sighed. "I do hope I get a fox, one with a big fluffy tail, that I can cuddle in bed at night." She looked at Stella and said, "I suppose you've got a unicorn you cuddle in bed, haven't you? What with being a princess and all."

"I do have a unicorn," Stella agreed. "But she sleeps in the stable. I've got a pygmy T. rex I cuddle in bed sometimes, though. Buster is an excellent cuddler." She reached into her pocket to give his scaly head a rub.

"Goodness, how lovely! A unicorn and a dinosaur!" Drusilla exclaimed. "It must be great being a princess. Well, I'm sure the spells goblin knows what's right for me and has picked out the very best familiar there ever was." She glanced at the broomstick in her hand. "I haven't quite gotten the hang of this thing yet, though."

The words were barely out of her mouth before the broomstick shot straight up into the sky a few feet. Drusilla had kept her grip on it, so her feet left the floor altogether, leaving her dangling in the air. "Oh drat," she said. "Sometimes it seems to have a mind of its own." The broomstick started to float lazily around the clearing, taking Drusilla with it. "I hardly know whether I'm coming or going," she complained.

"Well, we need to be going," Cadi said. "We have a rescue mission to mount."

"Follow me," Drusilla called over her shoulder. "I'll take you through the witch gate, but first we need to get you out of the forest. Don't worry. I know the best way to avoid the swampy marsh gnomes, the singing hex beasts, and the snarling troll-face trees."

She was already disappearing from the clearing, still dangling from her broomstick. The others had to scramble to keep up with her, leaving the teddy bears to finish their picnic in peace.

CHAPTER EIGHTEEN

A S THEY CONTINUED THROUGH the forest, Beanie hopped up onto Nigel's back to tend to the jungle fairies, who were moaning, groaning, clutching their stomachs, and generally feeling very sorry for themselves. Beanie fashioned some little blankets out of monogrammed hankies he had in his pocket, and also took out the Polar Bear Explorers' Club medical kit, which contained two miniature rescue dogs with brandy barrels around their necks.

"We did try to warn you not to eat the enchanted gingerbread," he told them. "But perhaps a drop of brandy will make you feel better?"

The jungle fairies didn't seem too interested in the brandy, but they were happy to cuddle the dogs.

A short while later the group emerged from the broomstick forest and found themselves blinking in the sunlight sparkling off the snow. It had been so dark and gloomy that Stella had quite forgotten it was actually daytime, but now they found themselves out on the mountainside, surrounded by elegant frost trees and more iced pumpkins. After the swampy fumes of the forest, it was rather nice to be breathing in the cold, sharp air once again. Three paths stretched away from them.

"We need to take that one," Drusilla said, pointing with her spare hand at the left path.

"What's down the other two?" Beanie asked.

"The middle one leads to a field of argumentative mushrooms," Drusilla said. "They're extremely nasty, actually, and poisonous, too—you wouldn't want to tangle with them. They'll fungus you if they get half the chance. And the right-hand path leads to a steep drop into a bottomless chasm, so you really don't want to go tumbling into that, especially given that there are biting rock heads with very sharp teeth on the way down. But the left path leads to the witch gate, which'll take you straight to the top of the mountain."

"And that way is safe, is it?" Ethan demanded.

"Well, you know, nothing on Witch Mountain is entirely safe," Drusilla said. "But it's certainly the least perilous."

"The least perilous," Ethan repeated. "Oh good."

And with that Drusilla's broomstick set off down the path, with the witch dangling beneath it.

"Are you just going to dangle from your broom like that the whole way?" Ethan demanded.

"So what if I am?" Drusilla replied over her shoulder.

"It's absurd," Ethan said.

"Well, personally, I think your ringlets are quite, quite absurd," Drusilla replied. "Whatever have you done it for? Perhaps you thought to disguise yourself as Little Red Riding Boot, but it won't work, you know. Any witch would see straight through that."

Ethan scowled and tugged his fingers through the ringlets, but they stubbornly refused to uncurl.

"Your arm will get yanked right out of your socket, and it'll serve you right." Ethan sniffed.

"Witches don't get tired arms," Drusilla said cheerfully. "It's one of our many strengths. We could walk around on our hands all day long if we chose. In fact, my sister, Cordelia, once walked around on her hands for an entire week, but I rather think she did that only to annoy me."

"Witches are a weird bunch," Ethan said.

Shay sighed. "You know what, Prawn? You'd make a heck of a lot more friends if you weren't so antagonistic to people all the time."

"I have plenty of friends already, thank you," Ethan said.

"You're my friend, aren't you, Ethan?" Beanie piped up from the camel. "You told me so on our last expedition."

"That's right, Beanie," Ethan said. He tilted his head in his loftiest manner and said, "You're worthy of being my friend. There's nothing wrong with being particular about it, though." He gave Shay a withering look and said, "I expect you'd make friends with a worm given half a chance, but one can't expect much else from a wolf whisperer, I suppose."

"You are still coming to my birthday party, aren't you, Ethan?" Beanie said. "Only you haven't responded to the invitation I sent."

Ethan sighed. "Beanie, I've told you a million times I'll be there. Magicians always attend their friends' birthday parties. It's one of our golden rules. But your birthday is weeks away. Isn't it a little early to be sending out invitations?"

"You haven't told me a million times," Beanie said at once. "You've told me fifty-six times."

"Well, why do you keep asking me, then?" Ethan grumbled.

"Because you haven't replied to my invitation," Beanie said. "You need to fill in the little slip at the bottom and tick the box to say you want to come. That's how it works. Also, I need your reply to show Uncle Benedict. After Moira said she didn't want to be my friend anymore, Uncle said it wasn't worth throwing birthday parties for me because no one but Stella ever turns up. He said it was a waste of good cake, and piñatas, and whistles, and balloons, and paper hats. Uncle says it's too pathetic for words, that's what Uncle says. So unless I can guarantee that at least three people are going to come, then I'm not allowed to have a party on my next birthday."

"What a mean old crank." Ethan grunted. "I'll reply to your invitation the moment I return home."

"Gosh, it sounds like a smashing party, though, if there's to be cake, and piñatas, and whistles, and balloons, and paper hats," Cadi exclaimed. "Could I come, do you think?"

Beanie gaped at her. "Would you?"

"I've never been to a birthday party before," she replied. "Witch hunters don't tend to have too many friends. Nor do witches. That's why Drusilla and I were very glad to make friends with each other." Cadi strained forward in Gus's saddle to call to the little dangling witch. "What about you, Dru? Have you ever been to a birthday party?"

"I've been to a lot of teddy bear picnics," Drusilla said. "Does that count?"

"Well, you're both welcome to come to my party," Beanie said.

"I think the jungle fairies want to come too," Stella said. Mustafah was tugging at Beanie's sleeve and pointing at himself and the others in an energetic fashion. "Looks like they're feeling better," she said. "And if the jungle fairies were to come as well as Cadi and Dru, then you'd actually have nine people at your birthday party."

Beanie looked as if he literally couldn't think of anything more wonderful in the whole world. He glanced back at the pumpkin strapped to Nigel's back and said, "And if this pumpkin makes Moira like me again, then it'll be ten!"

Stella sighed and shook her head.

They traveled on up the mountain for the whole morning, stopping only briefly to snap up the magic fort blanket for lunch. Stella hated having to stop at all—she simply wanted to get to Felix as quickly as possible. Every time her thoughts turned to him she felt an awful tangle of worry, fear, and guilt deep down in her stomach.

The moment the fort sprang up around them, however, Ruprekt was there with packed lunches lined up on the table for each of them, including the jungle fairies, and nose bags for Nigel and Gus.

"I would have made a sit-down lunch, but I guessed you'd prefer to keep moving," he said. "Explorers just need to keep going sometimes, don't they?"

"Oh, Ruprekt, you're marvelous!" Stella said, throwing her arms around the genie in a tight hug. "Absolutely marvelous!"

The genie flushed to the tips of his pointed ears. "It's really no problem at all, Miss Stella," he said. "I'm only too glad to help."

They collapsed the tent and continued on their way. Their boots crunched in new snow, and more flakes started to fall as they went, so they were all glad to find that the genie had packed flasks of piping-hot soup in their lunch bags. The jungle fairies seemed to have fully recovered from the gingerbread incident, because they wolfed their lunches and then had to be constantly batted away from Gus's and Nigel's nose bags.

The path wound quite close to the side of the mountain at times, and Stella saw that they were now incredibly high up. High enough to make your head spin, in fact. It was a good thing that none of them were afraid of heights. The mountain dropped sharply away in places, while in others it sloped out more gently, covered in snow and frosted pumpkins.

"There's Weenus's Trading Post. Look," Stella said, pointing it out to the others. They could see the striped awning all the way at the bottom, with the Jungle Cat Explorers' Club dirigible floating above it.

The dirigible made Stella think of Gideon, so she turned to Shay and said, "You've still got that bag of frogs, haven't you?"

"Yep." Shay hoisted the bag more firmly on his shoulders. "They're wriggling around like anything in there. It's rather nice, actually. They keep kicking at my back, and it feels like I'm having a massage."

"Oh, could I carry it for a while?" Cadi asked. "My back muscles are terribly stiff."

Shay handed the bag over. The hunter slipped it onto her shoulders and then sighed with pleasure. "Gosh, you're right," she said. "This is lovely. And not even that heavy. You should go into business selling frog massage bags. You'd make a fortune."

"Just don't lose it," Shay said. "One of the frogs in there is an explorer. Probably."

"How are we going to escape from Witch Mountain once we find Felix?" Beanie asked, suddenly joining the conversation. "I've been thinking about it, and I'm a bit worried, seeing as we had to trade away our dirigible and we're surrounded by dangerous, monster-infested oceans on all sides."

"Perhaps we could steal that hot-air balloon we saw?" Stella suggested. "Remember? The big black one with the 'Be gone! Witches only!' sign hanging from it? Actually, I'm surprised we can't see it by now—I would've thought it should be right here."

"Oh, it is," Drusilla said from her broomstick. "It's just around this corner, actually. You can't see it because the mountain is blocking it from view, but it's here—in fact, the balloon marks the witch gate."

The explorers turned the corner in the winding mountain path and suddenly found themselves face-to-face with the witch gate, set right into the rocky wall of the mountain. It was a looming, formidable thing, all black iron and frosted metal. The iron bars were so tall that they would have kept out even a yeti, and images of broomsticks and bats twisted around on themselves in the curling metal. As Drusilla had said, the hot-air balloon floated high above the gates, tethered to one of its vast posts by a long rope. Any one of them could simply untie it if they wanted to.

"There isn't even anyone guarding it," Shay said, looking around. "We could take it on the way back down."

"Oh, you don't want to escape in that," Drusilla said.

"Why not?" Stella asked. "It looks perfect."

"No, that's the Balloon of Death and Madness," Drusilla said. "Anyone who flies in it will go mad and die, you know."

Everyone stared at her.

"Why on earth would anyone invent such a depraved thing?" Ethan demanded.

"It was Mad Agnes who did it," Drusilla said. Then she added, "Oh dear, you're not after Mad Agnes, are you? She really is completely mad—even madder than that bag of frogs you're carrying around. And any witch who's madder than a bag of frogs is probably better off left alone, I'd say."

"You can all come back with me in my father's ship," Cadi said. "It's moored just offshore. You probably saw it when you arrived. I've got a flare gun to signal when I'm ready to be picked up."

"That's great," Stella said. "Thank you."

"So, are you after Mad Agnes?" Drusilla pressed.

"No. We're after a witch called Jezzybella," Stella replied. "Have you heard of her?"

Drusilla tilted her head. "Is she the one who turns children into matchsticks?"

"I don't think so."

"Or the scarecrow queen? She's the one who gave life to all the scarecrows, which then went on a rampage." Drusilla shuddered. "Gosh, the night of the rampaging scarecrows was pretty awful, from what I hear."

"No. She didn't do that either," Stella said. Then she frowned and added, "At least, I don't think she did. But I don't really know much about her except for the fact that she murdered my parents."

"Why did she do that?" Drusilla asked.

"I don't know for sure," Stella replied. "My parents were very cruel to her. And the magic mirror in my castle said she did it because she was evil."

Drusilla frowned. "There must have been more to it than that. Even bad witches don't go around murdering people without a reason. The thing is that a bad witch doesn't believe they're bad, you see. To them, everything they do makes perfect sense and is quite reasonable."

Stella would have liked to protest this and say that her parents couldn't possibly have done anything bad enough to give a witch reason to kill them, but she'd seen the iron slippers and the burned feet of the puppet.

"Nothing excuses murder, though," she said. "And my parents were the snow queen and king, so this witch must be very powerful."

Drusilla stared at her with big eyes. Then she glanced at the gate and said, "Look, are you sure you want to go after her? Just because not all witches are evil doesn't mean that some of them aren't really dangerous."

"I don't want to go after her, really," Stella said. "In fact, I didn't choose this at all. She's the one who came after me with a vulture. So Felix went chasing after her, and I can't let him face her alone. If anything happened to him, I don't know what I would do."

She could feel all her fear and panic rising up in her chest at the thought, and was glad of Shay's comforting hand on her shoulder.

"Nothing will happen to Felix, Sparky," he said. "Not when he's got such a superb rescue party racing after him."

"Well, this might be your last chance to reconsider," Drusilla said. "Once we go past the witch gate, there's no knowing what will happen or what we might come up against."

Stella glanced back at the others and said, "Listen, I'm so grateful to you all for coming with me this far," she said. "But if anyone wants to stop and wait here, I really will completely understand. There's no obligation to continue on."

But the boys were already shaking their heads.

"You know, you really talk rubbish sometimes," Ethan said. "Of course we're coming."

Beanie folded his arms over his chest. "Friends don't let friends face dangerous, murderous witches alone, and you're the best friend anyone could ask for, Stella."

Shay just lifted her up in a great big hug, her boots coming right off the ground. "Beanie is quite right," he said, setting her down. "You're one of the best friends anyone could ask for, Sparky. We love you, and there's no way we're letting you do this by yourself."

Stella suddenly felt a bit like she might be about to cry, but an expedition was no place for crying and carrying on, so she swallowed the feeling down and smiled at the other explorers instead.

"Thank you," she said. "If I can ever repay you, then I will." She glanced over at Cadi and Drusilla and said, "I expect you two would like to stay behind, though?"

"Not me." Cadi shook her head. "I want to be an explorer, remember? And what kind of explorer turns down the chance to explore a part of Witch Mountain they've never seen before? I've still got three days left before Father mounts a search party in case I've been captured by a witch or gobbled up by a swamp ogre."

"You mean rescue party, don't you?" Beanie asked.

Cadi gave him a look. "Really not much rescuing that can be done if you get gobbled up by a swamp ogre."

"Well, I've got to come with you because the witch gate will only open for a witch," Drusilla said. "Besides, now that I'm a witch in training, I have every right to finally see what lies behind these gates. I can't promise to stick around if some furious witch comes after you, though. In fact, I'll probably fly straight off on my broomstick if that happens."

"That seems fair enough," Shay said. "Let's press on, then. The days go by fast, and there's no time to lose." He glanced at Drusilla and said, "How do we get past the gates? They look like they're locked pretty tight."

Stella saw that he was right. A huge chain was wound through the iron bars, with the most gigantic padlock fastened at the front. Strangely, there was a small plume of smoke twisting from the top of it.

Drusilla noticed this too and said, "Perhaps there's a dragon key in there." She stepped up to the lock and pressed her eye right up to the keyhole. "Oh, it's a fairy lock," she said. "Yes, I can see that there's a spells fairy in there." She stepped back, gestured to Stella, and said, "Take a look."

Stella stepped up to the padlock eagerly. Although she had grown up with a fairyologist and had been surrounded by fairies her whole life, she was always eager to see a new one. She squinted through the keyhole and immediately saw that this wasn't just a padlock but was, in fact, a little house. There was a fireplace with a tiny fire crackling in it (which accounted for the smoke), a thick rug, and a line of bookshelves filled with fairy tales. There was also a table, on which sat a spotty teapot and a dainty teacup, and a wing-backed armchair, in which sat the spells fairy herself, who was just in the act of pouring herself a cup of tea. It looked ever so cozy, especially as there was a tiny white fairy cat curled up in a ball on the rug before the fire.

Stella would have loved to peer in for longer, but just then she felt a whiskery face pushing her out of the way as Gus muscled in, pressing his eye up against the keyhole.

"Sorry," Cadi said. "He just wants to see what all the fuss is about."

Unfortunately, the excellent lunch Ruprekt had pre-pared for him (consisting mostly of clams, clams, and more clams), caught up with Gus just then, and he produced a loud, long belch that absolutely stank of fish and walrus breath and went straight into the spells fairy's house.

She was out within seconds, gasping and choking for breath as she clutched on to the iron bar. She was similar to the fairies Stella had seen at home, except for the fact that she wore a robe rather than a dress. It was fur-trimmed and covered in glittering gold stars. She also wore a pointed hat, beneath which frizzed a mass of dark ringlets. She carried a tiny wand with a star at the end of it, which she gripped in one hand as she gasped for air.

"Gracious me, what is this?" she demanded. "Is the witch gate under attack?"

"Oh dear, I'm sorry," Drusilla said. "You're not under attack. It was an accident. Our walrus had a little too much lunch."

"Walrus!" The fairy gasped. "Is that what that was?" She gave a shudder and said, "You almost killed my cat!"

"We really are very sorry," Cadi said. "Gus doesn't have the best manners. He is a walrus, after all—"

The fairy held up her hand and said, "I don't care. What do you want? Why have you come to the witch gate?" She looked at them properly for the first time then and seemed startled. Stella supposed they did make rather a strange group. It wasn't every day that you saw four explorers, four jungle fairies, one hunter, one witch in training, one camel, an entire bag of wriggling wonky squish-squish frogs, and one walrus wearing a pith helmet.

"Um . . . we'd like to pass through the witch gate, please?" Drusilla said. "I'm a witch in training, you see." She pointed at her hat and waved her broomstick.

"And who are these other people? And beasts and things?" the fairy asked.

"They're my prisoners," Drusilla said promptly.

The fairy looked them up and down. "You've taken an awful lot of prisoners for such a small witch," she remarked.

"They're all very stupid," Drusilla said. "Quite remarkably so. Just look at their walrus. And this one thought he could disguise himself as Little Red Riding Boot," she said, pointing at Ethan, whose hair was still bunched up in tight ringlets. "It wasn't very difficult to take them prisoner at all. So, will you open the gate for us?"

"Fine." The fairy shook her head. "Anything as long as you take that walrus away with you."

She tapped the padlock with her wand, and it clicked open. The chain magically unwound itself, and the big iron gates swung slowly forward with a creaking sound that was loud enough to make the snow on the mountain tremble and had everyone thinking about avalanches.

Gus immediately dragged himself forward across the snow, tongue lolling happily. The others passed with a little more trepidation, trying not to feel too intimidated as the gates of Witch Mountain swung shut behind them with a loud *clang*.

CHAPTER NINETEEN

N O ONE REALLY KNEW quite what to expect from the top of Witch Mountain, but they were all fairly sure that it wouldn't be anything good. Stella felt a renewed sense of urgency—there'd been no sign of any confetti vultures for a while, and Felix could be confronting the witch right at this very moment for all they knew. Reluctantly, she took the magic tiara from her cloak and put it on her head. She had no wish to wear it really, but she needed to be ready in case some awful witch or monster came bursting out at them unexpectedly.

They set off along the snowy path leading through a gorge in the rock, the dark sides of the mountain looming overhead in a threatening sort of way. Stella saw that the sides were covered in dramatic frozen waterfalls, which would have been quite pretty if it weren't for the sight of the glow-piranhas trapped inside the water, still glowing softly, their bulging eyes staring out from behind their ice prison.

As they made their way deeper into the chasm, they saw other things trapped within the frozen water, including a pith helmet, a set of false vampire teeth, a cascade of star-tipped, sparkling fairy wands, a picnic basket full of chocolate broomsticks, and a teeny-tiny (definitely fairy-size) raft with a Jungle Cat Explorers' Club flag attached to it. Upon seeing this last one, Stella felt obliged to return the drums to the jungle fairies so they could resume the chant of doom they were clearly desperate to perform.

"It was a Jungle Cat expedition that first discovered Witch Mountain," Beanie said. "There must have been some jungle fairies with them too. Some of them must have gotten past the witch gate, after all. It was headed by Captain Archibald Primrose Perkins, you know, and he's generally seen as being one of the most determined and intrepid explorers ever."

"And what happened to him?" Cadi asked eagerly. "Showered with accolades when he got home, I expect?"

"No," Beanie said. "He was killed by witch wolves on the mountain."

As if on cue, a lone witch wolf howled in the distance—a high, keening sound that ripped through the cold air. Shay immediately flinched, and Koa tipped back her head and howled as well.

"Oh dear. You'd better stop her from doing that, if you

can," Drusilla said, looking worried. "We really don't want the witch wolves to know where we are."

"Sshhh. It's okay, girl. It's okay," Shay said to Koa in a soothing voice. He glanced at the others and said, "Everything about those witch wolves feels wrong, dreadfully wrong. Koa must feel it too, which is why she's reacting like that."

"How do you mean?" Stella asked, frowning at the sight of Koa, who had her tail between her legs and was cowering at Shay's side once again.

"Well, when normal wolves talk to me, I hear their words inside my head and it feels . . . kind of warm. But when the witch wolves howl like that, it feels icy cold, and sharp, and it actually hurts. Like having shards of ice packed inside your skull."

He rubbed at his temples with the tips of his fingers.

"Don't worry," Ethan said. "If any witch wolves come our way, I'll turn them into wonky squish-squish frogs. I'm getting quite good at that now."

"Yes, but you really ought to be trying to remember how to undo the spell," Stella said. "Poor old Gideon is going to forget how to be a human if he stays a frog for much longer." She fixed the magician with a stern look and said, "You are trying to remember the spell, aren't you?"

"Naturally," Ethan replied. "My every waking moment is consumed by it, in fact."

"You're such a liar," Stella said with a sigh.

"Well, you won't be able to turn a witch wolf into a wonky squish-squish frog, or anything else, for that matter," Drusilla piped up.

Stella turned and saw that the little witch was perched on her broomstick, ankles slowly kicking back and forth. The jungle fairies were all settled in a pile on her lap.

"The curse that turns them into wolves prevents them from changing shape," Drusilla went on. "They're trapped as witch wolves for all time. For ever and ever and ever. Their souls are frozen in there, you see, and there's nothing in the world that can change them back."

Somewhere in the distance, a witch wolf howled once again—a long, low, mournful sound that made the hair on everyone's arms stand on end. Koa whimpered, and Shay put his hands to his head with a groan.

Ethan and Stella were immediately at his side.

"It's all right," the magician said. "Even if they can't be turned into wonky squish-squish frogs, they're still just wolves."

"They're not exactly just wolves," Drusilla began. "They can rip your soul right out of your—"

"Thank you," Ethan snapped. "That's very cheerful." He turned back to Shay. "Look, didn't we face frosties, carnivorous cabbages, ferocious outlaws, and rampaging yetis during the last expedition and live to tell the tale? A bunch of wolves aren't going to be any problem to us."

"That's right," Stella said. "And if needs be, I can freeze them." She glanced at Drusilla and said, "There's nothing to prevent witch wolves being affected by ice magic, is there?"

The witch shrugged. "I don't know," she replied. "I don't think we've ever had an ice princess on Witch Mountain before."

They walked on—and before long the dark chasm opened out onto the cliff top.

"Well, would you look at that," Cadi said.

The others followed her gaze and saw, to their dismay, that six witches stood right at the cliff top with their backs toward the explorers. Stella knew immediately that they were the ones the group had seen from halfway up the mountain— the witches who had sent the snow hands after them. This close, they were even larger than she had realized—six feet at least. Beside her, Stella felt Beanie shudder.

"Let's go," Shay whispered. "Before they see us."

"No. Look," Cadi said again. "They're not real."

Finally, Stella saw that the witches didn't have legs poking out from beneath their coats, but broomsticks instead. And those weren't fingers sticking out from the ends of their sleeves, but long, dead twigs, all brittle and black, like they'd come from a diseased old tree. The figures were hunched over more than they should be, and their pointed hats were crooked on their heads.

"They're—" she began.

"Scarecrows, by gad!" Cadi exclaimed. "Not real witches at all."

"They don't look right," Shay said. "We should leave them alone."

But Cadi was already marching up to them. "I can't believe I was taken in by a pile of dead sticks!" she exclaimed indignantly.

The others followed Cadi and peered up at the tall scarecrow witches. They had lumpy sack cloths for faces, black buttons for eyes, and slashed charcoal lines for mouths.

"Those are the scarecrow queen's scarecrows!" Drusilla exclaimed. "And if they're here, then the scarecrow queen herself is probably nearby too. She can smell children from miles around, you see."

No sooner had she spoken than a witch came shuffling out from a nearby cave. She was dressed in a coat that seemed to consist entirely of crude little scarecrow dolls clumsily stitched together. Her hair ran in a long gray curtain down her back, and she carried a stick, which she pointed in their direction as she yelled in a croaky voice, "Intruders! Intruders!"

The nearest scarecrow immediately whirled around, grabbed a handful of Cadi's robes with its long twig fingers, and lifted her clear off the ground. The others watched in horror as the creature leaned close to Cadi and a hissing voice came out, even though its charcoal mouth didn't move at all.

"Turn back!" it said. "Turn back!"

"All intruders will be eaten by scarecrows!" the witch shrieked gleefully. "All of them!"

Cadi gave a yelp of alarm and thrashed around in the scarecrow's grip, punching and kicking at it, but the creature held her at arm's length and she couldn't reach its scrawny body.

Ethan threw a spell at the scarecrow, but it must have been cast with a protection charm of its own, because the spell simply bounced back. Drusilla hastily conjured up a gingerbread man, but this simply ran up to the nearest scarecrow, who snatched it up and crushed it into a shower of crumbs.

Stella grabbed the first heavy object she could find from her bag—which happened to be her telescope—and ran up to the scarecrow. Being careful to avoid the outstretched fingers of the one next to it, she began pummeling Cadi's captor on its back and legs, as far up as she could reach. One of the other scarecrows pointed a broomstick at the ground, a spell shot from it, and the next moment, cold snow hands unfurled and gripped Stella's ankle.

Ethan threw fire magic at them just as Shay whipped his boomerang from his bag and sent it sailing through the air. It cut off the scarecrow's hand in one clean sweep. The scarecrow let out a dreadful squawk, and Cadi fell to the ground in a shower of broken twigs. Stella pulled her foot free from the crumbling snow hand, grabbed Cadi's arm, and dragged her back, out of harm's way. The scarecrows didn't pursue them as they retreated. Their broomstick legs appeared to be driven deep into the ground, pinning them there. All six scarecrows shook their arms and wailed up at the heavens, but remained right where they were.

The witch gave a furious cry of her own and began to advance upon the junior explorers. Before she could reach them, however, the jungle fairies flew about her in a flurry of leaf tunics and spiky hair, taking aim with their slingshots and pelting her all over with stink-berries.

The witch howled, which unfortunately meant that the next stink-berry to go flying went straight into her mouth. It must have tasted as awful as it smelled because the witch really did kick up a fuss then, shouting and screaming something terrible before turning around and racing back into the safety of her cave.

Seizing their chance, the explorers ran from the scene as fast as their legs could carry them. They'd been running for some time when they finally reached a snow-covered plateau. Here, they paused for a moment to catch their breath, leaning over on their knees and gasping until they could breathe easily again.

"Some hunter you are," Ethan finally snapped, glaring at Cadi. "You might have gotten us all killed."

"Sorry," Cadi said, holding up her hands. "You're

right—it was a stupid thing to do. Thank you for helping me." She turned to the jungle fairies, who were strutting about and looking pleased with themselves. "Thanks to you guys, too," she said. "You were wonderful. Bravo."

"That was a close shave," Stella said. "But we're all in one piece."

Now that they had calmed down a bit, the explorers examined their surroundings. There was a signpost in the middle of the plateau with dozens of little signs attached to it, all pointing in different directions. Myriad paths led away from it—all different colors, from purple to black to pink to glittering gold. Stella thought that the snow somehow hadn't landed on them to begin with, but as soon as they stepped on the first one, they realized that the paths themselves were actually warm—so warm they could feel it through their snow boots.

The jungle fairies were quite delighted by this and immediately started laying down the monogrammed hankies Beanie had given them, using them as beach towels on the hot stone. One of them even started optimistically fashioning some kind of umbrella out of a toothpick and a banana skin. Stella hadn't seen a single banana the whole time they'd been on the expedition, so she wasn't sure where that had come from, but there was no time to wonder about it as they set off to examine the post.

Some of the signs pointed toward things the explorers

had already come across, such as the Balloon of Death and Madness or the Forest of Enchanted Broomsticks. Others were unfamiliar and ranged from terrible-sounding places, like the Pit of Spikes and the Poison Shrivel Caves, to rather nice-sounding spots such as the Fizzy Sherbet Fountains and Iced Spiced Gingerbread Street.

"Ooh, I'm going to go to Iced Spiced Gingerbread Street!" Drusilla piped up at once. "That sounds smashing!" She gave a shudder. "I don't fancy being chased by any more incensed witches, or their scarecrows either, thank you very much. I'm sorry, everyone, but from here you're on your own."

At the mention of the word "gingerbread," one of the jungle fairies gave a dry heave, which immediately made Nigel spit in irritation. Stella thought this only fair, since no one wants a jungle fairy being sick on their back, after all, especially when they're so frightfully noisy about it.

"Good luck with your witch hunt," Drusilla said. "I hope you catch up with your father before a witch gobbles him up." And with that she plucked a hair from her head, passed it to Cadi, and then waved good-bye before grabbing hold of her broomstick and zooming off in the direction of Iced Spiced Gingerbread Street.

Cadi and the explorers watched her go and for the first time realized that the peak of the mountain was actually in sight. It rose sharp and black and jagged in the air, with snow scattered about in patches.

The next moment Stella spotted a stray confetti vulture hopping off down one of the paths.

"Look over there!" she cried, pointing it out to the others. "It's a confetti vulture!"

Everyone turned to look.

"What path is that?" Shay asked.

It was bright orange in color and was made from hundreds of tiny bricks. Embedded between some of them were black cats, bats, toads, and cauldrons.

"It's the path for Witch Village," Cadi said, pointing at the sign.

Just as she spoke, the confetti vulture lost the last of its magic and keeled over on the snow, fluttering limply.

"Witch Village it is, then," Shay said.

"Is it safe to just go walking straight into Witch Village, though?" Beanie asked, fiddling with his wooden narwhal anxiously. "Won't it be full of witches?"

"We'll just have to deal with that when we get there," Stella said. She knew it wasn't much of an answer, but she couldn't think of anything else to say. Yes, it was dangerous, but they had already been slowed down by the witch and her scarecrows, and they couldn't delay going after Felix another moment longer.

As the explorers walked toward the village, Stella wondered what kind of awful place Jezzybella might live in. Visions of haunted castles, freezing bat caves, and savage dungeons filled her mind, but she tried to push these away. They just had to concentrate on getting there for now. Still, the closer they got, the more terrible the thought became. Stella couldn't help thinking of the nightmares that had tormented her for years—the screaming; the shuffling, burned feet; the blood droplets scattered scarlet over the snow. She had never wished more fervently to be home, warm and safe with Felix, in her whole life.

It didn't take them long to reach the village, and they smelled it before they saw it—a heavenly mixture of spiced gingerbread and hot fruit punch. They came around the corner and were met with a collection of the most crooked buildings Stella had ever seen. There were wonky thatched cottages, leaning towers, and twisted shops selling all kinds of things. The cobbled high street was made from hard candies, and a fizzy sherbet fountain fizzed and frothed in the center.

As they had feared, there were, indeed, quite a few witches hurrying to and fro—but they didn't look much like the angry one the explorers had just encountered. Most of them were pleasant-looking old ladies who wore their hair neatly arranged in buns tucked beneath their hats and wore outfits similar to the one Drusilla had worn: black dresses, pointed hats, striped stockings, and buckled shoes. There wasn't a scarecrow coat in sight. Some of the witches carried broomsticks, while others had cauldrons swinging

from their arms. Stella noticed one or two with a bat, or a toad, or a newt balanced on their shoulder or curling around at their feet and realized the animals must be the witches' familiars. Stella could tell they were no ordinary animals, because every one of them wore a pointed black hat.

The first witch that passed them stopped immediately. To Stella's surprise, she was a kindly-looking old lady, with a hooked nose and twinkly blue eyes. She carried a cauldron with a raven in it. The bird wore a pointed hat and gazed over the rim at them with bright, beady eyes before squawking amicably.

"What's this, then?" the witch asked, looking them up and down. "How on earth did you manage to get past the witch gate? Never mind the flying sharks and biting pumpkins and whatnot? I mean, what's the point in us putting all these things there if they're not going to keep nosy children away?"

The raven squawked in agreement.

"We're not nosy children," Beanie told her. "We're explorers."

"But you're not supposed to be here," the old witch almost wailed. A couple of passing witches heard her and stopped to see what all the fuss was about.

"Are these explorers?" one of the new witches exclaimed. "But why have they come here? Surely they know that Witch Mountain is too perilous for exploring?"

"I thought the hunters said that to everyone they met, including the explorers' clubs," the third witch said. "To keep their prices high, you know."

Cadi blushed. "Well, everyone has to earn a living," she said.

"We don't mean any harm," Stella said. The explorers were already starting to inch away. "We're just looking for my father. As soon as we find him, we'll go home."

"But—" one of the witches began.

"And we'll write a fearsome Flag Report," Shay added. "Telling everyone about what a terrible place Witch Mountain is."

"Just see that you do," the witch with the raven huffed. "We've made a great effort to keep people out. Is it too much to ask for a little peace and quiet in your retirement?"

"Absolutely not," Stella said. "We'll be gone before you know it."

The explorers hastily took their leave before the witches could question them any further. As they moved away from the center and into the outskirts, the streets became darker and narrower, and the shops looked like they catered to those looking for hexes and curses and evil magic. The explorers started to avoid looking in through the windows in case they saw a rat nailed to the wall, a pile of warty toads, or a barrel of poisonous apples. Everything smelled of damp and rot and grease.

The witches shopping here were distinctly less kindly-looking too. If they acknowledged the explorers at all, it was to mutter about how visitors shouldn't be allowed on Witch Mountain, and the only thing children were good for was eating, and it was a shame it was generally frowned upon to hex people in Witch Village.

They all became rather eager to get out of the village as quickly as possible, but unfortunately, the streets had become quite mazelike, twisting around and around on themselves, veering off into little alleyways and side streets, all filled with the same unsavory shops.

"We're going around in circles," Ethan said eventually.

"No, we're not," Cadi said. "I'm sure this is the way out."

"I recognize the mask in that window," Ethan said, pointing at a nearby shop. "I noticed it the first time because of how snarly it is. Nigel noticed it too. He spat at it. Look." He pointed at what did, indeed, appear to be a large trail of camel spit running down the filthy window.

Right on cue, Nigel spat at the head again, and the big glob hit the window with a *splat*. A moment later a man came hurrying out of the shop. He had a bent back and was almost entirely bald, and he seemed very irritated. Stella thought he must have had some goblin blood in him, because his ears were slightly pointed and his eyes were huge.

"Can't you control your camel?" the man demanded. "Why do you even have a camel here anyway? It's absurd and I won't stand for it! It's an outrage! I've worked too long and too hard to build up this shop only to have camels come along and spit at it."

"I don't see what difference it makes," Ethan said, "given that the window's already filthy."

"We're very sorry," Shay hurried to apologize. "We're lost. We're actually trying to find our way out of the village. Perhaps you could direct us? We're looking for a witch called Jezzybella."

The shopkeeper stared—his eyes becoming even larger in his face. "No one goes to Jezzybella's house," he said. "No one. There's a frightful thing living there."

"Do you know the address?" Stella asked eagerly. "It's really very important that we see her."

The man was already shaking his head and backing away from them into the shop. "Mad," he muttered. "You'd have to be mad to go there. Jezzybella has a dangerous taste in pets."

"We already know about the vulture," Stella said.

"I ain't talking about the vulture, girl." The man grunted.

Stella wondered whether he had meant the poisonous rabbits, but before she could ask, he said, "Look, if it'll get you away from here, then just follow the path around the corner, turn right, and then right again. That'll take you out of Witch Village."

He stepped into his shop and was about to close the door when Stella said, "And how do we get to Jezzybella's house after that?"

The man glanced at her, his eyes like saucers in the dim light. "From there you just follow the blood," he said.

"Blood?" Stella repeated, startled.

"Saw Jezzybella's vulture going up there yesterday with some chap in tow," he said. "You'll see the blood trail all right. Can't miss it."

And with that he firmly closed the door.

CHAPTER TWENTY

S TELLA PRACTICALLY FLED FROM the village, and the others had to hurry to keep up with her. She could feel her hands shaking as she raced around the corners of the little cobbled streets.

A trail of blood . . .

That must mean Felix was hurt. Perhaps the magic cuff on the vulture had worn off. Or perhaps he had been attacked by something else on his way up Witch Mountain. And now he had an entire day's head start on them and was going to face Jezzybella alone—in fact, he might already have done so, and perhaps they were too late. . . .

They found a side exit in the form of an arched gate, and as soon as they stepped out, they saw the blood on the snowy path leading away from them. There was no time to lose, and the explorers followed the path quickly and in silence. They were too tense to talk—no one wanted to speculate about what they might find when they reached the witch. The path led steeply up to the very top of the mountain, where the air felt cold and thin and sharp, burning their ears and making their chests ache with the effort of breathing.

Finally, the path cut straight through a mountain tunnel. The explorers went through it with the icy wind whistling past their ears, sounding strangely like voices. Stella was reminded of the cold, frozen spirits she'd heard on their last expedition to the Icelands—the tormented souls of all the people who'd died feeling cold. As an ice princess, she didn't normally feel the cold too badly—and seemed to be feeling it less and less all the time—but she shivered now and drew her cloak closer about her.

When they reached the other end of the tunnel, it looked like a dead end at first—just a solid wall of rock rising above them.

"Perhaps we took a wrong turn somewhere," Shay said.

"But this has got to be it," Stella replied. "The . . . The blood trail continues through here."

There was, indeed, a trail of smeared blood along the stone floor.

"Perhaps Felix realized it was a dead end and turned around and walked back the way he'd come," Shay suggested.

"But there was only one trail going into the tunnel,"

Stella said. "There must be another way out of here some-where."

She lifted the pixie lantern higher, and the explorers examined every inch of the wall. Finally, Beanie spotted the narrow gap in the rock.

Cadi shook her head. "No way Gus is going to fit through that. He'll have to wait here for us."

"So will Nigel," Ethan said.

Gus didn't like not being able to follow Cadi, and there was a great deal of fuss and bellowing as they left. They distinctly heard the *thump* of his pith helmet hitting the rock multiple times as he tried to follow them, with zero success.

"Gus, you can't come through here. You're not going to fit," Cadi said. "You're ginormous, and this gap is tiny. Look." She reached an arm through to pat him on his whiskery face. "We'll be back to get you before you know it. Promise."

After squeezing through the gap, the expedition found themselves in a larger tunnel, and they followed this to the open air on the other side. They stepped out not knowing quite what they would find, but fully expecting it to be bad.

In fact, it was worse than they'd thought.

They were surrounded on all sides by spiderwebs. Only these were no ordinary webs. For one thing, they were absolutely huge—far bigger than the explorers themselves—and for another, they were made of ice. The frozen webs glittered

dangerously at them, blocking their view of whatever lay ahead.

"Gosh," Stella finally said. "I wonder what could have made these."

"Ice spiders," Beanie said in a low voice at her side. She glanced at him and saw that he looked a little sick. "They're extremely dangerous."

Stella recalled what the goblin man had said about Jezzybella's taste in pets.

"Of course they are." Ethan sighed.

"No wonder that man back at the village said no one ever comes here," Stella said.

She couldn't help thinking the webs were rather beautiful, though. They were fantastically delicate and intricate, reminding her of the way each individual snowflake was completely unique and special in its own way. But she shuddered at the thought of a spider large enough to build webs this big—they towered over the explorers, chilling the air and blocking out the sunlight, which filtered through, pale blue and ghostly. The space around them was freezing cold and utterly still and silent, like all the air had been sucked out of it, as if something was crouching close by, holding its breath, and watching them . . .

"We can climb through the web," Stella said. "The gaps between the strands are big enough to squeeze through. I don't think we should touch it, though—"

Unfortunately, the jungle fairies were perhaps a little too intrepid for their own good and had already started forward. Before Stella could finish speaking, Humphrey had brushed up against one of the icy strands. It was so cold that it gave him a frost burn on his hand, and he snatched his arm back with an aggrieved cry. Unlike a normal web, this one wasn't sticky and didn't ensnare the jungle fairy. Instead, it rang out at his touch with a chiming sound that echoed from one strand to the other, until the air seemed full of peals, like hundreds of frozen bells all ringing at the same time.

The explorers stared around in dismay as the jungle

fairies fled to the safety of Stella's cloak pockets, poking their heads over the tops and peering around wildly. They all realized instantly that the chiming was an alarm system designed to alert something to their presence, and moments later there was a frantic scrabbling sound as something rapidly clinked and chinked its way toward them, sending off more chimes—echoes upon echoes of them—that were almost deafening.

The next second the creature had arrived, and a shadow fell across the expedition as a huge ice spider, easily the size of a house, loomed over them, its spindly ice legs ending in points as sharp as daggers, its pincers pinching together in frenzied excitement, and its eight burning red eyes staring down at them with an awful look of greed.

There is only one suitable response when faced with such a monster, and that is to scream and shout and run for your lives. The explorers raced through the icy strands of the web, trying not to notice that their boots were crunching on a deep carpet of bones as they went. Every time one of them knocked against part of the web, the chimes and peals set off all over again, ringing out so loudly it hurt their ears. A couple of times one of them bumped into the web so hard that a strand of it shattered, and this made even more of a din, like a trumpet going off beside their heads.

It was impossible to outrun the spider. It was there at every turn, using the web to climb up above them and drop down onto the path before them, cutting off any route of escape. The explorers fled deeper into the web and hunkered down together in one of the clearings as the spider scuttled to and fro above them, trying to work out where they had gone.

"What are we going to do?" Cadi gasped. "Didn't you bring any weapons with you?"

"Didn't you?" Ethan replied.

"Nothing big enough to work on an ice spider," the hunter replied.

"Ice spiders are blind," Beanie said. "If we tiptoe through without touching the web and don't make any noise, then it might not find us."

"That could work," Shay said. "If we just take it slow and don't panic, then we can avoid touching the web."

Stella made sure the jungle fairies and Buster were all securely tucked in her pockets before they continued on, carefully ducking and weaving and stepping over each icy strand. For a while it seemed to be working. The spider ran back and forth above them but had lost their trail and, finally, it came to a halt in the middle of the web, its legs trembling with anticipation as it waited for someone to make a sound and give away their position.

Shay nudged Stella and pointed ahead. Through the last strands they could make out a house. It had to be the witch's. Stella nodded at Shay. They were almost there. . . .

And then Beanie stepped on a bone that broke with a loud *snap* beneath his boot. Everyone immediately froze, but it was too late. The spider had heard them and came racing over, the web ringing and pealing around it as it skittered right up to them, stopping just a few feet from Beanie.

Stella held her hands up to her friend, wordlessly warning him to stay still and silent. The medic stayed absolutely motionless, although Stella could see that the pom-pom on the top of his hat was trembling slightly. The spider clinked ever closer, its pincers clicking briskly together in irritation. Finally it was so close to Beanie that he could see each individual frost hair on its chin and the cloudy milk spots in every one of its red eyes.

They all held their breath, and Stella prayed that no one would choose this moment to suddenly sneeze. Even the jungle fairies seemed to understand that this was no time to start doing the chant of doom.

Finally, the ice spider pulled back from Beanie, turned around, and began to move away from them, back to its lookout perch. They all let out a sigh of relief, but the next second Cadi gave a yell. The others turned to stare at her in appalled horror, only to see a razor-sharp fin had burst through the bag on her back. This was closely followed by another fin, and another, and another.

The witch hunter tore it off and threw it to the floor. The bag ripped apart as the frogs started turning back into glow-piranhas, all gnashing teeth and flailing fins. They seemed particularly furious—perhaps as a result of being turned into frogs and then stuffed into a bag filled with even more frogs—and the explorers had to jump back quickly in order to avoid their biting, snapping, teeth-filled jaws.

Unfortunately, all this commotion created a huge amount of noise, which immediately brought the spider racing straight back over to them. It was just about to sink its pincers straight into Shay's back when Ethan plucked one of the piranhas from the ground by its tail and hurled it at the spider. The furious fish immediately clamped its jaws on the spider's leg, causing great hairline cracks to spread all the way down the limb.

The others quickly followed suit, grabbing the piranhas by their tails and throwing them at the ice spider. Cadi started throwing frogs at it too, which mostly just bounced off and hopped away, although a couple of them clung to the spider, eyes bulging, as the great monster thrashed around, trying to dislodge the piranhas that had clamped their teeth into it.

"Stop throwing the frogs!" Stella gasped. "One of them is an explorer!"

"That one wasn't," Cadi pointed out. The frog that had been clinging to the spider's back was now a bemused-looking vampire troll, blinking and squinting in the sunlight.

"It's not working anyway!" Shay cried. "The piranhas are just making it even more angry."

"There are some sharks in there somewhere too," Ethan cried. He threw a magic spell at the nearest frog, and there was a soft *pop* as it abruptly turned into a boy—a boy with glossy chestnut hair, wearing a nightcap and a green dressing gown stamped with the Jungle Cat Explorers' Club crest.

"Gideon!" Stella exclaimed, beyond relieved that one of the frogs really was the explorer and that they hadn't left him back in the flying-shark cave or in the murky swamps of the Forest of Enchanted Broomsticks.

"Oh, blast," Ethan said. "This one's no use to anybody."

Gideon Galahad Smythe's hair stuck out wildly in all directions, and his dressing gown was crumpled and creased, but other than that he looked no worse for wear. He did, however, give an awful groan as soon as he turned back into a human, blinking around at them with an outraged expression.

"I can't believe you turned me into a frog! I just can't believe it! I can't—"

Before he could go on, Ethan threw magic at another frog, and there was an explosion of ice as it abruptly transformed not into a piranha, or an explorer, or a vampire troll, but a flying shark, which seemed to be every bit as angry about the frog fiasco as the piranhas had been. It bared its impressive teeth, thrashed its muscly body as it readjusted to its new form, blinked its cold, killer's eyes, and then looked around, determined to attack the first thing it saw—which happened to be the spider.

The shark flew at it with a vengeance, closely followed by another shark that Ethan transformed back into its natural shape. They were both equally desperate to bite and attack and reassert their mighty sharkness after the terrible indignity of being a frog. They tore great chunks out of the spider, which thrashed back into its web, legs flailing and pincers snapping, as it fought against the attacking sharks.

Shards of ice showered down around them, and it was hard to tell what was web and what was spider, but the explorers didn't stay to find out. They turned and fled as fast as they could, leaving the monsters to their ferocious battle and running, full pelt, toward the witch's house.

CHAPTER TWENTY-ONE

THEY EMERGED FROM THE web—which sounded like it was being smashed to pieces by the monster battle taking place inside it—and entered a snow-covered clearing, in the middle of which sat a house. They knew at once that it was a witch's house, although it was nothing like the gloomy castle Stella had anticipated. Instead, what lay before them was a magnificent ice-cream house.

It had a mint roof, liberally scattered with chocolate chips; a fudge chimney stack that scented the entire clearing; chocolate-flake windowsills; swirled-vanilla walls; and window boxes full of strawberry ice-cream roses and banana ice-cream sunflowers. An ice-cream-cone path led all the way to the front door, surrounded on all sides by different-colored ice-cream flowers—along with some rather odd-looking ice-cream cabbages—and there was also a scarecrow wearing a bowler hat, made entirely from pink sugar.

It was, in fact, one of the prettiest houses Stella had ever seen, and it was almost hard to believe that an evil witch lived there. She even wondered whether perhaps they had the wrong house after all. But then she noticed the blood trail leading around to the back of the house, proving they were in the right place.

"Good Lord, that's a witch's house, isn't it?" Gideon cried. "A witch's house, probably filled to bursting with all kinds of terrible—"

He didn't get any further, however, because Ethan threw out his hand and turned him, once again, into a wonky squish-squish frog.

"Ethan!" Stella groaned. "You really can't keep turning him into a frog!"

"I can't stand his whining," the magician replied, scooping up the frog and stuffing him back in his pocket.

"You didn't say you'd managed to capture a Prince Charming," Cadi said, clearly getting the wrong end of the stick due to Gideon's good looks. "There'll be a princess somewhere looking high and low for him, you know."

"He's not a Prince Charming," Stella said with a sigh. "He's an explorer."

"You said you couldn't remember the spell to turn him back," Shay said, giving Ethan an accusing look.

"Well, I couldn't at the time."

"Amazing how being faced with a giant killing ice spider focuses the mind," the wolf whisperer remarked, rolling his eyes.

"Quite."

The front door opened just then, with such force that it smacked against the ice-cream wall with a *thud*. The monster battle in the ice web behind them was continuing to set off all kinds of chimes and rings, so it had not exactly been the stealthiest approach, but they were all still quite dismayed to see a witch emerge from the house. Stella knew at once that this was the one they were looking for, because she had several puppets clutched in her hands—all made in the same style as the witch puppet Stella had taken from her room back at the snow queen's palace. The witch also wore an enormous pair of bright yellow rain boots, and Stella realized this must be to protect her feet, which she knew to be horribly burned.

She was ancient—far older than Stella had expected her to be—all knobby knees and elbows, wrinkled skin, and frizzy gray hair that flew out behind her as she ran, rather awkwardly in her huge rain boots, down the path toward them. Stella was even more horrified to see that she was almost incoherent with fury—crying and muttering unintelligible words under her breath. It was impossible to know whether she was angry about the destruction of her ice spider and web, or just furious at the mere sight of Stella.

Automatically, everyone reached for whatever weapons they had to hand. Shay grabbed his boomerang, Cadi pulled a potion bottle from her bag, and Stella reached up to check that the ice tiara was still on her head.

The witch was only a few feet away from them when she tripped over her big rain boots and toppled over, face-first, into the snow. Stella saw her chance and lifted her hand, intending to freeze the witch solid before she could murder them all.

But then a familiar voice rang out from the doorstep. "Stella, don't!"

She looked up to see Felix emerge from the house and hurry down the path toward them. After all that blood on the snow, she had feared that he might be awfully wounded, and relief rushed through her at the sight of him now, apparently completely unharmed. He stopped just in front of the sprawled witch, both hands raised in front of him.

"It's all right, Felix," Stella said. She assumed he was panicking in case she froze her heart with the ice magic. "I can do this."

"The witch isn't dangerous, Stella," Felix said. "It's not what we thought. Trust me."

Stella was extremely confused by this, but she trusted Felix unquestioningly, so she lowered her hands and watched in surprise as he turned back to the witch, crouching down in the snow before her and gently helping her upright.

"It's all right, Jezzybella," he said. "Just slow down for a moment. Take a breath. Now, look at me. Have you hurt yourself anywhere?"

The witch shook her head as Felix helped her back to her feet and offered her his arm. She moved the puppets to one hand, placed her gnarled hand in the crook of his elbow, and allowed him to help her hobble the rest of the way down the path to the explorers.

When she stopped in front of them, Stella saw that her eyes were full of tears, which ran freely down her wrinkled cheeks—only they didn't appear to be tears of anger, as Stella had first thought, but some other emotion that she couldn't quite identify yet. And then she saw the charm bracelet and sucked in her breath in shocked recognition. She had seen it before, a long time ago, on the wrist of someone who'd been reading her a magical bedtime story about unicorns.

"Princess," the old witch said, making a clumsy attempt at a curtsy.

Stella actually heard her knees pop and was glad when Felix hurriedly raised her back up and said, "There's really no need for that, dear. Stella doesn't expect anyone to stand on ceremony."

"I've kept them safe for you, Princess," the witch said, holding out the tangle of puppets with her shaking hands.

Stella looked at Felix, who nodded, so she cautiously reached out and took the puppets from the witch. They were handmade, and just like the witch puppet, they were magical. As soon as Stella touched them, they came to life and untangled themselves, the strings stretching upright as the puppets moved around of their own accord.

First there was a polar bear, covered in soft white fur, with bright blue eyes, that padded around, roaring, at Stella's feet. Then there was a unicorn, with a pearly horn and a silky smooth mane and tail, which pranced happily in the snow. The third puppet was a yeti covered in bobbly white wool, which beat its huge fists against its chest and stamped back and forth. There was also an ice dragon puppet made of smooth white wood, which flew around Stella, blowing out little plumes of steam. And, finally, the last puppet was obviously an ice princess. She was made from polished gold wood, just like the witch, and wore a powder-blue dress with a puffed-out skirt. A long white braid trailed down her back, and a sparkly tiara sat on her head. She curtsied to Stella and then went running after the unicorn.

Stella frowned down at the puppets, feeling a strange tug of memory. She could see herself playing with them when she was a little girl in her nursery.

"I left the witch puppet in the nursery," the witch said. "To watch out for you. In case you ever came home. I kept this for you too, Princess." Jezzybella dropped the silver charm bracelet into Stella's hand.

Stella stared down at it for a moment before looking back up. "But . . . I don't understand . . . ," she began.

"Jezzybella didn't kill your parents," Felix said. "In fact, she's the one who took you from the castle and placed you in my path."

"But why did she send the vulture after me, then?" she asked.

"Ah, the vulture," Felix said. "That's Oswald. He's not a bad old thing, really. He wasn't trying to attack you, Stella. She sent him to bring you back to Witch Mountain to check that you were safe. It seems the puppet caught sight of you and Gruff playing in the backyard, and Jezzybella mistook it for an attack. She was afraid you were going to be gobbled up by a polar bear if you stayed at home. When I tried to stop the vulture, he thought I was a threat. Jezzybella was your nanny when you were small, you see. She cares for you a great deal."

"But then . . . who really killed my parents?" Stella asked.

The witch burst into tears again then. "The magic mirror," she sobbed. "Oh, the mirror, the mirror! It ruined everything!"

"Magic mirrors can be tricky like that," Cadi said, patting her on the arm sympathetically.

"The Collector came, and he killed everyone and he took everything," Jezzybella went on. "He even took the Book of Frost. I could do nothing to stop it and saved only these poor trinkets."

She gestured at the puppets, and the yeti immediately roared in outrage at being called a trinket.

"You saved the princess's life," Felix said, squeezing the witch's bony old hand. "You were completely heroic, my dear."

The witch gave him a wobbly smile, but then her mind seemed to wander away from the conversation because she suddenly said, "I must go and count the cabbages."

She hobbled away, her huge rain boots shuffling a trail through the snow.

"Felix, I don't understand. What's going on here?" Stella asked.

"Excuse us for a moment, would you?" Felix said to the others, before drawing Stella to one side. "You know, I'm a little confused myself, since I distinctly remember telling you to stay at home and wait for me to come back," he said.

Stella lifted her chin a little. "Yes, but you might never have come back," she said. "I wasn't about to take that chance. And I don't think you can really tell me off for that, seeing as I only did exactly what you would have done.

Besides which, President Fogg had a report that Jezzybella had been bringing poisonous rabbits onto the mountain—he told Ethan's father, but he never got the chance to tell you about them."

"Oh, those." Felix sighed. "Yes, Jezzybella bought them as treats to feed to her ice spider. She put on her gloves and threw him the last one just yesterday. You know, I really feel I ought to be angry with you, but I suppose I have only myself to blame for setting a bad example. How on earth did you get here?"

"Oh, we . . . We kind of stole a dirigible," Stella said.

"A dirigible!" Felix exclaimed. "Who from?"

"The president of the Jungle Cat Explorers' Club," Stella said in a small voice.

"That's . . . not particularly good timing," Felix said. "He's a little nervous about you at the moment."

"I know, but we had to get here somehow," Stella replied. She decided that now probably wasn't the time to mention that they'd also broken into the Polar Bear Explorers' Club, stolen some things, and been chased out by guards.

"Are you hurt?" she asked instead. "We followed your trail to get here and it was all bloody."

"Oh, that was Oswald," Felix said. "We got a bit lost in Witch Village, and I'm afraid he found something dead and horrible in one of the back alleys there and insisted on dragging it home with him. I think it might once have been some kind of swamp rat, but it was quite hard to tell—" He broke off as the jungle fairies suddenly started tugging at his sleeves. The fairies back home absolutely loved Felix, and it seemed these were no different.

Stella introduced them, and Felix looked delighted. "I've never met a jungle fairy before," he said. "What marvelous fellows, and equally marvelous ladies. Delighted to make your acquaintance."

The fairies flew off to investigate the sugar scarecrow, and Felix turned back to Stella. "Listen, I arrived here yesterday all set to capture the witch and drag her back to the Court of Magical Justice for a trial, but she was absolutely delighted to see me, welcomed me into her home, and has been making me little ice-cream houses ever since I arrived. She didn't kill your parents. I don't think she's ever hurt anyone in her life. But she's extremely old now and doesn't seem to quite have all her marbles left, I'm afraid. It took a lot of rambling, roundabout conversations, but I think I've got the gist of it.

"The magic mirror you described isn't actually a mirror at all, but an enchantress. Your parents trapped her in the glass for some reason. Jezzybella thinks she displeased them in some way. But this enchantress was able to communicate with another magic mirror on the other side of the Black Ice Bridge. It belongs to someone the witch knows only as the Collector. She coaxed him to the castle, thinking that he would free her, but he killed your parents and stole this Book of Frost instead."

"What's the Book of Frost?" Stella asked.

"You know how witches have a Book of Shadows?" Felix asked. "A book that contains all of their spells? Well, it seems that snow queens have something similar, only it's called a Book of Frost. He took this book with him and left the mirror behind. She didn't realize that the castle would shut itself down if there was no snow queen or ice princess there. Jezzybella seems to think that snow queens and ice princesses have their own intrinsic magical powers that can be used even without the tiara. That's why ice princesses normally have witch nannies—albeit they're treated like wretched slaves—so that they can help young ice princesses master their magic.

"Your parents used the iron slippers on her because she tried to run away one time, many years before you were born. Apparently Jezzybella had been with your family for generations. She knows all kinds of things about snow queens, and if I've understood her correctly, this inner magic won't run the risk of freezing your heart like the tiara would. It seems to be something to do with the difference between ice magic and frost magic."

Stella felt a growing sense of excitement. "I think I've already done a bit of frost magic," she said, and then proceeded to tell him about the snow unicorn back home, the yeti guard on the dirigible, and the snow trolls in the magic fort.

Felix grinned at her, sharing her excitement. "How absolutely smashing," he said. He gestured at the charm bracelet in her hand. "This is magical too, apparently. You touch the different charms for different spells."

Stella glanced at the silver bracelet. There was a yeti charm there and a unicorn, a sleigh, a fairy, an ice goblin, and more.

"You have a lot to learn," Felix said. "The study of magic is quite involved, from what I hear. I've asked Jezzybella if she'd like to come and stay with us for a while. She will be able to help you master your frost magic."

Stella could think of nothing she'd like more, but a dark fear niggled away at her. "Do you think I should?" she asked.

"Don't you want to learn magic?" Felix asked, looking surprised.

"I would love to," Stella replied. "But people won't like it, will they? Those people who wrote those horrible letters and the president of the Jungle Cat Explorers' Club. President Fogg left all these papers on your desk at home before he went—a whole load of reports about evil snow queens. If I start learning how to do magic, it's probably going to upset people even more, isn't it?"

Felix gave an easy shrug. "My darling thing, if we spent too much time worrying about what narrow-minded people thought; then we'd really never get anywhere at all." He crouched down in front of her and took her hand. "You mustn't ever let anyone stop you from feeling like you can be yourself, you know. So if you would like Jezzybella to come home with us and help teach you your ice magic, then that's certainly what we shall do."

"But the President of the Jungle Cat Explorers' Club—"

"The President of the Jungle Cat Explorers' Club can go and jump in the Tikki Zikki River for all I care," Felix said cheerfully. "This has got nothing whatsoever to do with him, so he can keep his overlarge nose out of it."

Stella grinned at Felix. "I love you so much, Felix," she said.

Felix wrapped his arms around her in a tight hug. "I love you too, sweetling," he said. "More than anything."

They were interrupted then by Jezzybella wandering over to them with a huge basket full of ice-cream cabbages.

"Cabbage?" she said, thrusting one out to them. "You must each take a cabbage with you. Cabbages for everyone!"

"They're not biting cabbages, are they?" Ethan demanded, as the others joined them. "Because I was attacked by one of those on the last expedition, and I don't care to repeat the experience."

"I don't think so." The witch stared down anxiously at the bundle of cabbages in her arms. "They've never bitten me, at least."

"Of course they're not biting cabbages, Ethan—they're made of ice cream," Stella said. She took the cabbage the witch held out to her and said, "Thank you very much. That's very kind."

Jezzybella squeezed Stella's arm tightly, emptied the rest of the cabbages onto the ground, and then proceeded to climb into the basket. She whistled through her teeth, and instantly a broomstick flew out of the house, hooked under the basket handle, and lifted it right up off the ground.

"Jezzybella is ready to go," the witch announced, beaming at Stella.

Felix scratched the back of his neck. "Ah, yes," he said. "Well, the problem now is how are we going to get home? Oswald can't carry all of us." He glanced at Stella. "Can we use the dirigible?"

Stella shook her head. "We traded it back at Weenus's Trading Post," she said. "But Cadi is a hunter and her father has a ship that she says we can travel back on." She quickly introduced Felix to her new friend.

"We should press on," Shay said. "It's a long trip back down the mountain."

"Not long," Jezzybella said cheerfully. "There's a witch hole in the tunnel that'll take us to the bottom. I'll show you."

They made their way back through the shattered ruins of the ice web, hurrying quickly past the flying sharks, which were feasting on what remained of the ice spider. Remembering what the shopkeeper had said about it being Jezzybella's pet, Stella was suddenly terribly worried that the witch would be heartbroken. In fact, she didn't seem to notice and just called out a cheery good-bye to the spider.

"So long, Marvin," she said. "I've found my Stella, and I'm leaving for good."

When they squeezed back through the gap in the rock, Gus gave a great bellow and practically flattened Cadi in welcome. Nigel tried to pretend that he didn't care whether they'd come back or not, but Stella noticed that he nibbled affectionately at Ethan's hair when he thought no one was looking.

It didn't take long for Jezzybella to locate the entrance to the witch hole. This time they made Nigel go first, since no one fancied having their heads bashed in by a flailing camel hoof. They gave him a little bit of a head start, and then the others followed one by one. Stella jumped in last and immediately discovered that this witch hole was even steeper than the first one. Her skirts and petticoats puffed up around her as she slid downward, and she couldn't help laughing, for it really was tremendous fun. Besides which, she was so relieved that they had found Felix unharmed, that the expedition had been a success, and that the witch wasn't actually evil at all. Everything had gone far better than she could have hoped, and in no time at all she'd be safely back home with Gruff, learning how to practice frost magic. . . .

But the thought was too soon. She flew out of the end of the witch hole, her boots landing with a crunch in the snow. Then she looked up, and fear turned her blood to ice.

They were surrounded on all sides by witch wolves.

CHAPTER TWENTY-TWO

THE EXPLORERS FOUND THEMSELVES on a snowy shoreline. There was even a little pier made of frozen wooden planks, stretching out into the sea. Stella saw that Cadi had already released the flare to call her father's ship. The glittering red light still fizzed above them like a dying firework, calling the witch-hunting vessel that, even now, was turning in the water and sailing slowly toward them.

But between the explorers and the pier was an entire pack of witch wolves, and they were monstrous. Far bigger than any ordinary wolf, they were at least as large as Koa herself, and their coats were entirely white, from snout to tail. There must have been a dozen of them, and they all had ghostly silver eyes, frozen solid and coated in frost, giving them a look of blindness. Their frosted eyes reflected the light back strangely, making it hard to meet their gaze.

When Stella tried, a throbbing started in her temples, and she had to look away, confused.

Shay was on his knees, both hands clutching his head, with the others grouped around him. Koa stood in front—a lone dark shadow wolf facing the white witch wolves—her hackles raised, her lips pulled back in a ferocious snarl. But the witch wolves were not in the least bit afraid of her and padded closer and closer, their strange, silver eyes shining with cold, murderous intent.

Ethan threw a spell at the nearest one, but it bounced off harmlessly, and Stella remembered what Drusilla had said about how it was impossible to change a witch wolf's form. The wolf briefly bared its teeth at the magician, but Ethan wasn't the one it was interested in. It only had eyes for Koa, and the next second, the witch wolf took a flying leap toward her.

Stella whipped the tiara from her pocket and put it on just in time to throw out her hand and freeze the witch wolf mid-jump. It was much, much harder than she was expecting—and she felt the wolf's magical resistance shudder all the way up her arm at the same time that the ice magic chilled her from the inside, pushing away thoughts of warmth and love and friendship. Stella snatched off her tiara, and the frozen witch wolf fell to the ground with a *thump*, one of its paws snapping off on impact.

The other witch wolves all attacked at once then, and

the expedition fell into position around Shay and Koa to try to ward them off. An awful sound of howling carried through the air, which suddenly seemed full of teeth and silver eyes and iced fur and frost-tipped fangs. Cadi produced more spell bottles from her bag, which she threw to the ground in front of the wolves, but they just created a thick fog that slowed the wolves down only for a few moments. Felix had a crossbow tucked away in his cloak, with which he managed to take down one of the wolves, but this used up every single one of his arrows. Beanie, as usual, was not much use in a crisis and only tugged at his pom-pom hat, muttering unhelpful facts. And Shay had his boomerang gripped in his hand but didn't seem able to use it. In fact, he didn't appear to be able to do anything other than hunch in the snow and gasp for breath as the wolves closed in.

Stella saw immediately that their only hope lay with the ice magic of her tiara. All that mattered in that moment was saving Shay, Koa, Felix, and the rest of the expedition. Even if she froze her own heart solid in the process and became the evil snow queen everyone said she was destined to become, it would be worth it if she could save her friends.

She summoned every ounce of her energy, strength, and determination, replaced the tiara, and threw both hands up in front of her. The ice magic fizzed and crackled around her fingertips for a moment before she drew in a deep breath and then blasted it away from her, directly into the path of the approaching witch wolves. Immediately, she felt as if her whole body had been plunged into icy water, and her hands fell to her sides.

The ice magic coated them one by one, and they fell heavily into the snow, some of them losing tails or legs as their frozen limbs snapped on impact. The spell raced all the way along the pack but wasn't quite strong enough to reach the very last wolf, which remained snarling and unfrozen as it advanced toward Koa.

Stella lifted her hand to freeze the wolf, but then hesitated. The final burst of ice magic had chilled her heart, and in that moment she didn't care what happened to Koa, or to Shay, or to anyone.

Shay saw the expression on her face and gave her a desperate look. "Stella, please!"

Stella was about to walk away, but some inner part of her was screaming, and with a gigantic effort she fought off the effect of the tiara and threw one last burst of ice magic at the final wolf.

But that moment of hesitation meant she was just a fraction too late. The witch wolf dodged her spell as it fell on Koa, and they became one ball of tooth and claw, black and white fur merging together, terrible howls filling the air around them. Shay groaned, doubling up on the snow.

Stella strode forward and grabbed the witch wolf with both hands. It froze instantly at her touch, and its rigid body fell down harmlessly, but the damage had been done. Koa limped, bleeding, back to Shay's side. Where her fur had once been completely coal-black, now there was a streak of white down one side of her back. A matching streak had appeared in Shay's own dark hair.

Jezzybella came to stand at Stella's side. They both watched as the others crowded around Shay and Koa in concern, trying to work out whether they were okay and what the white streaks meant.

"I can tell you what it means," the witch piped up. "That shadow wolf will turn into a witch wolf."

"Koa? Into a witch wolf? When?" Beanie cried.

"Hard to say," the witch replied. "Could be one month, could be a year."

"And what about Shay?" Ethan asked. "What'll happen to him?"

The witch shrugged. "I don't know," she said. "But one thing's for sure—it'll be nothing good."

Stella knew she should feel upset about this, but in fact, she felt nothing at all. The witch hunter's ship was almost at the pier, but Stella didn't care about that either.

"How do you feel?" Ethan asked, leaning down toward Shay, who was shaking from head to foot.

"Cold," the wolf whisperer replied as Koa lay down at his side.

"If she's going to turn into a witch wolf, then that's

almost the same as dying, isn't it?" Beanie said. "Isn't there anything we can do?"

"Nothing," Jezzybella said. "A witch wolf's bite can't be undone."

Felix appeared beside Stella suddenly and plucked the tiara from her hair.

"You did well, Stella," he said quietly. "The witch wolf might have killed Koa if it hadn't been for you."

"I'm not sure I care," Stella said. She gazed at her friends and felt nothing. "In fact, I don't care about any of you."

"Not right now," Felix said with a sigh as the witch hunter's ship docked at the pier. "But you will."

When Stella's heart thawed on board the ship an hour or so later, the remorse she felt was so bad that she almost couldn't breathe with it. She knew that she'd had the power to stop the wolves, but—for those few seconds—she had chosen not to use it.

She buried herself away in a cabin and refused to come out. She was too ashamed to face anyone—even Felix. When he told her through the door that Shay wanted to see her, she shuddered at the thought. How he must hate her! She remembered what she had said to everyone back at the witch gate:

"If I can ever repay you, then I will."

Well, this was a pretty poor way of repaying the friend who had risked everything for her.

When night fell, Stella couldn't stand being cooped up in the cabin anymore, and sleep was quite impossible, so she snatched up her tiara and went up onto the deck. She found a quiet spot right at the back and stood there alone at the railing. Even though they'd been sailing for hours, she could still see the orange glow of Witch Mountain far away on the horizon.

Stella had come up without her cloak and wore only her pale blue dress and fur-topped boots. Snowflakes swirled around her, patches of ice floated on the surface of the sea, and her breath smoked in the freezing air, but she wasn't cold. She was becoming more and more of an ice princess every single day, and there was nothing she could do to stop it.

She clutched the tiara tightly and stared down at the icy water churning into frothy white foam below. Perhaps she should drop the tiara straight into the sea. She might almost be able to pretend that she wasn't an ice princess at all then, that there wasn't this evil lurking inside of her. . . .

"You came up for air at last, I see," a voice remarked behind her.

Stella turned to see Felix standing there, his hands buried in the pockets of his explorer's cloak, a striped scarf wound around his neck in the blue and white colors of the Polar Bear Explorers' Club.

"Please don't try to comfort me," Stella said. "I hate

myself. I hate everything about myself, and there's nothing you can say that will make me feel better."

"Well, it certainly sounds like you've made up your mind," Felix said. He joined her at the railing and gazed toward the glow of Witch Mountain. "So, what next?" he asked. "Now that you've decided to hate yourself?"

Stella shrugged. "Just . . . try to keep away from people as much as I can, I suppose. So that I don't hurt anyone else."

Felix was silent for a moment. "You surprise me," he said at last. "I never would have thought to hear you say something so cowardly."

"Cowardly!" Stella exclaimed. "How is it cowardly to try to protect the people I love? There's something wrong with me. What else can I do? I wish I could just be good and kind like you, but I'm not."

"Stella, my darling, you are good and kind," Felix said. "We all have dark sides to ourselves that we must learn to fight against."

"You don't," Stella said. "You don't have any badness in you at all."

"Dear me, you can't really believe that, can you?" Felix asked.

"I bet you've never in your whole life done something so awful you couldn't forgive yourself for it."

"On the contrary," Felix replied sadly. "You know, I broke somebody's heart once, and that's about the worst thing one person can do to another. And I don't even have any ice magic to excuse my behavior. I am wholly responsible for the pain that I caused."

Stella turned to look at her father. He was gazing out to sea as snowflakes settled in his brown hair. "I don't believe it," she said, shaking her head. "I don't believe that you would ever break someone's heart."

"But I'm afraid I did, my dear," Felix replied. "Falling in love is the greatest adventure there is, but it takes an enormous amount of courage as well, and I was too much of a coward in the end. It's my greatest regret."

"What was his name?" Stella asked, and then immediately wondered whether she should have pried.

Felix didn't seem to mind, though, and simply said, "His name was Oscar."

She saw a flash of pain cross his face before he turned back to her and said, "Everyone makes mistakes, my darling. No one is perfect, I can assure you—least of all me."

Stella looked down at the tiara, sparkling in the starlight in her hands, and said, "On that first expedition to the Icelands, when I almost let Ethan fall down that ravine, Beanie said that it wasn't me talking; it was the ice magic. But the ice magic is me, isn't it? I can't choose not to be an ice princess."

"No," Felix acknowledged. "You're an ice princess, and it's part of who you are, but it's only a part. It doesn't have to

define you. Nor does it have to be the biggest, most important thing about you. That's for you to decide."

"Everyone thinks I'm going to turn into an evil snow
queen, and maybe they're right," Stella said. "The ice magic
makes me feel like I'm not really me. That I don't even
know who I am. Like I'm losing myself. It makes me so
afraid that I'm just going to . . . to disappear."

Stella struggled to find the right words to explain how
she felt. The tiara made her feel like a non-person, like a
drawing that was being slowly rubbed out.

After a moment Felix said, "You know, Stella, you don't
have to be an ice princess to feel that way. I've felt it myself."

"You have?" she asked doubtfully.

"Many times. Most often back in those days when I was
trying to fit in and be rather ordinary. And failing miserably, of course." He looked at her. "It's a great pity that we all
spend so much time trying to be exactly the same as everyone else when, in fact, we should be celebrating those things
that make us different and uniquely ourselves. So I know
how you feel. When you lose faith in who you are, it can
feel as if bits of yourself are being chipped away, and that's
a terrible thing."

"What can I do about it?" Stella almost whispered. She
desperately wanted to feel like herself again, but the bad
feeling was so big and horrible that it felt like it would crush
her, and she was completely powerless to stop it.

"Plenty," Felix replied. "There's plenty you can do. First, and most important, you mustn't water yourself down. You must never allow other people to make you feel worthless or small. You must hold on to what you believe in. You—"

"But, Felix, that sounds really hard."

To her surprise, he laughed. "Naturally. It's devilish hard. Most worthwhile things in life are. You just have to pick yourself up when you get knocked down. And you must allow yourself to feel sad sometimes, and lost, and perhaps a little defeated as well. And you must accept that sometimes you are definitely going to make an absolute mess of things. But the only way we ever fail is if we stop trying. And ultimately, all those mistakes and wrong turns are how we find out who we really are, deep down. It's how we strengthen our souls."

"But what if my soul is just bad?" Stella cried. "What if I'm just a horrible, unfeeling, worthless—"

Felix dropped down to Stella's level, took hold of both her arms, and turned her around to face him.

"My dear girl, you are the best and most wonderful thing that has ever happened to me," he said, reaching up to wipe away a tear that was trailing down Stella's cheek. "You think you feel this way because of being an ice princess, but that's not true, you know. Almost every person in the world has felt wretched and worthless at some point in their lives. But shutting yourself off from other people only leads to misery. We must allow others their flaws, accept our own imperfections, be brave enough to share our souls anyway, and always, always be kind."

"But I wasn't kind back on Witch Mountain. I could have saved Shay—"

"If it weren't for you, Shay would probably have been turned into a witch wolf there and then," Felix said. "You did what you could at the time. And all you can control now is what you do next. How is refusing to talk to Shay going to help matters?"

"I don't want to see him because I'm afraid he'll hate me."

"Oh, my dear one, never make decisions from a place of fear," Felix replied. "Nothing good ever comes from that, trust me. Our bonds of love and friendship with other people are not always as simple or as straightforward as we would like them to be, but that doesn't mean they're not worth it in the end, warts and all. We must fight for our loved ones with everything that we have, and yes, sometimes that means pushing through the fear of being rejected, or looking foolish, or getting hurt, or having our hearts broken. You can break your own heart, you know, and that's even worse. It's something I wish I'd learned a little earlier in my life, Stella." He kissed her on the cheek. "Don't lose hope just yet. There may be something that can be done for Shay. When we get home we will find out all there is to know about witch wolves. It's not over until it's over." He squeezed her hand. "Now, why don't you come and get some sleep?"

"I'd like to stay here just a little longer, if that's okay?" Stella replied.

"All right, but don't stay up too late, and come straight in if the weather turns." He paused, then added, "I was going to wait until we got home, but you might as well have this now." He pulled a thin silver chain out from under his collar. From the end there dangled a tiny telescope. Stella had seen this necklace before and knew it was a fairy telescope that the fairies had given Felix. He'd worn it ever since she could remember.

"We each have a star in the sky that shines only for us," he said. "We might lose track of it from time to time, but

it's still there nevertheless. Sometimes we just have to find a way to get ourselves back on track, to be reminded of who we really are. The fairies gave me this telescope at a time when I'd lost my way a bit. I haven't needed it for a long time, but it might be useful to you now." He put the chain over Stella's neck. "Just search in the sky for your star and you'll see what I mean."

"How will I know which star's mine?" Stella asked, picking up the telescope to examine it.

Felix smiled. "You just will," he said. "Good night, my dear."

After he left, Stella stood examining the telescope, which felt cold and heavy and solid in her hands. Finally she lifted it to her eye, peered through the tiny lens at the night sky, and gasped. She could see hundreds of thousands of stars up there—far more than she'd been able to see with her own eyes—as if the sky were full of glitter. But there was one that blazed a bright, fierce, sparkling white, and Stella knew immediately that this was the star Felix had mentioned—the one that burned only for her.

The moment she saw it, a whole flood of thoughts and feelings and images raced through Stella's mind. She was reminded of all the things she most liked about herself: the fact that she had a polar bear who loved her; she was friends with dinosaurs; she knew how to read a map, skate on ice, make balloon unicorns, and build a snow bear. She recalled all the things that brought her the greatest pleasure: things like globes, and purple macarons, and ice flowers, and penguins, and unicorns, and beautiful dresses with petticoats underneath them, and exploring unknown lands, and being with her family and friends. Her flaws and imperfections were there too, but they no longer seemed to matter so much, or even at all, really. They were just part of who she was, and it was okay that she wasn't perfect.

And as she looked up at her star, she no longer felt like a black-and-white drawing that was being rubbed out, but instead she felt like a painting created in hundreds of glorious, wonderful colors. Deep inside her soul she felt a star that was the exact twin of the one in the sky, blazing strong and fierce with all the things that made her uniquely herself, including being an ice princess, and strangely, it felt okay, and she was glad that she was Stella Starflake Pearl and no one else.

Finally, she lowered the telescope, only to find that the air around her had filled with dozens of tiny snow stars, sparkling with the same blue magic that fizzed from her fingertips. Stella smiled at the stars, glad to see something beautiful come from the magic inside her.

Surrounded by the light of the twinkling snow stars, she stood and thought for a long time about all that Felix had said. He'd always told her that when a task seemed too big, or too difficult, or impossible to even begin, then you shouldn't think about the whole thing in its entirety, but should focus instead on doing just one thing, no matter how small, to get started.

Stella knew what she had to do and went belowdecks to find Shay's cabin. When he answered her knock on the door, she couldn't help flinching at the sight of the white streak in his hair, and a feeling of shame burned through her. She was afraid that he might shout, or demand an explanation, but instead he simply stepped forward and wrapped his arms around her in a tight hug.

"I'm sorry," Stella said. "I'm so sorry. I'm going to do whatever I can to put this right. I hope you can forgive me."

"But, Sparky," Shay replied, "there is nothing to forgive. Nothing at all."

CHAPTER TWENTY-THREE

Two Weeks Later

STELLA THREW THE BOOK across the room in frustration. It hit the wall and fell to the floor with a *thud*, narrowly missing Gruff, who was snoozing on the rug with the jungle fairies sleeping off their lunch on top of him.

"It's hopeless," she said to the room in general. Jezzybella was warming herself in a chair by the fire, yellow rain boots stretched out toward the heat, and Felix was going through a stack of books on the other side of the room. "There's absolutely nothing in here about what to do for someone who's been bitten by a witch wolf. Everything says there's no known cure. But there's got to be something I can do! There just has to be!"

Over the last two weeks she and Felix had had much of their time taken up with complaints from both the Polar Bear and Jungle Cat Explorers' clubs, attending disciplinary meetings and providing explanations for their behavior. Quite aside from the theft of the dirigible, the Jungle Cat president had been incensed by the treatment of his son— who Ethan had returned to human form as soon as they had arrived home. Despite the wheedling of the others, the magician had refused point-blank to change him back into a boy during the journey, and it wasn't until they were on the docks at Coldgate that he shot a spell at the frog, and Gideon appeared sprawled on the floor before them.

His hair was a terrible mess, and there was some indefinable air of "froggishness" that hung about him still in the way that his eyes bulged and his mouth seemed just a little wider than it had before. His fancy dressing gown was terribly crumpled and dirty too. Stella had never seen an expression of such hatred as when Gideon, still sprawled on the wooden pier, glared up at Ethan and said, "I'll get you back. I don't care when, or where, but one day, I swear I'll get you back for what you did to me."

Ethan dismissed the threat with a wave of his hand, but Stella felt a little chill of worry deep in her stomach. They didn't have too much time to worry about Gideon just then, however. The investigation rumbled on, and Stella and Felix had both been warned that they might face expulsion from the Polar Bear Explorers' Club.

Cadi, meanwhile, had returned with her father to their home on Yeti Island to await the decision as to whether she would be allowed to join any of the explorers' clubs. She and Stella had stayed in touch by letter, but most of Stella's remaining time was completely consumed with feverishly researching witch wolves. They'd learned that, like snow queens, witch wolves had frozen hearts and that their bite put a shard of ice into the bitten person, which would gradually spread, until they finally became a witch wolf themselves. At least, that was how it worked with an ordinary person. No one was quite sure how a wolf whisperer would be affected. Shay had been to many kinds of doctors, but they all said the same thing—there was nothing that could be done for him. Beanie had even tried magical healing, but to no effect.

"He seems like such a nice young boy," Jezzybella said from her chair. "Such a shame the Collector took the Book of Frost. That ice-melting spell would have been just the thing."

Stella and Felix both looked up sharply.

"What do you mean?" Stella asked. "Are you saying there's a spell in the Book of Frost that could help Shay?"

The old witch nodded. "Yes. Didn't I mention it? But it makes no difference, because the book is long gone, dear. The Collector has it, you know. Whisked it away with him to the other side of the Black Ice Bridge."

Stella and Felix looked at each other. Stella could feel a smile spreading across her face for the first time in two weeks.

"Felix," she said. "I have a plan. We must organize an expedition to the other side of the Black Ice Bridge. Then we must find the Collector, take back the Book of Frost, and use it to save Shay's life, and Koa's."

Felix smiled back at her. "Indeed, my dear," he said, already reaching for his hat. "That is exactly what we must do."

Acknowledgments

A great big thank-you to all of the following:

My agent, Thérèse Coen, and the Hardman and Swainson Literary Agency, who have continued to be fantastic champions for my books.

The lovely team at Faber, who've been as wonderful as ever in their support and enthusiasm for the Polar Bear Explorers' Club books. Special thanks to Hannah Love for looking after me on the promotion trail.

My two Siameses, Suki and Misu, who provided cuddles.

My fiancé, Neil Dayus, who provided cocktails, as well as some of the ideas for this book, including Weenus's Trading Post and the magic fort blanket.

All of the children's booksellers and teachers I've met, either online or in person, over the past year, whose passion for reading and books never fails to reinvigorate my own.

And, finally, a massive thank-you to all of the children who have read and enjoyed *The Polar Bear Explorers' Club*. When you dress up as the characters, or write letters to me, or create things in the classroom, or share your amazing ideas at events, you remind me of what a special thing it is to be a children's writer. I hope you enjoy this book too.

About the Author

ALEX BELL has always wanted to be a writer but had several different back-up plans. After training as a lawyer, she now works at the Citizens Advice Bureau, a legal advice firm in the United Kingdom. Most of her spare time consists of catering to the whims of her Siamese cat.

About the Illustrator

TOMISLAV TOMIĆ graduated from the Academy of Fine Arts in Zagreb, Croatia. He started publishing his illustrations during his college days, and since then has illustrated a great number of children's books. He lives and works in Zaprešić, Croatia.